DEAD
Week

KELLY BRAKENHOFF

Dead Week

A Cassandra Sato Mystery

Copyright 2019 by Kelly Brakenhoff

Cover Design and Artwork by Melissa Williams Design
University building © MSSA, Shutterstock; Dog © a7880ss, Adobe Stock; Trees © andreusK, Adobe Stock; Acorns © aliaksei_7799, Adobe Stock; Leaves © venimo, Adobe Stock

Interior Formatting by Melissa Williams Design

Author Photo by Susan Noel

Editing by Sione Aeschliman

Published by Emerald Prairie Press

kellybrakenhoff.com

DEAD
Week

KELLY BRAKENHOFF

Emerald Prairie
PRESS

To Dave.
Let's be saints together.

From: Terrance Zimmerman <tzimmerman2@mortoncollege.edu>
to: All Morton College Faculty and Staff
subject: Dead Week and Finals Week policies
security: Standard encryption (TLS)
date: November 19

Good afternoon Colleagues!

Several social media posts have come to my attention regarding alleged plans for an unrecognized student organization to stage a campus demonstration, thus disrupting students' ability to complete end of semester projects and prepare for exams. Rumors of professors moving Final Exam dates have also surfaced.

The last full week of classes before final examinations is designated as Dead Week. The intent of this policy is to establish a one-week period of substantial and predictable QUIET study time for undergraduate students.

Instructors are reminded that violation of the Dead Week policy can cause excessive student workloads.

We recognize that playful shenanigans help students blow off steam, however we ask you all to remain vigilant in strictly enforcing the 23/7 quiet hour policies during Dead Week and Finals Week. With your cooperation, we can ensure a peaceful ending to the semester.

Incidents of disorderly behavior should be referred to the Office of the Vice President for Student Affairs. For more serious misconduct, please contact Campus Security immediately.

Please refer to the website for complete Dead Week and Finals Week policies and procedures. www.mortoncollege.edu/exampolicies

Best regards,

Terrance Zimmerman
Professor, Agriculture Sciences
Faculty Senate Examinations Committee Chair

Chapter One

If Cassandra Sato had to pinpoint the moment enthusiasm for her dream job faltered, it was when her weather app displayed a morning temperature of thirty-eight degrees with a predicted high of forty-two. Morton College in mid-November had more in common with the arctic tundra than a tropical paradise.

No one in her native state of Hawai'i would consider forty-two degrees a high temperature. Ever.

After three months, Cassandra had grown accustomed to Nebraska and the college, if not the frosty weather. Hard work and a good plan had gotten her to this point in her higher education career so quickly: a thirty-four-year-old Vice President of Student Affairs. A student's tragic death in October had been unsettling, but with the help of friends she'd passed her first professional test.

Fast walking from the Faculty Senate meeting back to the Osborne Administration Building, Cassandra slid Professor Zimmerman's printed memo into her leather portfolio and drew her numb hands inside her coat sleeves for protection. Only two weeks earlier, her boss, President

Nielson, had announced his retirement then left on an extended vacation with his wife. In his absence, Cassandra felt added pressure to prevent shenanigans or disorderly behavior during the remaining weeks until the holiday break.

Inside the gloriously warm lobby, she climbed three flights of stairs to her office suite and paused to check her reflection in the elevator's mirrored steel surround.

Winter hadn't officially begun, yet Cassandra's red cheeks stung with cold. Her watery eyes had loosed a small mascara trail near her nose that she wiped away before entering her office suite.

Facing the doorway, four student workers deep in animated discussion crowded around a laptop screen on the reception desk. Since the September budget cuts and hiring freeze, Cassandra's secretarial needs had been cobbled together by part-time work study students whose primary concerns were passing Chemistry and getting dates for Saturday nights. She longed for a permanent assistant someday soon.

Logan Dunn, a dark-haired senior, quickly typed while the others dictated.

Rachel Nagle's voice rose above the hubbub. "I think a hunger strike is way better than blasting really loud heavy-metal music!" Then she slowly signed in American Sign Language to Lance Erickson, the deaf student standing near Logan's desk.

"I was gonna suggest a smoke grenade," said Logan, "but I love the irony that loud music irritates hearing people and the deaf people don't care. Weaponized sound . . . now *that's* style."

"Skipping meals makes my blood sugar drop." Bridget's French-manicured hand daintily rested over her heart. "I think we should nix the hunger strike and just have people sign a petition."

Logan leaned away from the keyboard, allowing Lance to read their ideas on the laptop screen. "Petition drives are too easy. No one pays attention to them. We could always just boycott class. Preferably on Tuesday during my European History test at 11:30." He acknowledged Cassandra's entrance with a charming smile.

"What are you future felons up to now?" Cassandra crossed her hands in front of her chest. "Please tell me this is for a class?" Normally their amusing antics involved breaking office machinery or mixing up appointment times, not planning terroristic threats.

"Yeah, my Deaf Studies class has been working on an advocacy project." Rachel said, "We've recruited students to support our cause, and we have to follow through with one of our ideas. Lance took the class last Spring so he's helping me decide our final tactic."

Lance put his two palms face out at Cassandra and shook his head no. Then he made a bomb gesture and his cheeks mimed an explosion. His head shook again.

The "no grenades" denial didn't reassure Cassandra. Professor Zimmerman's memo hadn't mentioned the Deaf Studies class by name, but hunger strikes, smoke grenades, and boycotts sounded like *alleged* demonstrations.

Rachel's eyes shone with excitement. "Professor Bryant told us that if we wanted things to change on campus, we had to advocate for them. Like back in the 80s. Another freshman in my class complained that Morton isn't accessible for us deaf people. So, we're going to protest and get them to change it."

Since Cassandra was likely the "them" who'd deal with their student misconduct charges if they crossed the line, she needed to set them straight from the beginning. Cassandra knew deaf students could have a classroom interpreter from talking to her friend Meg O'Brien. What more did they need?

"Wait." Laying her portfolio on the reception desk, Cassandra held up a hand. "Let's back up. Did you say, 'us deaf people,' Rachel? What do you mean?"

Rachel raised the left side of her long blonde hair, showing Cassandra a hearing aid behind her ear.

Cassandra's eyes widened. "I've never noticed that before. I thought you could hear."

"I could until tenth grade. Over six months, I completely lost my hearing on the right side, but my left still has a little bit. I started learning some signs my senior year because if I'm going to be deaf the rest of my life, I might as well use ASL. I've been trying an interpreter in my classes, but I don't understand enough yet to really learn that way."

"If you don't understand ASL well yet, how do you keep up in your Deaf Studies class? Does an interpreter tell you what Dr. Bryant is signing?" asked Cassandra.

"Everyone in my class is learning ASL," said Rachel. "Our professor uses sign, his PowerPoint, and gestures to communicate with us."

"Is any of your family deaf?" Logan asked.

"I wish I knew. My dad's family can all hear, but my mother was adopted. I want to research her birth parents, but it's kind of a sensitive subject for my mom."

Bridget frowned. "Your mom doesn't know her birth parents' names?"

"When I asked in high school, Mom said she believed her birth mother had made the best decision she could. She didn't want me to search for her birth parents, but I need to know about their genetic history."

"Nothing about adoption is easy. I understand why your mom is sensitive about it," said Cassandra.

"We studied about causes of deafness in my class with Dr. Bryant." Rachel bit her fingernail. "There's even one called Usher Syndrome 3 where people lose their hearing in their teens and twenties. Like me! Then when they're 40 or 50 years old, they also go blind."

Cassandra knew enough from Meg to know that being deaf didn't have to be a barrier to a great job and family and life. Adding blindness would definitely be harder though.

Rachel fought back tears. "What if I have that? Or what if I carry a gene that means my future children will become deaf, too?"

"Surely the odds of you having that specific type of syndrome are very, very small, Rachel," Cassandra reassured. "Don't get ahead of yourself in worrying."

"I'm going to convince my mother to let me take a DNA test over semester break to check for the genetic syndrome." Rachel added, "I found my mom's birth certificate and searched my birth grandmother's name. She was a student here at Morton in the 1970s."

"What a coincidence," said Cassandra.

Rachel's eyes flickered off to the side before meeting Cassandra's. "Not really. One reason I chose Morton was to find out more about my birth grandparents' families. My grandmother is dead. I saw her online obituary from 1976."

Cassandra had heard of students choosing a college because it was near the beach or they'd been offered a good scholarship. Following your dead grandmother's footsteps was unusual, at best.

"Promise you won't tell my mother I know all this!" Rachel pleaded, "I may have snooped for that birth certificate."

Cassandra didn't want to tangle with anyone's mother. "I won't tell your mom."

Rachel blew out a sigh. "Thanks, Dr. Sato."

"No worries, Rachel. But what if she finds out you went behind her back?"

"She'll be mad for a little while." Rachel shrugged off the warning.

"Now, for the rest of you lot..." Raising a finger, Cassandra made eye contact with each of them in turn. "Smoke grenades are *not* a joke. The college frowns upon blowing up stuff."

Lance showed Cassandra his phone screen where he'd typed a list for the class advocacy project titled: "Things on campus that aren't accessible. Public TVs not captioned, public announcements spoken in English only, classroom videos not captioned, no emergency alert or 9-1-1 text system."

If they presented their concerns appropriately, Cassandra would be happy to help. "I look forward to seeing your advocacy proposal when it's finished." She stopped short in her inner office doorway. "And Logan, you'd better study for your history test, because no way is a class boycott going to happen."

"It worked before at Gallaudet University in Washington, DC." Rachel looked eager to start right now. "They got out of classes for a week, got the president fired, and pressured the board to appoint the first Deaf President in school history."

Cassandra advised, "In any negotiation, it's better to make your requests privately first before you escalate to more serious and public moves."

"That's not what Professor Bryant told us. He was at Gallaudet in 1988, and he says deaf people are tired of fighting this battle."

Professor Bryant's student advocacy project had the bones of a great learning experience, but campus anarchy was not how Cassandra planned to end her first semester. Demonstrations and boycotts were the last thing the college needed after the difficulties of last month. With Nielson's exit, it fell to her to keep the peace. She'd have to keep a close eye on this project.

Chapter Two

The contented feeling of knowing she was in the right place at the right time, doing a job she loved, settled over Cassandra during the Faculty Senate meeting and while guiding her student workers back on track. The glow lingered oh... maybe fifteen more minutes while the Diversity Council brainstormed activity ideas for the first campus-wide Diversity Day. Taking a deep pull of hot chamomile tea from her Morton College travel mug, she smiled expansively at the hand-picked representatives seated around the scarred oak boardroom table in the executive administration suite.

To her left sat Dr. Shannon Bryant, chair of the Deaf Studies department. Cassandra guessed he was in his late forties by the deep wrinkle between his large, dark-brown eyebrows that threatened to grow together if he didn't follow a strict grooming schedule. His face was tanned like a guy who spent a lot of time outdoors.

Bryant raised his hands and signed in ASL, and Cassandra's best friend, Meg O'Brien who worked the meeting as his interpreter, spoke in English, "I'd like to see a small group discussion forum where students learn how it feels to be a person of color or a person with a disability at Morton." Rocking back in his chair, he crossed his arms.

Cassandra wrote Bryant's idea on the large whiteboard that filled one wall of the conference room. One British professor, one assistant admissions director she'd never met who looked Korean, and two African American men also sat at the table. Ben Dawes, she recognized from the housing department. The second gentleman, Cassandra knew worked in the athletic department, but she'd never spoken to him before. Shawn Armstrong was printed on the cardboard name tent in front of him. Others present represented academic departments or student clubs around campus.

President Nielson had appointed Cassandra as the Diversity Council chairperson upon her hiring in August, entrusting her with the opportunity to make an immediate impact on students and the campus climate through leadership of the institution's most progressive colleagues. She relished the chance to hit the reset button on last month's negative publicity.

"No-Nonsense Nielson" was an odd mix of small-town traditionalist mentality and bumbling dreamer who often made Cassandra cringe. He'd recognized the importance of bringing their small, private college into the current decade of institutional diversity. Since 83% of their students, faculty and staff were Caucasian, administration had a long way to go in making the remaining 17% feel more at home on campus.

Before announcing his intention to relax on a fishing boat somewhere warm during retirement, Nielson had forged a new connection with Hangzhou Commerce College in China to increase the number of international students studying at Morton and to open study-abroad opportunities for Nebraska students visiting Hangzhou.

Piggybacking on his success, Cassandra planned to prioritize their 6-month action items before Nielson's replacement was named. Substantive events and discussion at all levels of the college were important first steps for making quick and visible positive impressions.

"Maybe after the Diversity Day events, we could add an evening activity," suggested Gia Torres, a Latina Political Science professor. "A Poetry Slam would be a great opportunity for diverse voices to be heard. Set up a small stage and microphone at the coffee shop where it would attract the most attention."

Dr. Torres had attended the inaugural meeting of Cassandra's pet project, the Women of Tomorrow leadership academy, over a week earlier and seemed full of creative ideas. With only three female members—Cassandra, Gia, and Cinda Weller, the Counseling and Career Center Director—even their Diversity Council wasn't exactly the pinnacle of diversity.

Cassandra nodded encouragingly at the fifteen faces turned her direction hoping for a few more ideas. She thought, *this process was going well!*

"How about a Hobby Fair where people bring in items related to their hobbies and share stories about them," said John Park.

Cassandra added his idea to the board then wrote, *Deaf Studies Advocacy Project.* "Thanks. I'd like to address Dr.

Bryant's students' proposal about increasing accessibility on campus for deaf and hard of hearing students.

The point of Diversity Day was to include members across campus, raising awareness among all the stakeholders. Incorporating students in the planning process might head off any wild ideas they had about smoke bombs or protests while also elevating the Diversity Council's visibility. It was a win-win solution.

Bryant's head nodded slowly while he watched Meg signing.

From a corner of the table, Dawes said, "Morton receives federal aid and grants. We must already be accessible. That's the Americans with Disabilities Act."

Cassandra noted the smirk on Dr. Bryant's face. He signed, "Just because we have the ADA doesn't mean Morton is accessible." His lips twitched into a quick smile in Cassandra's direction, then he resumed watching Meg. "It's about time someone took us seriously."

"Depending which weekend we choose, I could check with the guys in my band and see if we're available to perform after the Poetry Slam," offered Dr. Simon Harris.

A loud scoff erupted from Bryant and his dark eyebrows nearly met, hooding deep-set eyes.

Cassandra had noticed Harris texting on his phone earlier during the meeting. It didn't surprise Cassandra that the leatherjacket wearing, Indiana Jones look-a-like teacher moonlighted in a band. But his comment had no relation to the student advocacy project or the ADA.

"Dr. Harris—"

"—How do deaf people hear music?" The British prof without a name tent in front of him interrupted her. She'd met him once but forgotten his name. "I couldn't live without the Beatles."

Wait. Seriously?

The guy next to the Brit rolled his eyes, "They feel the vibrations. *Everyone* knows that."

Cassandra thought some deaf people probably felt musical vibrations, but now was not the time to ask. She opened her mouth to redirect the conversation but stopped short when Dr. Bryant raised his hands.

His vigorous signing and animated expressions captivated everyone's attention. Meg's voice could hardly keep up with his fast-moving hands. "I'm tired of re-explaining the same tedious assumptions to people with no imagination. Being deaf is about more than whether or not our ears work. Instead of looking for ways to embrace the Deaf Community's unique communication and cultural assets, you're splitting hairs about music appreciation."

Bryant stood up so quickly his chair rolled against the wall and he walked out. In the momentary silence following his departure, Cassandra's stomach dropped like an elevator skipping several floors at once. Looking around the room, most of the council members appeared confused or uncomfortable.

Cassandra fought to keep her astonishment hidden while she adjourned the meeting and promised to schedule the next one soon. She'd expected her life experience growing up on Oahu would be an asset to the Diversity Council. Hawai'i was a crossroads of races, ethnicities, and incomes where ideals like aloha and ohana were treasures. Instead, she had hesitated when she should have led by example.

Only Meg hung back after everyone else had left the board room. "That could have gone better," said her friend.

Cassandra squinted hard and shook her head. Meg was the master of understatement.

So much for relationship building and preventing student unrest. Restoring her confidence would take more than a mug of hot tea.

* * *

After lunch, Cassandra was several paragraphs into reading the meeting minutes to salvage the useful Diversity Day ideas, when Rachel Nagle glided into her office and closed the door.

"Do you have a minute, Dr. Sato?"

Her timing was perfect. Rachel was exactly the kind of student Cassandra wanted to include in Diversity Day planning. "Sure, Rachel. How can I help you?"

Hesitating a few seconds, Rachel said, "Remember earlier when I showed you my hearing aid?"

Cassandra nodded.

"Well, my friend Taylor Phillips works for the *Maple Leaf* college newspaper, and she's writing a story about our Deaf Studies advocacy project," said Rachel. "Our booth at the Student Center has been pretty popular this week. Lots of kids have signed up to support us. We even have hashtags."

Cassandra had less than twenty Facebook friends and didn't post on social apps. Still, she knew about hashtags and was relieved she had other things to worry about besides creating clever phrases to describe her daily activities.

"Taylor wants to interview me. Like, my personal perspective."

Rachel's situation was unique, but other students might be inspired by her battle to overcome her hearing loss obstacles. Cassandra said, "Good for you." Studying Rachel's oval face, Cassandra noticed a slight frown. "Are you worried about the article?" she guessed.

"I'm not 100% sure I want to tell Taylor everything." Rachel squirmed in the armchair facing Cassandra's desk. "Not everyone here knows about me . . . uh my, um hearing thing. Sometimes in Dr. Bryant's class I feel inspired that I can still do anything I want even if I can't hear. Look at him. He's traveled the world, testified in front of the state legislature, and teaches college classes."

Cassandra nodded. "Yes, he's a very successful person."

"The thing is, I'm not sure I want the whole world to know me as deaf. "

"Honestly, I couldn't even tell until you showed me your hearing aid. What you've done is pretty amazing." Cassandra leaned forward at her desk. "In fact, I'd like you to attend our next planning meeting and present the accessibility issues your class has identified. Your Deaf Studies project is a great example of how Morton could be more responsive to students. It'll need to be a complete proposal including justifications and estimated costs. Email me a draft, and I can help you organize your ideas."

"Me? I don't know if I need any more clubs." Rachel's shoulders hunched up. "I just like being able to talk to you." Her wide set green eyes gazed in open awe of Cassandra. "You left everything behind in Hawai'i and moved to Carson, Nebraska. I mean, it's crazy right? But also, so brave."

Cassandra's cheeks heated slightly. She was encouraging Rachel, not holding herself up as completely together. If Rachel's work on the advocacy project succeeded, she could join Cassandra's Women of Tomorrow leadership group her junior year. "Sometimes bravery isn't a bold cross-country move. Sometimes bravery is embracing your unique gifts and talents to help those around you. Overcoming your hearing loss obstacles makes you a role model for students with similar experiences." Cassandra saw an intangible light within Rachel and wanted to open doors for her. "Getting involved with Diversity Day planning would look great on your résumé." Cassandra's reasons weren't entirely unselfish. Rachel's positive, feel-good story would be a big improvement over last month's negative news articles. Cassandra wanted to highlight what was going right at the college instead of dwelling on Morton's shortcomings.

Rachel put up two hands. "Whoa. I'm not role model material. I don't get the best grades. Half the time I don't even know what's going on."

"Can I ask, how *do* you know what people are saying?"

"I can hear which direction the talking is coming from. Then I look at people's lips or the situation and . . . pretty much guess what they're saying."

"What happens when you guess wrong?" Cassandra wondered.

"I either fake it or ask them to repeat."

Meaning she'd gotten this far by observation and winging it. "Wow. I imagine that feels super stressful," said Cassandra. "You don't have to help with Diversity Day if you don't want to. Think about it and let me know. Now, you had asked about whether you should tell Taylor your whole story, or just keep it limited to the class advocacy project?"

"If I tell everyone, how will people treat me once they find out I'm deaf?"

"Maybe some people will treat you differently, but —."

"Will deaf people assume I know sign?" Rachel's hands fluttered up in exasperation. "Will people who can hear ignore me because it's a pain to repeat things to me?" Her eyes welled up. "I'm not culturally Deaf-with-a-capital-D, and I'm not fully hearing. I'm in between. I don't fit anywhere."

Cassandra had no idea it was so complicated. Her throat constricted. "Rachel, you control who knows your personal medical information and which details are included in the newspaper article your friend publishes. If you aren't ready yet, that's okay."

"I want to tell my story and fight for my rights like Dr. Bryant." Rachel wiped under her eyes with a Kleenex from the box on Cassandra's desk. "I want to help people. But I don't want to lose my friends."

"All I can tell you is that you've opened my eyes about how it feels to be in your shoes. When you're ready to tell everyone, I'll have your back. Whenever you need me."

Chapter Three

The next morning, with a satisfied smile on her lips, Cassandra set out on the two-block trip from her house. In Hawai'i, she would have been fifty before she could have afforded a two-story, three-bedroom 1940s bungalow.

Her brother, the numbers guy, had advised her to commit to five years before moving to reap the benefits of homeownership. If all went according to plan at Morton, five years gave her time to learn the administrative ropes enough to apply for president jobs at small to medium institutions.

Cassandra wasn't used to arriving at work in the dark. Growing up in Waipahu, Hawai'i, sunrise varied only an hour or so all year long, but climate was different in Carson, Nebraska. As in, two hours less daylight in November different.

Mama Sato would shake a wrinkled finger at her if she could see her now. "Eh, forty-five degrees is too cold to walk to work," she imagined Mom scolding. "You get sick, who's gonna cook for you and do your laundry?" Mom's top worries were that Cassandra would die of starvation or run out of clean underwear.

The final uphill stretch before she turned onto campus near the football field brought her alongside a beautiful old Craftsman-style cottage double the size of her own. For weeks, a metal "for sale" sign had been mounted on a large berm of half-dead weeds and untended flowers.

When a close, sharp, "Woof," came from a large bush along the driveway, Cassandra's heart skipped, her toe caught something hard, and her knee buckled. Her over-stuffed Kate Spade tote slipped off her shoulder and threatened to pull her off balance into the dewy grass near the street. A furry, white dog launched out of the bush toward Cassandra's shins. Swinging the tote around in a wide arc, she successfully planted it on the sidewalk between her and the snarling, yipping dog with tiny bared teeth.

"Back off, you rude . . ." Cassandra grumbled, squaring up against the dog and standing feet wide apart with hands on her hips. The morning light had brightened enough that she could see the creature weighed little more than a bag of rice.

A door slammed in the shadowed front porch of the Craftsman cottage and a woman wearing slippers and a thick fleece bathrobe hurried toward them. "Murphy . . . Mur-phy! Murph–! Stop barking." She held out a small rubber toy and squeaked it a few times to distract the dog. Finally it heard her, turned, and trotted away from Cassandra.

The older woman leaned over and scooped up the dog, holding it like a toddler.

"Murphy's bark is worse than his bite," she said, petting his head and straightening the black-and-white-plaid bow tie fixed to his collar. Cassandra was pretty sure the stinging scratch on her bare leg was from a long doggie toenail and not teeth, but she wasn't convinced he was exactly safe.

Managing a weak smile, Cassandra said, "He, uh … surprised me."

Cassandra picked up her tote bag and Murphy growled again. Despite the frumpy bathrobe, the woman's fluffy layered gray hair was styled and sprayed. Carefully penciled-in eyebrows met in a deep frown. "I saw from my porch. Did you *hit* my dog with your bag?"

Excuse me? The evil dog was the attacker here. She replayed the whole scene quickly in her head. She'd swung the bag around to catch her balance and defend herself, but she hadn't even touched the animal.

Cassandra deliberately disengaged, keeping a neutral expression on her face. "No, ma'am. I was walking past, and he jumped out at me."

Her eyes quickly swept up and down the street. Were any neighbors outside witnessing this silly exchange? "I walk by here every day … I didn't know anyone lived here."

"Moved in yesterday," said the woman. "You must have looked suspicious to him." She gave Cassandra the once over from head to toe, as though agreeing with her dog. "I'll try to keep him in the back yard."

Turning abruptly, she stepped back into the shadows.

"That would be great, thanks."

She adjusted the bag over her shoulder, resumed walking, and thought silently "Namo Amida Butsu, Namo

Amida Butsu," and hoped the calming prayer would reverse the inauspicious beginning of her day.

* * *

Forty-seven emails, two Housing Director hiring interviews, and one Intramural Sports Advisory Committee meeting later, Cassandra sat across her desk from Dr. Bergstrom.

"Thanks for coming by. I thought we were meeting in your office," said Cassandra. Her stomach low-key growled, but lunch was at least an hour away.

Bergstrom was an emeritus philosophy professor who looked every bit the part of old school academic, right down to the leather elbow patches on his brown tweed jacket. One of the first people to introduce himself when she started work in August, they'd developed a fatherly, informal mentoring relationship.

"I was already in the building." Bergstrom's gray beard partially hid his tobacco stained smile. "No sense both of us fighting this wind." His chin lifted up, indicating the picture window behind Cassandra's desk, where gusty winds bent the bare treetops surrounding the large field carpeted by orange, gold, and red leaves.

"Right. Much appreciated." She congratulated herself on today's wardrobe choice of a heavy cardigan over her blouse and skirt. "I asked to meet with you because I wanted to get your take on a dust up in yesterday's Diversity Council meeting."

She gave Bergstrom a quick recap of the brainstorming session, including the ADA comments, Dr. Harris's musical offer, and Dr. Bryant's abrupt exit.

Bergstrom relaxed in the armchair, his folded hands resting on his Santa Claus-shaped torso. "I've heard Dr. Harris's band play before and they're not horrible. If you enjoy middle-aged men singing radio covers and acting like 30-year-olds."

"I like good music as much as anyone, but what does it have to do with diversity? I don't know whether Dr. Bryant was more upset about the insensitive disability comments or Harris's band offer." Cassandra glanced right, eyeing her framed University of Hawai'i degrees between the two large bookshelves. "In my six years of employment, no one's ever stormed out of a meeting before. I thought the entire point of collegial discourse was to debate viewpoints and understand others' experiences."

Bergstrom remained quiet, nodding slowly.

"Is there some small-town Nebraska cultural thing I'm missing?" Cassandra asked.

"I know nothing about deaf people's musical tastes." Removing his glasses, Bergstrom wiped them on the bottom edge of his shirt. "However, street bands often perform at small-town cultural festivals all around the state during the summer county fair season. Lots of local people think diversity means sharing ethnic food and musical traditions without taking it to a deeper level."

"That's what I mean! They're missing the point." A frustrated sigh escaped. "It's more than a food day, wearing a costume, or celebrating your heritage. Now instead of forward momentum, the council will have to repair internal relationships before we're ready to engage the broader campus community." Cassandra's shoulders dropped.

"Dr. Sato, you are far too wise to give up so easily. Where's your energy and good humor I've come to expect? You must know that things worth having require hard work. If there are no obstacles in your path, where's the fun of overcoming them and basking in the glow of sweet success?"

His habit of spouting philosophical platitudes usually endeared him to Cassandra, but not today. Her eyes rolled towards the ceiling. Putting her palms together as if praying, she dipped a little bow towards him. "Thank you, Yoda, for the pep talk."

Two loud beeps sounded over the public address system signaling the daily announcements. Cassandra and Bergstrom paused their conversation while a female voice enthused over the ceiling speakers. "Good morning, Morton Maples! Today is Friday, November 20th. Expect a partly cloudy day with a high of fifty degrees. Temperatures will drop this afternoon bringing a slight chance of rain or sleet."

Cassandra frowned. She hadn't brought her umbrella to work.

The announcer's voice was polished, like a radio DJ. "Have you made Thanksgiving break plans yet? Check the bulletin boards in the Student Center if you're looking for a carpool ride home. There's a Runza lunch special available today. Get-'em while they're hot. Remember to wear white on Saturday if you're attending the football game. That's all for today, folks."

Bergstrom opened his mouth to speak but was interrupted by two sharp raps on Cassandra's office door.

The students knew better than to interrupt her meeting.

When Cassandra opened the door, she immediately recognized the new board of directors chairman, whose perfectly groomed hair was sculpted to a disproportionately large head for his average-sized body. "What a surprise Dr. Hershey!"

Cassandra stepped back to invite Chairman Hershey into her office. She'd met him briefly during her first week at Morton, but Hershey had only recently been elected Chair.

Luckily Cassandra kept her space tidy enough for unexpected VIP visits. Trailing several steps behind him was a slim lady with backcombed gray-blond hair wearing a cream tweed suit who looked old enough to be Hershey's mother.

Placing a large hand on the woman's shoulder, Hershey said, "Dr. Winters, may I present Cassandra Sato, the Student Affairs Vice President. Dr. Sato, this is Deborah Winters our new interim President. She has graciously agreed to come out of retirement and lead us while we conduct a nationwide search for a permanent President." Hershey smiled, "You already know Dr. Bergstrom."

Chicken skin crept up Cassandra's arms. She threw Bergstrom a wide-eyed glare over her shoulder. Standing, he had the grace to shrug apologetically while mumbling something like, ". . . meant to tell you the news."

Cassandra had assumed it would take weeks to fill Dr. Nielson's position. Apparently not.

Staring into her small blue eyes while they executed a firm handshake, Cassandra imagined her new boss wearing a thick fleece bathrobe. The ill-mannered dog's owner smiled, "Dr. Sato, it's a pleasure to meet you."

Their morning encounter had been decidedly *unpleasant,* and Cassandra had the battle wound to prove it. "Yes, it's nice to see you again," Cassandra fibbed.

No recognition sparked in Dr. Winters' eyes. No contempt showed on her face. Either she was an excellent actress, or she sincerely had forgotten their driveway moment only hours earlier. Neither option boded well.

"Dr. Winters taught here for nearly thirty years. She retired..." He raised a questioning eyebrow, "two years ago, I believe?"

Winters said, "I thought when my husband Charlie and I disconnected the land phone line at our retirement home in Arizona that meant Alan here wouldn't be able to track me down." The wrinkles around her eyes deepened as she smiled warmly. "Harder to stay hidden nowadays than it used to be."

Hershey held up a palm in a mock oath. "She made me promise we'd complete the permanent search in time for her to be back in Arizona by next December."

Winters gently patted Hershey's arm, the veins on the back of her thin hand sticking out like she'd been pumped full of purple Kool-Aid before arriving. "Morton was good to me. Since losing Charlie, I find I've got plenty of free time on my hands."

Winters made a slow 360 turn, taking in the crisp white walls, dark bookcases and small seating area. "Dr. Sato, your office is lovely. That colorful undersea painting is especially eye catching. I saw similar artwork during our vacation in Maui years ago."

"Thank you, that was a graduation gift from my parents. It's by a Hawaiian artist named Wyland. His style is distinctive."

"Charlie and I saw four whales on a glass-bottom boat tour." Winters' blue eyes misted. "Who'd have guessed that would be our last vacation together?"

Hershey placed a hand on Dr. Winters' back to usher her out of Cassandra's office. He seemed uncomfortable with the emotional memory. "We have to move on. Lots more introductions to make. Thanks for your time, Dr. Sato, Dr. Bergstrom."

Moving with them into the outer office, Cassandra's hospitable smile slid off her face. The waiting chairs were empty and *two* students played with their phones instead of the work she'd assigned them earlier.

Winters looked closely at each student, her mouth pursed slightly. Stepping forward, she stopped directly in front of Rachel and Logan. The intense scrutiny made Cassandra's heart thump.

"Does your secretary have the day off?" Winters gestured toward the students and the reception desk stacked with files and papers.

"My assistant, Connie McDermott, retired in September right before the hiring freeze was instituted."

Winters smile was wry. "Connie? She put the 'old' in old school."

Bergstrom made a strangled laughing sound behind Cassandra, and she dared not make eye contact.

Hershey steered Winters back towards the hallway and chuckled. Cassandra overheard Dr. Winters, "Alan, students staffing the vice president's office simply won't do. Oh, we're going to fix that."

Would she finally get a real assistant? Cassandra repressed a celebratory whoop.

The elevator down the hall had barely closed on Hershey and Winters when Cassandra rounded on Bergstrom, arms folded over her chest. "Why didn't you warn me!" Cassandra stage whispered.

"I got distracted. You know, I had that job before Nielson." Bergstrom mumbled.

"I remember reading that somewhere. Why'd you resign?"

Shoving his hands into the pockets of his pleated dress pants, Bergstrom shrugged. "Too much responsibility. Faculty complaining about the limits on their academic freedom; students complaining about cafeteria food. All I want now is to open young minds to the wisdom of the ages, play some chess, and linger awhile before I pass into the next world."

"Maybe dial back the 'passing into the next world' talk, could you?" Cassandra said, "Who'd teach your Philosophy of Batman class?" Teaching awards filled an entire wall in Bergstrom's shoebox-sized office. "The students would riot.

Besides, I need your help getting through to the old guard faculty."

"Do you really believe you can change the world through your councils?" Stepping out of Cassandra's office, Bergstrom said, "The worst form of inequality is to try to make unequal things equal."

"Why is talking to you always a memory test of my ability to recall famous philosophers? Okay, I should know that one. Plato?"

Behind wire-framed glasses, his eyes twinkled in pleasure at the game. "Very close. Aristotle. Well done!"

"Yes, I believe one person can change the world," she said. "Inequality might be a necessary part of life, but groups like the Council are one way to promote equality of opportunity." A worthy goal. Pausing on his way outside, Bergstrom's bushy eyebrows knitted together, and he stared transfixed at Logan and Rachel for several long seconds.

"You... your name?" He reached a hand towards Rachel. She instinctively cringed backwards.

"Uh... Rachel?" She said slowly, as if to a child. "We haven't met."

Cassandra touched him gently on the shoulder and he flinched. "Dr. Bergstrom? Rachel works for me. Are you feeling okay?"

Was that sweat on his forehead? Cassandra hoped he wasn't having a medical episode.

Bergstrom's face quickly resumed his usual charm. "Forgive an old man, folks. When you're my age, all the students start looking like someone I've taught before."

He and Dr. Winters were nearing the end of their careers, while Cassandra was just getting started. Learning from a female boss might be a good opportunity and she intended to make the most of this development.

Chapter Four

Monday morning Cassandra entered the bustling Student Center, relieved to escape the dark clouds and chilly breeze that swirled orange leaves against the glass entry doors. She headed for the student organization hallway where on any given day groups set up booths for recruiting new members, publicizing upcoming events, and selling baked goods or similar fundraising items.

In particular, Cassandra zeroed in on the Deaf Studies advocacy booth where Rachel was scheduled to work. Cassandra had read the *Maple Leaf* article published Friday afternoon and needed to clarify some misinformation included in the article.

Rounding the final corner, she spotted Rachel, Bridget, and two guys standing behind a table covered in a blue cloth surrounded by a knot of students talking or signing papers on a clipboard. A hand-lettered poster board rested on an easel behind the table with the slogan, "Deaf Rights are Human Rights."

From her left, Cassandra heard a familiar drawl, "Well, bless your heart! Aren't you the talk of the town? Can I have your autograph?"

Cinda Weller, Counseling and Career Services Director, was tall and unfairly thin for having popped out three kids in four years. An Air Force brat, the Arkansas accent was the one that had stuck.

Cassandra smiled at Cinda's distinctive voice then winced at the meaning behind her teasing. "You must've seen the newspaper article, eh?" How embarrassing to be in the news again without her cooperation.

"Rachel made you sound super badass for moving here from Hawai'i. You inspired her." Cinda stepped aside from the busy walkway and they sat on a bench against the wall.

Cassandra set her bag on the floor and eyed the scabbed over gash across her bare calf. *Stupid dog.*

"I bawled like a baby when I read Rachel's story about becoming deaf in high school. The kids actually teased her!" Cinda scoffed, "Like being deaf was a lifestyle choice. No wonder her mother is so protective."

"The Diversity Council thing wasn't a done deal," She needed Cinda to be clear that Rachel had exaggerated their conversation. "I only meant to encourage Rachel. I would have gotten the members' consent before adding her to our meeting agenda. I don't want people thinking I'd go behind their backs. And I never offered Rachel a seat at the table. I wish the reporter had called me directly for a quote instead of relying on Rachel to give accurate information."

Cinda waved a hand in the air between them. "Including student input on the Diversity Council wouldn't bother me. Although at the last meeting, I don't think everyone was super excited about making the Deaf Studies advocacy project one of the action items. Probably there will be push back now that Rachel announced that she intends to take their class's demands to the college president."

Cassandra cringed. "I don't know how Rachel thought I'd invited her to join the council."

"Probably just a misunderstanding. But now that the article has gotten traction, it's more complicated."

Cassandra's eyebrow shot up. "Gotten traction?"

Cinda was her go-to friend about academic politics and everything social media. "Hello? Haven't you seen all the re-posts about the Deaf Studies project? The AP picked up the *Maple Leaf* story and it's been shared to regional newspapers. They've gone viral."

Cassandra's heart gave a big thump. "Uh, no. Please, no."

"Just the messenger." Cinda held out her hands and pointed back at her chest.

"I don't blame you. Remember what happened the last time my name was plastered all over the news? I almost lost my job. Not going there again." Cassandra's plan to keep the semester ending low key was rapidly slipping away. "Hey, what did you mean when you said Rachel's mom was overprotective?"

"I've spent hours on the phone with Rachel's mother this semester. Patty Nagle makes helicopter moms look soft. I told you and Meg about her before, I just didn't mention her name."

"Is she the one who passed out her kid's resume to the career fair employers because her daughter was too busy to attend?"

Cinda nodded. "And called the dorm cafeteria to ask how they'd prepare the food to her daughter's food allergy specifications. It's amazing she sent her baby girl to school an hour away from home."

Cassandra's eyes widened as she imagined her new boss's reaction to all of this. She glanced at her watch, noting the temperature had dropped to 36 degrees with a little raindrop icon. An involuntary shiver ran across her shoulders. "Thanks for telling me. I need to talk to Rachel before my next appointment."

The crowd at the Deaf Advocacy booth had thinned. Rachel saw Cassandra and beamed. "Hey, Dr. Sato! Want to sign our petition? We could use more supporters to get the word out."

Wasn't the AP enough exposure? The article had included a copy of Lance's list from the other day, but Cassandra had thought those were just brainstorming ideas. The students hadn't submitted their formal advocacy project request yet.

Cassandra waved and beckoned to Rachel so they could have a private conversation. The hallway was loud with students heading to the coffee shop and cafeteria or seated in pods throughout the main floor. Rachel left her classmates behind the booth and they moved to a quieter corner. "I noticed in the newspaper article that you changed your mind and told your whole story."

Rachel's face was flushed. She seemed a true extrovert who loved the interaction with groups of people. "I was nervous when I talked to you last week, but you gave me the courage to go for it. So far everyone's been really nice! With all the shares and news coverage, I feel like we can make a real difference here."

Cassandra had meant to support Rachel as an individual, but quickly the college had become the main focus of attention. Cassandra hadn't foreseen this possibility.

Cassandra crossed her arms in front of her chest. "Rachel, I think you misunderstood me last week when we talked about the Diversity Council. I only suggested you *might* be able to present your accessibility ideas at our next meeting. We didn't even agree on that part, let alone making you a student representative on the Council. I don't have the authority to decide alone."

Rachel looked confused for a few seconds. "Oh, yeah. I never told Taylor that exactly. She kinda got the Council part wrong." More breezily, she said, "It was just that one little error though. Otherwise she wrote a solid article. Dr. Bryant teaches that getting grassroots supporters to share our story helps pressure the decision makers to pay attention to our cause."

Knowing that the reporter had gotten the details wrong did little to relieve Cassandra's unease. Rachel might be unconcerned about an exaggeration in the article, but Cassandra now had a new decision maker in her life. She could only hope Dr. Winters would be too preoccupied with getting herself up to speed to pay attention to a small student group's class project.

* * *

By lunch time, Cassandra had been on the receiving end of several old-fashioned pink paper phone messages from Dr. Winters asking for status reports on the Student Affairs department, her procedures, and workflows. The most recent one had a subject line that said, "Please stop by my office when you have a minute."

Cassandra squinted at the summons.

Taking a deep breath, she decided to face her new boss right away. Winters had seemed like a reasonable woman on Friday. She'd understand being misquoted. Maybe Cassandra could ask the newspaper to print a correction in the next edition.

Julie, Dr. Winters' assistant, greeted Cassandra warmly when she entered the president's suite a few minutes later. "Dr. Winters is expecting me. She asked me to stop by."

Dr. Winters, wearing a rusty-colored tweed polyester pantsuit with a wide, brown cashmere scarf wrapped around her shoulders, met Cassandra just inside the door. Cassandra hardly recognized the office. Only a month ago, Cassandra had finalized plans with Dr. Nielson here before his goodwill trip to China. Then, the room had looked like a British men's club filled with heavy, dark leather furniture, wood-paneled walls, and an imposing walnut desk and bookshelves. The only remaining feature of the decorating transformation was the dark wood paneled walls. Everything else had been replaced by stark white mid-century modern furniture. Winters' empty desk was small and sleek with narrow legs centered on a large plush white rug in the middle of the room. Behind a white leather seating area, cardboard computer boxes were neatly stacked atop several bankers' boxes awaiting unpacking. Gone were the squeaky antique armchairs and mahogany conference table.

"Pleased to meet you, I'm Deborah Winters." Her boss enveloped Cassandra's hand in both of her warm palms. "Mr. Hershey told me many good things about you Dr. Sato. Welcome to Nebraska and Morton College. I hope you are settling in and adjusting to our lifestyle," she beamed. "Quite a bit different than living in Honolulu, I imagine."

The formal greeting left Cassandra speechless. They'd already met. Twice. Cassandra did a quick check over her shoulder to make sure she was in the right office.

Had someone else called requesting the status updates? Staring at Winters' delighted, yet somewhat vacant facial expression, Cassandra wondered how many times they'd meet before it stuck in Winters' mind.

"Yes, ma'am . . . especially the weather here," Cassandra laughed tentatively. "I've heard it might snow. I'm not ready for that yet."

"What brings you by my office today, Dr. Sato?"

Cassandra raised an eyebrow. "You . . . left a phone message asking me to stop by, Dr. Winters." Maybe one of her student workers had mixed up the name on the message?

"Call me Deborah, please. Your department . . ." she paused long enough that Cassandra filled in the blank.

"Uh, Deborah . . . I'm the Student Affairs VP?"

"Oh yes, of course, Student Affairs. You keep up the good work over there.'" Her laugh was deep and melodic. "I've met so many new faces and sent so many emails the last week."

Cassandra smiled back, relieved that Dr. Winters was obviously unaware of the news article's viral publicity. Maybe it would all go away in the next news cycle.

"Now dear, we do need to talk about your little committees," said Winters. "Back in the day, we expected students to follow the Golden Rule. We didn't need special councils telling us how to behave. Nowadays parents want to be friends with their children instead of disciplinarians."

Cassandra didn't know where she was going with this, so she remained silent.

"Student Affairs is a critical department and we need good people like you leading it," said Winters. "We could do without the fancy titles and committees, though. I hate extra meetings that take away valuable time that should be spent directly serving students. We've had too much negative publicity the last month. I'll scrutinize every council, committee, and subcommittee. Cut the fat." She patted her slim waist. "What's good for healthy bodies also makes a positive, healthy workplace!"

Winters wanted fewer committees and planned to micromanage her administrators. Cassandra's shoulders tightened more with every sentence. She didn't want a boss who second-guessed every move. "I appreciate your focus on students, ma'am. I believe you'll find most committees like the Diversity Council and Women of Tomorrow are an important key to building positive relationships among all students, faculty, and staff. Dr. Nielson felt the council would provide vital guidance on areas of improvement."

"I'll be the judge of that." Dr. Winters held up both hands to indicate the redecorated room. "This is my office now."

She turned away without another glance at Cassandra and returned to her desk.

Winters was hard to read. Alternately confused and focused. Invested, yet opinionated. Clearly the Diversity Council sat on her chopping block and negative publicity would make it easy for her to cut it out before they started. Cassandra needed to patch things up between the members and get moving on providing tangible benefits to students to keep her good reputation intact.

* * *

Cassandra inhaled the earthy scent of decaying leaves. The misty rain had begun mid-afternoon, then turned to solid icy chunks somewhere between rain and snow for less than an hour. Luckily, by the time Cassandra carefully walked home, the sidewalks had dry patches.

A soft ping sounded from her tote bag and Cassandra groped for her phone, eyeing Marcus Fischer's name on the display. "Hello?"

"Hey, Cassandra." Her heart skipped upon hearing his deep voice. Was he calling for business or personal reasons?

Fischer said, "Is now a good time to talk?"

Good news usually didn't follow that question. Her vision of a relaxing workout and eating dinner while seated at her table evaporated. She'd felt so adult having an evening off, like normal people.

"Just walking home. This is fine. What's up?"

Fischer had only recently been promoted from Housing Director to Facilities and Maintenance VP. Though she was no longer Fischer's boss, Cassandra still didn't like mixing personal feelings with professional relationships. Not that one date made an official romance, no matter how much Meg and Cinda teased her.

"I just talked to Hannah Chapman from Communications, and an Omaha TV station's film crew is coming tomorrow to the Student Center. They saw the AP story about the advocacy project and want to interview students for their reactions. The increased traffic around the Student Center will be a problem. Once people see the news truck parked out front, the whole town will show up to check it out."

Cassandra slowed to a snail's pace and stared at the slightly rotted pumpkin adorning her front porch. Online news articles were bad enough. Every busybody in Carson on Morton's doorstep would be another nail in her career coffin.

"Everyone goes home in a couple of days for Thanksgiving." Was she a fool to hope that widespread turkey comas would make the hype go away?

Opening her bungalow's front door, Cassandra's big toe connected with the 50-pound bag of rock salt she'd hauled home from the hardware store when the first severe weather watch had appeared on her phone. "Augh—" A strangled gasp escaped as her tote bag dropped. One hand cradled the front of her shoe while she hopped around, finally leaning against an entryway wall.

"Are you okay?" Cassandra heard the concern in his voice. After last month's surprise stalker visits, maybe Fischer thought she had an intruder.

"Yeah, I'm fine." Kicking off her shoe, she wiggled her toes enough to see they weren't broken. "I was attacked by a bag of rock salt that some idiot left in front of the door."

Cassandra could almost hear him tilting his head at her. "Some idiotw...?"

"Uh, yeah, that would be me who forgot to move the rock salt out of the way. Also, I'm the one who just kicked—never mind."

"You don't wanna use rock salt on your steps and driveway."

"I thought it melted the ice." Cassandra frowned.

"It also ruins the concrete."

Why did the store sell bags of stuff that ruined your driveway?

Retrieving her tote, she laid it on her desk and headed to the master bedroom. "Can you monitor the news crew situation tomorrow? If they interview a few students about their 15 minutes of fame, that shouldn't hurt anything, right?"

Two, then three heartbeats of silence over the phone. *God, how did one toe throb so much anyway?*

"Hard to predict what the reporters think is worth filming." Fischer was a conversational minimalist. She admired how he didn't embellish the facts with unnecessary emotion. "It's not like the students are protesting us. It's just an information booth and petitions, right?"

Unless their professor encouraged them to go further. Her eyes squinted. "We need to talk about how to address their accessibility concerns. I'll keep in touch."

About an hour later, Cassandra took deep, steady breaths as she sank deeper into Pigeon Pose on the padded yoga mat in her living room. Ocean waves pounded the rocky shore in the background of the video she followed. Her glutes and hamstrings burned slightly as they stretched. Each inhale carried the savory blend of thyme and rosemary that she'd sprinkled on the chicken thighs baking in the oven. The rice cooker beeped its completed cycle. She'd timed her workout perfectly.

The doorbell chimed.

Unwinding her legs, Cassandra opened the inner door and turned on the light in the little entry foyer. She recognized the blonde buzz-cut hairdo showing through the high window of her front door and unlocked it.

Walking on her still tender foot reminded her to move the salt out of the way. She opened the outer door to Andy Summers. "Andy! I'm surprised to see you at this hour." She turned around to shove the salt bag into the corner.

Usually the Morton Security Director and she were the earliest to arrive on campus. They'd forged a friendship since her first week of work over hot coffees and cinnamon donuts, and when she'd been temporarily suspended during the previous month's cancer research fiasco, he'd believed in her.

By the time Cassandra straightened and said hello, Summers' cheeks were pink, and his eyeballs took an extra couple of seconds to travel up to her smiling face. "I was on my way home—" Summers glanced down at the bag of rock salt and frowned. "Hey, you aren't using that stuff on your front walkway, are you?"

Cassandra narrowed her eyes. "The hardware store sold it right next to the snow shovels."

"It'll ruin your sidewalk."

First Fischer, then Summers.

Summers shrugged, "Anyway, sorry it's late, but I just got off work."

Should she invite him to sit down? After all, they were sometimes work breakfast buddies. But were they join-me-for-dinner kind of friends?

"Is this about the Omaha television crew coming tomorrow?" she asked.

She stood just inside the living room. In the overhead light, his high, wide forehead had a faint sheen of perspiration.

He shook his head, "How did they find out about the accident already?"

"Wait, what accident?" she asked.

Frowning, he said, "She's on the way to the hospital now. There's nothing to show on TV."

Cassandra raised her hands waist high. "Hold on. Who are you talking about?"

He shifted his weight. "Rachel Nagle. An ambulance is taking her to the emergency room in Wahoo."

"Rachel Nagle?" she parroted. *Her* student worker. In the ER?

"Yeah. She slipped on some ice near the football stadium parking lot and must've gone down hard. She's breathing and everything, but mostly out of it. They took her in to check for concussion."

Cassandra took a moment to digest that.

"How do you know the television station is sending out a crew?" Summers scratched his head. "They already took her away. There's nothing to film."

"The film crew was scheduled for tomorrow. About the Deaf Studies advocacy booth in the Student Center, not this accident." She frowned, "Although they're interviewing students so I'm sure people will mention Rachel's situation. I hope she's going to be okay."

"I'm just a security guy, not a doctor." Summers made a quick wry smile at his own Star Trek joke. "Depends how hard she hit her head, I guess. Tomorrow's gonna be a busy day if the TV crew draws people to campus."

"I appreciate you telling me in person, Andy." Sometimes Summers acted like a Midwestern version of her older brother, Keoni. Others, he seemed on the verge of asking her for a date.

Pausing a few seconds extra, his eyes again traveled from her head to her bare feet. Pointing at the corner, Summers bent down. "I'll take this back to the hardware store and trade it for ice melt." He hefted the rock salt bag onto his shoulder. "Trust me, you'll like it better."

"Thanks," she said, softly closing the door behind him.

All the peaceful, calm yoga energy she'd felt earlier had changed with Andy's news. Now too many variables were out of her control. For starters, Cassandra needed a plan to address the advocacy concerns. Then, she'd find a way to spin the latest news positively to Dr. Winters.

Chapter Five

Wide awake from drinking strong Kona coffee, Cassandra spent the early hours before the office opened studying online articles about the Deaf Community, Deaf rights, and emergency management software systems. There was so much to learn about accessibility before she saw Dr. Bryant again or met with Fischer or Winters.

"I'm heading out to a meeting," Cassandra told Devon, her student worker, soon after he arrived. "I don't have scheduled appointments, but if anyone walks in needing help right away, try Dr. Hansen." Cassandra tilted her head towards her officemate's closed office door.

"Sure," Devon looked up from his phone. "Have you seen how much Rachel's story has spread!"

"You mean yesterday's accident?" Cassandra zipped up her coat and pulled on knitted gloves. "Someone put that online?"

"Her roommate Sarah asked for prayers and then it just kind of took off from there." Devon showed her Sarah's post on his Facebook newsfeed. Over one hundred comments had been added by classmates and family.

Cassandra hoped Rachel's doctors were simply being cautious and careful.

Good thing she'd arranged a morning meeting with Lance Erickson before he left town for Thanksgiving break. Not only could he help Cassandra understand the advocacy project, he might know more about Rachel's medical condition.

As soon as the Student Center coffee shop's rich, hazelnut-roasted aromas hit her nose, Cassandra's stomach rumbled. Breakfast had been hours ago, and time for a real lunch wasn't guaranteed.

She ordered espresso and an apple muffin, then joined Meg at a wrought iron corner table. "Hey, there. What kind of teachable moment does Dr. Bryant think he's orchestrating? First my student workers got all wound up with glamorized civil rights stories. Now the AP and TV stations are involved. This news coverage is killing me."

Her long, wavy hair piled into a messy red bun, Meg's lightly freckled face smiled impishly, "Good Tuesday morning to you too, friend. How are you? I'm fine, thanks for asking. Although I'm a little worried about Rachel Nagle, as you obviously are too. I'm sure you meant to mention her before you got all hangry about being in the newspaper."

She and Meg had been friends for more than ten years and knew each other's personality quirks well. Cassandra had worked with Meg at their first real jobs at Oahu State College back when Meg and her husband, Connor, had been stationed in Hawai'i. Cassandra and her fiancé, Paul, had spent many days together with the O'Briens at Waimanalo Beach or hiking near Makapu'u. One of the best things about taking the job at Morton and moving to the middle of Nowhere, Nebraska, was spending time with them again.

"Maybe I'm antsy, but I've got a lot on my mind." Cassandra blew out a big sigh. "Rachel's interview in the newspaper started the whole thing. Then the word spread. Now my student worker just told me everyone's posting good thoughts and prayers for Rachel online."

"There's the compassionate, supportive vice prez I know and love."

"No, really. I hardly slept from worrying about Rachel. I'm hoping Lance can give us an update. Before he gets here, I thought you could clue me in on Bryant. Will I be able to work with him?"

Meg shrugged, "Bryant's a good guy. The Intro to Deaf Studies class teaches about the history of deaf people, their languages, and culture. The advocacy project required them to choose an issue they felt strongly about and plan events or social media campaigns to bring awareness to the topic. Dr. Bryant's role is strictly an advisory support person."

"I thought talking them out of boycotts or protests would be less disruptive for the college," grumbled Cassandra. "One little news article seemed so trivial. I never thought they'd make the national news."

"Dr. Bryant had a great new quote in that national AP article. Did you see it?" Meg thumbed open her phone and read aloud, "Equal access isn't a bunch of entitled whiners begging for extra favors. We demand access to the same basic human communication rights and services offered to the rest of the public."

Cassandra broke off a piece of muffin. "Look, I'm willing to learn about Deaf rights, but I can't change any policies before I understand the issues better. Bryant could have educated us all at the Diversity Council meeting last week instead of storming out."

"I wouldn't take that personally, if I were you," said Meg. "Bryant likes the occasional grand gesture to make his point. Sometimes drama is the only way to get attention."

"Well, now we have both drama and attention. So that isn't helping solve the situation."

Lance Erickson entered the coffee shop, then waved in Cassandra's direction when he noticed her and Meg. Tall and lanky, his puffy vest layered over a navy hoodie, Lance approached the serving counter, held up his phone, and pointed to the screen. The barista read his order and gave him a thumbs up before making his drink.

Cassandra was proud of how quickly Lance had stepped into a leadership role within the student government. Only a few weeks earlier, his roommate and childhood friend had passed away. Instead of letting it derail him from doing well for the semester, Lance had focused on bringing justice for his friend.

When Lance sat across from Cassandra, she signed, "Hi Lance. Thank you for meeting me here. I know you're busy."

She'd practiced maybe ten times in her office before walking over to the coffee shop. Cassandra's sign vocabulary was less than a toddler's grasp of the language, but she tried her best.

"I have a study group soon, but I can be a few minutes late."

Cassandra put her hands in her lap and nodded at Meg to take over interpreting. "Have you heard how Rachel's doing?"

"I texted her roommate Sarah this morning. She knows Rachel's brother, who said Rachel fractured her ankle when she fell plus the concussion." Lance shook his head. "The doctors put her under sedation all night. She must've really hit her head."

All three of them exchanged grim nods.

"I'm so sorry to hear that. I hope she feels better today." Cassandra's skin felt itchy with anxiety, but she needed to get control of herself. "I need to talk to you about the Deaf Studies advocacy booth before the TV crew comes here later today." Sipping her espresso, she nearly laughed at the irony of being over-caffeinated but attempting to chill. "I've read both the school newspaper and the national AP articles. I support making positive changes for students with disabilities, but we can't fix everything overnight."

"Your support means a lot." Lance paused to drink his coffee.

Cassandra opened her mouth, thinking his pause meant it was her turn to speak.

Instead, he put down his cup and signed, "No offense, Dr. Sato. But I'm not 'disabled.' I'm not broken or impaired. I prefer to communicate in ASL, but I can also use English. I've spent my life figuring out how to get around in the world with people who think that hearing is super important. Or that *I* should always be the one to adapt to *their* way of doing things. My ears don't work the same way yours do, but I'm fine. I can do anything."

Cassandra waited a few extra seconds after Meg stopped talking to make sure Lance was finished. "I'm sorry if I've offended—"

"I'm not offended, Dr. Sato. I think you really do want to help. If I didn't like you, I wouldn't tell you the truth. I'd just let you keep saying the same stupid things over and over without correcting you."

Wait, stupid things? She studied his expression. Lance didn't seem upset.

"I want the campus accessible for all students. I just need a little time," Working with him was hard because he experienced the world so differently than she did. "I told Rachel before she got hurt, and I'll tell you, too. The *Maple Leaf* reporter kind of overstated my ability to make policy decisions alone. I never promised Rachel could serve on the Diversity Council."

"I have just over two years left of school. I'm tired of waiting around for basic campus communications that should already be happening." Lance let out a sigh and checked the time on his phone. "We had no idea it would go national. We'd asked for these changes before you started working here, but nothing happened before."

"We're on the same side, Lance. But keep in mind today that going through proper negotiation channels will gain more administrative support than protest signs and dramatic TV interviews. In fact, I'm not even sure there will still be a Diversity Council once my new boss finds out about all of this news coverage."

"If negative newspaper or TV stories get it done, then I don't really care if your bosses like it or not." Lance's face was animated, but respectful.

Why did the people she was trying to help insist on doing things their own way instead of listening to her experienced, educated advice?

"I gotta go study." He zipped his vest and hoisted his backpack on his shoulder. "Logan's boycott idea to cut classes and change the world could make for a fun ending to the semester..." He smiled impishly, then waved good-bye and left the coffee shop.

Was he joking? Cassandra's face reddened, and she stared at Meg for a few moments.

Residual tension filled the silence between them. Even though she knew Meg did her job speaking what Lance signed, it was hard to separate the two in Cassandra's mind. Meg's personal opinion wasn't mixed in with Lance's words. But since it was her friend's voice speaking, it took an intentional act of will to keep them straight.

Meg broke the spell by taking a long pull from her coffee cup. In her normal voice, Meg said, "Sooo, who do you like for Friday's football game?"

Like an actor shedding their character, Meg became herself again in Cassandra's eyes.

Cassandra wrinkled her nose. "Which game? I'll cheer for Morton, of course."

"Nah... I meant Minnesota versus the Huskers," said Meg. "I love Morton, but... hello? Are you even listening to me?"

Cassandra frowned, "Sure, I am. Football, blah blah, Huskers, blah blah."

Slipping into her coat, Meg mimicked Cassandra by mouthing, "blah blah." Meg leaned sideways and gave Cassandra's three-inch heels and bare legs a long look. "You know about the severe weather watch, right? It's gonna snow this week."

"These are the work shoes I keep in my office." Cassandra raised a palm in exasperation. "Yes, everyone keeps talking about snow. But no one can tell me exactly when! I need to plan my schedule."

Meg and the others teased her for constantly asking about the weather and the temperature. They had no idea how many outfit changes she went through each morning trying to find the best combination of warm layers that could get her through an entire day and early evening. Just last week, she had arrived at work in the morning wearing a heavy sweater and skirt combo with thick tights and knee-high boots. By early afternoon, the sun had warmed the day up to 74 degrees. Walking across campus, sweat had dripped down Cassandra's back and torso, making her feel like she'd just finished an intense workout.

"You gotta ditch those shoes and wear the fuzzy boots we bought at the outlet mall."

Cassandra rolled her eyes. She'd seen snow before. She wasn't a complete winter novice.

Meg said, "Let's hope Lance and the students are just enjoying their moment in the spotlight. Probably they'll get distracted before they do anything rash."

"I can't count on that. I underestimated their story's popular appeal and had no idea my name would be included in the spotlight. I'm laying low until the new boss settles in."

* * *

By late afternoon, Cassandra had managed to steer clear of the TV news crew. She'd also ignored any phone messages that appeared to be from reporters. Now that Dr. Winters was in charge, she should field those phone calls. Cassandra wasn't sticking her neck out again so soon and have it chopped off.

She emptied her desktop piles enough to call Cinda for a media update. And she needed a quick, friendly distraction. They chatted for a few minutes about Thanksgiving—Cassandra's first holiday away from home—and the weather, while Cassandra scrolled though the Omaha newspaper feed on her iPad, seeing no mention about Morton.

"We'll have to watch the local evening news to see if anyone in the big city paid attention to Carson," said Cinda. "Wait! Here's a video still from the TV affiliate showing a group of people at the Deaf Studies booth this afternoon."

Cassandra tried to find the page but was much slower navigating.

"I sent you the link, Cass. The page counter shows 2,000 views already! They even made a hashtag #prayersforRachel." Cinda was quiet for a few seconds. "You'd better read the comments. Someone said Morton gave a public address announcement warning people about sleet and icy sidewalks, but never sent written warnings."

Cassandra waited to receive the link and thought back to Monday but didn't remember the morning announcements particularly. Used to the normally mundane bulletins, she often tuned them out. "Are we supposed to send written weather warnings? I thought people just looked at their phone apps." That's what she did.

"We don't warn people every time, but sometimes they mention it during announcements." Cinda laughed. "I got a voicemail from Rachel's mother. Wouldn't be surprised if she claims Morton should've cancelled classes because of the sleet."

"Shoot, it was pretty slippery for a while." She really didn't want to be on the helicopter mom's naughty list. "How often do we cancel classes during the winter?"

"Sweetie, this is Nebraska," Cinda drawled. "If we cancelled class every time it sleeted or dipped below freezing, there'd be no school from mid-November to April."

"Okay. Point taken." Cassandra closed her eyes. "Are we still on for drinks after work tomorrow?"

"If the creek don't rise."

Cassandra checked out her office window to see if it was raining again. "What creek? Does it flood in November?"

"Girl, you've gotta chill. It's just a Southern thing." Cinda laughed. "You're so literal."

Maybe Cassandra did take things too seriously, but online videos and parent complaints seemed worth worrying about.

Chapter Six

During the thirty-minute drive to Wahoo General Hospital, the nearest medical facility to Carson, Cassandra admitted her motivation for visiting Rachel wasn't 100% altruistic. Mostly, she wanted to see how badly her student was injured and provide support to the family. Truthfully, she also wanted to gauge how upset Mrs. Nagle was about the accident.

Turning a final corner down a maze of yellowed linoleum hallways, Cassandra pulled up short directly in front of room 321's open doorway. With no time to collect her thoughts or peek first, Cassandra put on her game face and extended her hand to the woman sitting in an armchair directly inside. "Good morning. I'm Cassandra Sato from Morton College. Are you Patty Nagle?"

Although the woman's hair was darker than Rachel's, the first words out of her mouth confirmed she was the notorious Mrs. Nagle. "It's about time someone from the college showed up here. Rachel's been in this God-forsaken dump for over 24 hours."

The dump in question was old and smelled like chemical disinfectant mixed with floral air freshener. Cassandra gazed at the bed where Rachel rested in dim light hooked up to two glowing monitors and an IV stand. A small patch of hair over her left ear had been shaved and covered with a gauze bandage. Multicolored circles under her closed eyes were tinged yellow around the edges.

"Ma'am, I came to see how Rachel was feeling and offer Morton's support for your family."

An unexpected memory squeezed Cassandra's stomach in a vice. Another hospital, another sleeping body on the bed. Machines beeping intermittently. Another distraught mother with dark, under-eye circles. All reminders that Cassandra hadn't stepped foot in a hospital room since her fiancé Paul Watanabe had died eight years earlier. Cassandra's breaths came in tiny sips, but it was too late to back out.

"I said that out loud, omigawd!" Mrs. Nagle covered her open mouth. "I'm so tired."

As beautiful as her daughter, upon closer inspection Cassandra noted Mrs. Nagle's red-rimmed eyes and pink edges of her nose where she'd wiped with a tissue until the skin was raw.

"My husband was out of the country for work. Weather delays in New York made him miss his connecting flight. The emergency room doctor looks seventeen years old, and that recliner," she pointed across the room at a burgundy vinyl chair whose lumpy, worn cushion was partially covered by a bunched-up pillow and institutional, beige blanket, "is older than I am, and feels like sleeping on a rock."

All the positive, cheery comments Cassandra had practiced in the car on the way over dried in her constricted throat like dust. Cinda had made Mrs. Nagle sound like a crazed control freak, but all Cassandra saw was a tired, helpless mother.

Cassandra held out the disposable coffee cup she'd brought with her and placed a small paper gift bag containing hand cream, lip balm, and granola bars on the bedside table. "Would you like some warm coffee? Have you had a chance to eat? I could bring you a sandwich from the cafeteria."

"No thanks, I couldn't eat. I'm waiting for the doctor to come through on rounds. They're supposed to wake Rachel up this afternoon."

Cassandra smiled encouragingly and prepared to sit quietly in support. Sometimes a shoulder to cry on was all you could offer.

Now that there was someone to listen, Mrs. Nagle wasted no time with idle chitchat. "I was so mad when I read that newspaper article about my daughter. Rachel's not deaf," she ranted. "The story made her look handicapped and pitiful. And she's not going blind either. She has a hard time in big crowds and loud restaurants. Heck, nowadays it seems like restaurants have all gotten louder with those high ceilings."

Her mother seemed out of touch with Rachel's frustrations. Cassandra said, "Rachel wants to make the world better for people who are deaf or hard of hearing. She's practicing advocating for what she needs."

"Rachel doesn't like being in the spotlight. I can't tell you how many times she's suffered an upset stomach or headache because she was allergic to food she was served but didn't want to complain or ask for a special diet plate. Rachel just needs to learn when to say no. Even in high school she joined every club possible."

"I thought it was brave of Rachel to speak up about an issue she feels strongly about."

Clear blue eyes widened in recognition. "That's right! You're the one who encouraged Rachel to spill her guts to the reporter. You and that professor."

The way she said "encouraged" made it sound like a curse. Cassandra's eyebrow went up. "Rachel told you she was pressured into the newspaper interview?"

"Rachel called home last week, excited about her project and the interview. I didn't realize she'd turn around and tell the whole world our private lives. I want to know who put her up to it. Rachel knew I grew up happy in my adopted family."

Regardless of what Mrs. Nagle believed, Cassandra had given Rachel neutral counsel. If anything, Rachel had told the reporter more than Cassandra had expected or wanted.

"Maybe I've held on too tightly. If it hadn't been for the scholarship, I wouldn't have let her go away to Morton. I thought she should stay home a year until she was more used to her... situation." The woman's face crumpled, and she plucked a tissue from the box on the mobile tray.

Wiping her eyes and nose, Mrs. Nagle sniffled, "I just want her to be safe. I don't know what I'd do if she—if she . . ."

Cassandra's heart still had a fiancé-sized hole that infinite time could not fill. Mrs. Nagle might be overprotective, but Cassandra totally identified with her fear of losing her precious daughter. "She'll get better, ma'am. You said yourself the doctors might wake Rachel up soon."

"You're right. I'm overreacting." Wrapping her arms over her chest, Mrs. Nagle heaved a big sigh. "Ever since junior high, when Rachel begged me to find out her grandparents' names, this has been a distraction. I never told her my mother's name was Susan Peters. She must've gone behind my back. If Rachel is determined to research our family's genetics and history, I'd support that. We could do it together. Not all over the internet for anyone to read."

Cassandra squirmed in her chair, knowing that Rachel had chosen Morton College specifically to research her grandparents' family histories. "We all want to support Rachel as best we can." Given what Cassandra had seen and heard, for Morton's legal benefit they needed to document that her fall was just an untimely accident. "If you don't mind, I'll contact the campus security director so he can take Rachel's statement when she wakes up."

"I understand. Sorry I'm such a hot mess." Mrs. Nagle had a way of always bringing the conversation back to herself. "Rachel must have known I'd disapprove. How could she do this to me? The doctors have assured me that they are just being cautious, and Rachel will be fine once she's had time to heal. Which is good. Because once she wakes up, I'm going to kill her."

* * *

Several hours later, Rachel was awake and talking. Cassandra was reading emails in the waiting room when Andy Summers appeared. She pointed the way to Rachel's room and followed him inside.

The hospital room was crowded. Rachel's father had arrived, and he stood by the elevated head of the bed. Next to him, Mrs. Nagle's hand rested on Rachel's shoulder. A nurse pushed a button on a monitor, straightened the IV tubing, then stepped out.

Rachel said, "Last thing I remember was walking down the ramp behind the ticket booth wall."

Andy said, "Can you start from the beginning, please?"

Slim, pale fingers tested the large bandage taped to her temple and she winced.

Rachel's roommate Sarah sat on Rachel's right side, holding her hand. Sarah asked, "So you don't know how you fell? Maybe from the ice?"

"My head is killing me, and y'all are giving me anxiety," Rachel said. "I don't remember everything yet. Omigod, I just woke up. Is there a mirror in here? This bump on my head feels like a baseball."

Truly it was sized more like an olive, but Rachel's brush with mayhem hadn't dampened her flair for the dramatic.

Brushing the blonde hair back from her daughter's forehead, Mrs. Nagle said, "Just try, dear. We need to know whose fault this is."

Now that Rachel was safe, her mother's focus had shifted from the newspaper's exposure of their family secrets to the accident itself. Leaning against the far wall, Cassandra took a long, slow breath. She wanted to hear this all first-hand. Cinda had laughed off her concerns about the weather making conditions dangerous, but she couldn't stand the possibility that Morton could have done more to prevent this incident.

Rachel ducked to the side to avoid her mother's hand. "I'm fine. Except for the headache. And how am I going to get around to classes with crutches?"

"I'll carry your books for you," Sarah volunteered.

"So, you left class at 5:00 p.m.?" Summers prompted, "Was it dark outside?"

Rachel frowned, "Not completely dark but getting there. The streetlights were on. I could see the path where I was walking. That damn dog scared me."

"What dog?"

Cassandra hadn't heard anything about a dog.

"Yeah, I was heading to my car to get some dinner. I planned to study all night for my Anthropology test." Rachel's hand moved up to cover her mouth, but the IV tubes stopped her progress. "Oh no! I missed my Anthropology test! Crap, I'm going to have to make that up."

Mrs. Nagle patted her daughter's arm. "Language, Rach. I can call your professor, dear. I'm sure he'll excuse you for a medical emergency. I'll talk to him for you."

Rachel pulled her arm out from under her mother's hand and rolled her eyes like a frustrated thirteen-year-old. "Mom! Will you stop calling my professors. Please. I can do it."

She mouthed "omigod" to Sarah and flicked her eyes upward as if to say, "Told you so."

Summers coughed uncomfortably. He seemed to want to get the questioning done quickly and run away from any family drama. He nodded at Rachel and motioned for her to keep talking.

"I hate walking across campus in the dark. I had my car keys ready." Rachel held up a fist like she had keys poking out between her fingers. "I was walking fast, but it was misty and kinda snowy earlier, so I was careful. I always look around and behind me for creepy guys."

Mrs. Nagle interjected, "Good for you, honey. But I thought we talked about always walking with a buddy at night."

"Mom, usually I do. But it wasn't really dark yet. And no one else needed to go to their cars." Rachel squinted hard at her mother. "Wait. Are you saying this is *my* fault? I'm the victim here, remember?"

Her father hadn't said a word. He just looked back and forth between Mrs. Nagle and Rachel like a tennis match.

"Anyway," Rachel resumed her story, her face more animated, "As I got closer to the hill, I heard loud barking. I mean it had to be loud if I could hear it, right?" She shrugged sheepishly. "I couldn't see him behind the bushes, but he sounded big."

Cassandra pictured the area Rachel described. The football stadium and main parking lot were downhill from the main campus buildings clustered around the quadrangle of green space in the middle. At the top of the hill, the wide sidewalk split leading either north towards the stadium or south to parking. "I've seen stray dogs around campus, and I don't need rabies, right? I pulled out my phone to call for help. But with the keys and my backpack, my hands were full," said Rachel. "I dropped the phone, and the screen cracked. You guys, it was so scary. I'm like, worried about getting raped but instead I was gonna get attacked by a dog."

Cassandra felt herself leaning forward.

"I didn't see the ice on the path until I stepped on it. I swear, something hit me hard. I slipped."

Patty Nagle's hand flew up to cover her mouth. Her eyes watered up listening to her daughter's story.

Rachel shrugged, "I don't remember falling or anything after that until I woke up here."

Summers quickly captured her words in his pocket notebook, and he let the silence stretch while he finished writing. "You felt something hit you. Did you see what it was"

"I know it sounds weird." Rachel's palms turned up on her lap. "I thought I was the only one walking that way, but there was someone else."

Summers finished writing and handed her his card. "Please call me if you remember anything more. I hope you feel better soon, Rachel."

Mrs. Nagle petted Rachel's shoulder, "It's not your fault, honey. The sidewalk was icy."

Cassandra's eyebrows lifted. The Nagle family probably had a lawyer. This was bad.

"Accidents happen," Summers said.

"You're not listening. I told you I didn't fall by accident," Rachel insisted with more confidence. "I was pushed."

Cassandra had assumed a lawsuit was the worst-case scenario. She felt upended, like when that big wave had swept her off her feet at the beach when she was eight. It had filled her lungs with saltwater until she'd fought her way to the surface.

Her mouth set in a hard line, Cassandra resolved to figure out who hurt Rachel and why. Cassandra was even more stubborn now than she'd been as a child. The only way back to shore was to swim, and she wouldn't stop until she had answers.

Chapter Seven

Cassandra returned to her office from the hospital by 1:00 p.m., pleased to find three student workers decorating posters for an upcoming intramural basketball tournament. Since it was the day before Thanksgiving, most students had already gone home, and she'd planned to close a couple hours early.

She'd arranged to meet with Dr. Bryant before he left for the day, thinking she could research more over the long weekend. Lance waved hello and resumed hand-lettering posters on the large worktable.

"Sarah posted a Snap picture to our office group. Rachel looks pretty banged up." Logan organized stacks of paperwork into team piles. "Seriously, someone pushed her?"

"You saw her, Dr. Sato. What'd you think?" Haley stood near the large copier.

"She was awake and talking. She said someone pushed her." Cassandra raised a shoulder. "The police will investigate and look for evidence."

Lance looked up and frowned.

Logan fingerspelled, "R-A-C-H-E-L" and did a palms-up shrug.

"This is so eerie," said Haley, "It's like a mystery!"

"Does that make you Nancy Drew and me one of the Hardy boys?" Logan said. "I'm Frank. I guess that makes you J-O-E." He fingerspelled Joe and pointed at Lance. Using his phone, Logan showed him a photo of a book cover for *The House on the Cliff.*

Lance smiled and typed, "Frank was too bossy."

"Everyone knows Nancy Drew was smarter than the boys," said Haley. "But the Hardy boys got to do more fun stuff, like outsmart art thieves and be secret government agents."

Cassandra's first instinct was to brush off their jokes, but maybe they knew something helpful. "Do you know of anyone who was mad at Rachel? Or bullying her?"

"Maybe she was just in the wrong place at the wrong time," said Logan.

Lance fingerspelled T-J and nodded at Logan.

Logan said, "Lance thinks a kid named T.J. was bothering Rachel. She said something a few weeks back about a fraternity formal that didn't end well."

Cassandra made a note in her journal to find him.

* * *

Dead leaves puddled at the base of the Student Center doorway where Cassandra met Meg. Nearly late, they hurried into the coffee shop without talking. Cassandra smiled as she slid into the booth after Meg and faced

Shannon Bryant. His impeccably groomed hair, dress shirt, and preppy sweater-vest were out of place with the sweat pant and hoodie-wearing students, as well as the frumpy middle-aged faculty and staff scattered around the seating area.

Cassandra had been tongue-tied at Bryant's confident aura the first couple of times he'd attended meetings with her. She was used to him now and the way female students stopped talking and stared at him quietly when he entered a room.

"Where do you want to start?" Bryant signed and Meg interpreted his ASL into spoken English. He didn't waste time on pleasantries.

Good. Talking about the weather only made Cassandra anxious anyway. "Thanks for meeting me, Dr. Bryant. Like I mentioned in my message, I wanted to learn more about your concern in our last Diversity Council meeting about Morton's lack of inclusiveness for students and staff who are deaf or hard of hearing."

"You read the newspaper article," he signed. "None of Morton's public communications are captioned, and there's no emergency alert or 9-1-1 text system. It's more than an inconvenience. Obviously, it's a safety issue."

"I'd definitely like to work with you and the students to upgrade our systems and provide better access. But for Rachel Nagle, the ice wasn't the issue. I saw Rachel this morning in the hospital. She said she was pushed."

His jaw tightened. "Someone pushed her?"

"I'm checking into it further. Could it have anything to do with the Deaf Studies class project? There've been rumors this semester about demonstrations and student disruptions."

"Advocating for equal access to their education isn't disruptive," signed Bryant.

Did he know her student workers had considered using smoke grenades and class boycotts? "So you don't know of anyone who disliked Rachel? Have you received threats against anyone working on the class project?"

Bryant's face shifted from watching Meg to giving Cassandra a deep frown. "Threats? None that I know of."

"Good. I'd appreciate it if you'd think about it more and let me know of anything suspicious." Cassandra looked back in her journal notes. "I'll research the emergency alert systems before our next council meeting. I'd like to meet again to discuss the project and other ways we can work together."

Bryant nodded.

"And do we always need an interpreter when we meet? Can we write notes, or maybe you read lips, too?"

"Not to be a jerk, but that's an example of you thinking of me in terms of dollar signs or as disabled. I resent that," signed Bryant. "You want me to read your lips or write in English because that's what you're comfortable with and it costs less money, right?"

Cassandra felt she was walking into a trap but didn't know what she'd said that was wrong. She plunged ahead. "Kind of. I just thought that if Meg was busy and we wanted to talk, maybe we could email instead or sit and write or type to each other?"

"Email's fine, but you're missing my point. Using American Sign Language as my preferred language to communicate does not make me disabled." Bryant leaned forward and took a pull from his coffee. Setting it down, his dark brown eyes homed in on hers directly. "It makes me bilingual," he signed. "I use English every day to negotiate the world. The fact is, *you're* the one at this table at a disadvantage." Bryant stopped signing and tilted his head towards Meg.

In the several beats of silence that followed, Cassandra looked back and forth between the two. "Yeah, I get it. I can't sign but you both can," she said. "When you two get going so fast, I can't even guess what you're saying. If you'd sign to me like a three-year-old, I could probably keep up."

Meg broke eye contact with Bryant to look at Cassandra, who sat up straighter. "I meant that sarcastically, eh?" Cassandra vaguely waved a hand in the air between Meg and Bryant. "You folks can do sarcasm in sign language?"

Meg's right eye squinted at her, and Cassandra leaned away in case an elbow was going to be shoved into her ribs.

Straight-faced, Bryant said, "No. We can't."

When Cassandra stared at his expressionless face for a few seconds, he frowned and shook his head. "Of course we can do sarcasm. We're not tapping out Morse Code. ASL is a language for God's sake! Trust me, deaf people's lives are filled with irony and sarcasm, and we are experts at conveying it in our language."

Cassandra liked to think of herself as inclusive and progressive. But every time she tried to understand why Bryant was upset, she just drew a blank. She needed his expertise and participation on the Diversity Council as much as she needed to avoid costly lawsuits.

"Forgive my ignorance, Dr. Bryant, but why are you so angry?" Cassandra asked him. "I've learned about ASL and Deaf Culture from my friendship with Meg, but no matter what I say or do, I feel like you think it's not good enough."

Bryant responded, "I never said I don't appreciate you trying. You know more signs than 90% of the hearing people I know. Does that mean I should thank you every time we have a two-minute exchange?"

Cassandra flung out her hand in frustration. "What I don't understand is why you get so upset with us hearing people? Like you said before, you deal with us every day."

"How many times since you've moved to Nebraska has someone met you for the first time and politely asked where you're from?" Bryant countered.

"*What?* Uhh... a couple of times a day. Depends." What did this have to do with his class project or the council? "Why do you ask?"

"Doesn't it get old when people assume that because you look Asian, you must not be from here? Plenty of Nebraskans with Japanese ethnicity were born in this state. How do the white people know you grew up somewhere else, and how many of them assume it was a foreign country instead of our 50th state?"

He wasn't wrong. In the past four months, she'd been asked where she was *from* more than she had her entire previous 34 years. "It's not like I wear muumuus and a flower in my hair every day," she nodded. Pausing a few moments, Cassandra gathered her thoughts. "I guess I thought something about me looked or sounded like I'm not from here. I don't think I have an accent, but I must do something different."

"Maybe you haven't been in Nebraska long enough for the constant questions to get old. I've been deaf my whole life. Most days I understand that people who can hear have never or rarely met a deaf person before, and they're curious what my life is like." Bryant leaned back in the booth. "If I had a dollar for every time someone asked me if I can lipread, I'd live in a mansion and drive a Corvette."

Cassandra connected the dots. "So you're saying you get mad because people ask you the same questions over and over?"

"Have you ever turned off the sound on your TV and tried to watch the news? You'd be lucky to understand 25% of the content. Not every deaf person reads lips. It's hard. And inaccurate."

She could see she'd hit a nerve. "Ok..."

Bryant was in teachable moment mode. "Wouldn't you appreciate it if people got to know you for five minutes before assuming you'd just stepped off a plane from Japan? For once, I wish people would respect my individuality instead of assuming deaf people are all the same."

Cassandra's mouth clamped shut while she processed his logic. She tried catching Meg's eye to get some clue of where this conversation had gone off the rails, but Meg was stubbornly looking at Bryant instead.

"I went to a mainstreamed high school. Which means I was one of two deaf students in the whole school. Everyone else was hearing, and I had an interpreter in my classes. My favorite sport was wrestling, and I was the 170-pound state runner-up my senior year." Bryant took another swig of coffee and smiled at his memory.

"At the winter sports banquet, my coach shared the story that when I first made the team as a freshman, he had called my father. Coach wanted to know how to communicate with me and teach me to become a better wrestler. At first, I was stunned. No one had mentioned that to me in four years. I was even kind of mad they'd gone behind my back. Later I realized the Coach had thought I was good enough to warrant the extra work to make me wrestle well."

His coach sounded like a good guy. "Aren't we saying the same thing," Cassandra said. "In order for students and faculty on campus to appreciate the diversity of others, they first have to get to know folks on a personal level. Remember the brainstorming we did at the first Diversity Council meeting? The college's role is to provide the venue and encouragement for students to get to know others who are different than themselves."

Their meeting wrapped up a few minutes later, and Cassandra watched Bryant and Meg walk away signing. Bryant had given Cassandra a lot to consider and research over break. He said he'd review his Deaf Studies class roster and think about who'd want to work against their advocacy project. She'd promised to bring an interpreter the next time they met. They had shaken hands before parting, but Cassandra felt uneasy about their relationship and uncertain whether the college was negligent regarding Rachel's injuries.

Chapter Eight

Already wearing her coat and carrying her tote bag, Cassandra had one last stop before meeting her friends after work. Dr. Winters needed to be in the loop. Julie's desk was empty, but the inner door was open, and a 60s Motown song drifted into the darkened lobby.

Knocking loudly on the doorframe, Cassandra smiled and tried to catch Dr. Winters' attention. She stood on a low stool shelving several books on the white wooden bookcase, her hips swaying to the music while she sang along. After several seconds, Winters looked her way. "Dr. Sato! You're still here? I thought everyone had already gone home."

Grateful that Winters remembered her this time, Cassandra moved closer to the desk in the middle of the spacious office. "I was just leaving but wanted to check in with you first. Are you aware that a student fell near the football stadium on the sidewalk Monday?"

Stepping off the stool, Winters scooped another armful of books out of the box on her desk. "Julie mentioned it yesterday, I believe. Accidents happen, I'm afraid."

"Here's the thing. She's a student worker in my office and I went to see her this morning at the hospital. She fractured her ankle and had a concussion. She's feeling better now but says someone pushed her on purpose."

A small gasp escaped Dr. Winters and her hand fluttered to her chest.

Immediately a raspy, snarling bark sounded and Cassandra startled. Her eyes widened when a furry white form separated from the white rug under the desk. The creature barked again, scrambling to stand at Winters' feet.

"Your . . . dog??" She pointed, confused.

What was her ill-tempered mutt doing in the presidential suite? And couldn't Winters make him stop sniffing Cassandra's grey suede pumps?

"Don't worry, Murphy's all bark but he only gets nervous around small children. You're pretty tiny, but you know better than to make any quick movements to pet him, right?"

Cassandra nodded, her eyes glued to the beady eyes and black nose over snarling teeth. "The security director has already taken the student's statement for his incident report. He'll investigate the episode."

"That's most unfortunate about the poor girl's injury." Winters set the books down and told Murphy to stay. A warm palm on Cassandra's shoulder guided her towards the door. "Thanks for letting me know. I'll send an email to my church prayer chain right away asking for her healing."

Although prayers were nice, Cassandra was hoping for more tangible action from the college president. "President Winters—"

Winters interrupted, "Let's hope her accident doesn't make the evening news. Morton has had plenty of publicity already this week, wouldn't you agree, Cassandra?"

So Winters did know about the viral AP article. Probably she'd seen the news truck yesterday, too. "If someone intentionally hurt the student, I'm worried what could happen next."

"And again, you seem to find yourself in the center of the news storm. Just like last month and the science lab situation. This has got to stop. It's almost like you seek ways to be noticed."

Winters' first impressions were all wrong. Cassandra valued her privacy. She needed a do-over to prove that she sought collaboration, not self-promotion. Dr. Winters cared about how it looked more than student safety.

* * *

Cassandra folded her thick, hooded parka and pushed it towards the wall, scooting all the way into the red leather booth. She'd forgotten to wear gloves, but luckily the jacket Meg had helped her buy from the outlet mall had deep, warm pockets and a fur-lined hood.

Carson's only sports bar was decorated in local high school memorabilia, Morton College jerseys and team photos, and Nebraska Husker fan items. Cozy and humble, it had become the place where Cassandra and her friends decompressed.

"I just came from Dr. Winters' office." Cassandra rubbed her chilly hands together and noticed her skin was drier than usual. "She thinks I'm an attention seeking diva."

Their drinks and a popcorn basket arrived.

"Winters called you a diva?"

Meg had found a booth with a view of the TVs mounted above the immense, dark wooden bar at The Home Team. Owner Margie Gallagher had once told Cassandra about its origin. Her Irish immigrant ancestor had brought the bar in several pieces cross-country from Philadelphia in a covered wagon and then pieced it back together to open this establishment. Three generations later, the menu had changed, and the booths had been replaced, but the main bones of the old brick building were intact.

"Not exactly, but she knows about the viral Deaf Studies article and that my name was mentioned specifically as someone who helped their cause."

Cassandra scooped popcorn into her mouth. "How's my favorite baby?"

Meg patted her belly where the slightest baby bump was beginning to show under her black sweater. "Squirmy. We're both good."

A few moments later, Cassandra frowned when she realized Meg's attention was fixed behind Cassandra's head towards the end of the bar. She checked over her right shoulder to see what she was missing.

Three men wearing heavy winter coats sat at the far corner of the bar, heads together, playing a trivia game on a small screen. The guy farthest away looked about sixty with a blue stocking hat, his weathered face lined from years working outside. The middle guy was so heavy, his behind spilled over the sides of the wide barstool. One leg extended to the floor where his cowboy-booted foot rested in a small pile of peanut shells. While she looked, he broke open another shell, popped the nuts into his mouth, and tossed the husks over his shoulder to the wood floor. The third man had his back to Cassandra, but she recognized the army-instilled posture and dark wavy hair that spilled over onto the collar of his jacket. His right hand rested comfortably on his thigh and the other held a beer bottle to his mouth. Marcus Fischer.

The older guy said something so funny the other two laughed loudly, the Peanut Guy spilled his beer, and Fischer jumped off his stool to avoid the splash.

Cassandra quickly looked back at Meg and shifted her shoulders a bit so Fischer might not catch her staring if he turned around right then.

Meg winked at her, "Subtle. Very nice. Uh ... why are we hiding from Fischer?"

"I'm not hiding from Fischer. I hadn't planned to meet him tonight, that's all. I'm here to see you and Cinda."

No sooner had Cassandra spoken when Cinda herself breezed through the front door bringing a gust of chilly air. Cinda walked past several other full tables to their booth and slid in next to Meg. Nodding towards the bar, Cinda smiled, "I'll have a Gin and Tonic and a hot Maintenance VP, please."

For someone working in career and counseling services, Cinda said remarkably inappropriate things about male colleagues when she was with friends.

Meg laughed, "Your husband might have an opinion on any extra hot men around your house. Cassandra's avoiding Fischer today, though. So don't make any embarrassing moves."

Before Cassandra could even scoff properly, Cinda popped back up again and approached the bar. The dark-haired bartender took her drink order while Cinda turned her back towards Fischer and pals and made juvenile kissy-face pouts at Cassandra and Meg.

"Why did I think it sounded fun to relax with friends at the beginning of our long weekend? Going out with you two is like reliving seventh grade."

It had been a stressful week. She should have just gone home, eaten leftovers, and watched Netflix.

Cinda returned to the table with her drink and a basket of peanuts. "Sooo ... how's Rachel doing? I got your text that she said someone knocked her down."

"No one said when Rachel will go home, but she was awake and gave a statement. At first, I was worried her family would sue the college, but now I wonder why someone would hurt her."

"Nothing that Helicopter Momzilla could do would surprise me. I don't think I told you about last week." Cinda rolled her eyes. "Mrs. Nagle called because she couldn't figure out how to pull up Rachel's course schedule online. I told her 'well, ma'am that information is private, so unless your daughter has given you her personal username and password, you can't see her schedule.' Mrs. Nagle has that phone app that lets her see where Rachel's phone GPS is, but she wanted to match it up to Rachel's schedule. To follow whether she's actually attending class, studying in the library, or goofing off."

Meg's jaw dropped, and Cassandra shook her head in disbelief.

Cinda said, "I don't know the real app name, but I call it iStalker. When I told her, 'Sorry you'll have to wait until your daughter is available to give you that information herself,' Mrs. Nagle did a big HUFF and hung up the phone on me."

"Yikes." Meg laughed. "I'm so glad I attended college before smartphones."

"Rachel's mother might be difficult, but we need to figure out who'd want to hurt Rachel. My work study students mentioned that Rachel had a run in with a guy at a frat party." Cassandra scooped a handful of popcorn and gestured at Meg. "Dr. Bryant said he'd think about if anyone in class disliked her enough to hurt her."

Meg wrinkled her freckled nose. "Maybe Rachel's wrong and it was just an accident. The sidewalk was slippery. For years, Morton has done these verbal announcements over the PA system, but never provided an equivalent message in print."

"I'm going to research newer emergency systems."

"The Student Center TVs could post captioned messages. You can have text alert systems that send out messages to anyone who subscribes."

"I want to know how Rachel got hurt, but I just learned of this advocacy project." Cassandra had assumed Meg would understand the constraints she was working under. "We haven't had time to implement anything new."

"Well, I've been here for years. Morton is really behind the current technology," said Meg. "Deaf and hard of hearing people have a right to know information at the same time that others find out. For them, that means print, captions, or texts. My point is that if you warn the hearing people verbally, how do the deaf people find out? You didn't know about the accessibility issue, but it's not the first time it's ever been suggested here."

Only last month they'd had plenty of scrutiny from parents, the board, and media for a student's untimely death. "I'm doing the best I can with the information I have right now."

"We know you are. Let me know what I can do to help," said Cinda.

"One more thing." Cassandra leaned towards the middle of the table. "Dr. Winters is kind of odd. Like remember I told you she met me four times before she remembered me?"

"Apparently you're not as memorable as you thought," said Meg. "You'll have to do something distinctive to stand out next time you talk to her. Like wear a muumuu and lei."

"I'm serious here. Winters leaves me super long voicemails at 5:00 a.m. Not a big sleeper, I'm guessing. She wasn't happy about the public criticism of Morton." She raised her eyebrows.

Cinda's eyes got super wide. "Dr. Winters, bless her heart, took matters into her own hands to stop the Deaf Studies project!" Her dramatic voice echoed Cassandra's own thoughts, but her tone dripped with sarcasm.

"Are you saying Dr. Winters, our college president, was involved in assaulting Rachel? What's wrong with you two?" Meg rolled her eyes. "No one likes public criticism but let's be logical." She held up her phone. "When did Winters even start working? Today's November 25th. Rachel was hurt on November 23rd."

"Our *interim* college president," Cassandra corrected. She tapped her phone calendar's appointment times and dates. "I met her last Friday the 20th, but I'm not sure exactly when she was hired."

"That would've been the same day the first newspaper article in the *Maple Leaf* was published." Cinda said, "Before it went viral on the national news."

"Right," said Cassandra. "She read that article and knew Rachel was the face of the advocacy project. Winters wanted to stop her before Morton's reputation was tarnished. I told you she takes her job as steward of the college very seriously. She once told me she wouldn't have allowed the cancer research lab thing to have gotten so much press last month like President Nielson did. She's a micro manager."

Meg squinted. "Do you hear yourselves? It took her four times to remember you, Cass, but she instantly remembers Rachel? Winters is a micro-manager, not a thug. You both need a vacation."

Cinda crossed her arms. "She is kind of old."

"Cass, you need to chill. Forget your fantasies about Dr. Winters thinking she's Wonder Woman."

Cinda patted Cassandra's forearm gently. "Oh well. Keep tryin', sweetie."

Cassandra's lips formed a hard line. She'd thought talking to friends would help her know what to do next. Instead she felt more unsure than before. And though she had plans to spend Thanksgiving dinner with the O'Brien family, she dreaded the homesickness that was sure to arise from a long weekend away from work.

Again, Cassandra noticed Meg's eyes shift to the bar.

Meg nudged Cassandra's knee under the table. "Incognito, no more, my Hawaiian sistah! Fischer's off the stool and lookin' around the room."

Meg smiled and waved vigorously. "He's coming this way. Wait . . . no, he's answering a phone call. He's walking towards the bathroom hallway with a finger in his other ear. Are we too loud? Is it another woman?"

Cinda smirked and whispered into Meg's ear.

Cassandra scooted her knees together out of the way of Meg's boots and ran a quick hand over her hair to make sure no big strays had fallen out of her bun. "I may be new in town, but I'm not so desperate for friends that I can't replace you two."

While they both sipped quietly from their drinks and ate popcorn, Cassandra's stomach tightened in anticipation. Their silence was only a pretense. Who knew what they'd do next.

Watching Meg's eyes, Cassandra knew when Fischer had returned, and that he was headed straight for their table. His face was unexpectedly serious when he appeared on her right side and sat uninvited next to her in the booth, bringing his woodsy scent with him. "My office called. There was a parent complaint about unsafe sidewalk conditions."

Cassandra told him about Rachel's allegation that someone pushed her.

"Sounds like Patty Nagle aka Momzilla is covering all her bases." Cinda was totally biased against that woman. "I can hear her now, 'I entrusted my daughter's safety to Morton.'" Her voice sounded eerily close to Mrs. Nagle's. "'There's a psychopath prowling campus, preying on unsuspecting freshmen.'"

Meg scoffed. "By pushing them on the icy walkways?"

Cinda held up both her hands.

"Monday wasn't a real snowstorm." Fischer frowned. "There's not much we can do about sudden freezing rain. I wonder why they're making a big deal about it. Students trip or fall sometimes."

Cassandra filled him in on the Deaf Studies student advocacy project. "The students in the class learn how to present their concerns to decision makers and convince them to make changes on campus. One of their suggestions is to make all the closed-circuit TVs in the public spaces accessible with updated messages."

Fischer nodded slowly. "Sure, we can turn on the subtitles on the TVs pretty easily. I'm not sure who updates the calendar events or other messages. Maybe someone from Communications or Marketing? I can check."

Meg pointed towards the large screen TV over the bar. "When we started coming here after work, that was my first request to Mrs. Gallagher. No point watching a silent TV in a noisy bar when we can read the captions and know what they're saying."

"Except when the little words overlap the football field and I can't see who's running with the ball," added Fischer.

Meg threw a piece of popcorn towards him, and Fischer opened his mouth and caught it perfectly.

"I'll check the logbooks showing what chemicals were applied on the sidewalks by the stadium and when." Fischer stood, buttoned his navy wool pea coat, and pulled a knit hat over his ears. "I'd better go."

Good. They'd need those logbooks if it came to a lawsuit.

Cinda drawled, "Oh, hey before y'all leave. I want to invite you to my house Friday. We're hosting a Husker football watch party. Cassandra's coming."

Showing remarkable restraint, Cassandra did not groan or smack a hand over her eyes. Fischer and she had been on one semi-awkward date, and these two acted like they were an official couple.

Cassandra felt her no-romance resolve crumbling in the face of spending her first holiday weekend far from home. She did not have time or energy for a serious relationship. Men were too much work. Even hot ones with translucent blue eyes. Cassandra glanced down at the table, trying to quell the tingly zip she felt under his gaze.

Fischer's smile made the corners of those eyes crinkle. "I think that'll work. Thanks for the invite. When's the game?"

Cinda said, "2:30 kickoff. Jacob's smoking a pork butt. Hopefully this time he'll remember to plug in the smoker."

There were now a few things to look forward to this weekend. Dinner with her local ohana tomorrow, soaking up authentic Nebraska football culture on Friday, and Saturday she'd research severe weather and emergency management systems. Draining the last of her beer, Cassandra conceded this outing was better than leftovers and Netflix after all.

Chapter Nine

Although Cassandra rarely slept in and never backed out of plans, by the time she was fully awake Thursday morning she was tempted to give up and stay in bed.

In the deepest level of sleep, she'd felt strong arms holding her close as her head rested on Paul's chest listening to his beating heart. Stretching in contentment, she had risen slowly through sleep layers, like peeling back a gauzy film.

One step up from a deep sleep, she was on the phone with Paul, listening to him cough. He'd been sick for a few days. "My back is sore, eh? But my throat feels betta today."

"I'll bring you umeboshi and hot tea. Maybe take some ibuprofen."

"I'm fine. My mom can bring it. Don't you have exams?"

"Ya, okay den," she said. "I'll stop after class and bring you soup. 'Bye now."

Up another layer, the next scene was a hospital room filled with family. Paul's dark head unmoving on his pillow. Machines flashing, IV tubes connected to his arm.

The scene splintered when a heavy pressure crushed her heart, emptying her lungs. Suddenly she was completely awake, breathless, and disoriented.

Panting, her eyes darted between the curtained window, her dresser, and her nightstand until Cassandra's consciousness caught up to her surroundings.

She crumpled back into the pillow and pulled the quilt over her head, weeping. Paul had waited too long to get help. And she hadn't urged him to see the doctor until it was too late. She missed his laugh. He'd never let Cassandra take herself too seriously.

She hadn't had that dream for months. Pretty sure yesterday's hospital visit had triggered her long-buried regrets. How could she help anyone else if she couldn't even solve her own problems?

* * *

Hours later, Cassandra opened the laptop on her galley kitchen counter and connected to FaceTime. Five years away from home stretched out before her like forever. It would be so easy to quit now and return to her old life. Her job at Morton had seemed like a dream come true, but quickly the nightmare had gone from bad to worse. The only people who could talk her down from the ledge were her parents, but admitting she was wrong would cost her.

"Aloha, Mom! Did you get my pictures of the snowy rain this week?" She forced a cheerful smile when her mother's face appeared on the screen.

"Aloha! Yes, I saw them. Did you have to shovel? Have you stayed inside all week? Daddy's out back working on the turkey."

"Nah, it wasn't that bad. Just slippery for a while."

Her mother's laptop was set up on the lanai's picnic table. Bright pink flowers in lush bushes framed the scene behind her head.

Waiting for the oven to preheat, Cassandra mixed enough flour and salt together for two pie crusts. She carefully stirred in vegetable oil and ice-cold water with a fork until the dough held together. Seeing her aunty's neat handwritten block letters on the recipe card cemented the connection with home.

"Your father and I once visited Seattle in February during a big snowstorm. After three days, I was ready to come home to the warm sun and beaches."

"I didn't know what to expect but Nebraska's landscape is surprisingly beautiful. In a different way. I did slip a little on the sidewalk though. I bought boots for walking to work in the snow. They have da kine with rubber bottoms here."

"You may think snow is beautiful now," her mom said. "But come March, you're going to want to come home."

"Ya, maybe when you come visit in March, we'll still have snow on the ground and you'll get to see it, too. Where's Daddy? How's the boys and grandma?"

"Grandma had a bad week. She got dehydrated. She's more forgetful when she's sick. When I went to see her Sunday, she didn't even know who I was. But she's the most stubborn woman I've ever known, so I'm sure she'll be back to her old cranky self soon. So what else happened this week?"

"Remember my boss retired? They found a temporary boss until they hire someone new."

"Wasn't he the nice man that hired you?"

"Yeah. He's still nice, but he wanted to be retired."

"Can you be the new boss now?"

Cassandra laughed. "No, they brought in a lady who used to be a professor at Morton."

"She sounds old."

"She's older than you, but she's only staying while they look for a new president. We got off to a rocky start. She thinks I'm a kid." Cassandra heard the whining in her voice but complaining to her mom made her feel better.

"Cassandra." The serious tone of her mother's voice made Cassandra's neck hairs raise in alarm. "To a seventy-year old woman with a lifetime of experience, you *are* a kid. She's your elder. You could learn from her wisdom if you'd stop worrying about your hurt feelings."

Cassandra's eyes widened and her jaw dropped. How dare her mother accuse her of disrespecting an elder? Hadn't Cassandra personally spoon-fed her Gran for months of dinners?? After her stroke?

Dr. Winters had simply waltzed into Morton's presidential office and issued orders without asking what already worked.

Stung, Cassandra knew not to argue this point. When it came to respecting elders, her mother didn't care if the elder in question was making Cassandra's life difficult. She'd expected talking to her family would make her feel better, not worse.

After placing both pies in the oven, Cassandra set the timer and moved the laptop screen so she could sit at the kitchen table to wrap the O'Briens' hostess gift. She tried another topic. "Did the boys like their birthday gifts?" Cassandra had missed her nephews' birthday party. "Did they fit?"

Cassandra had sent both of Keoni's keiki Morton College and Nebraska Cornhuskers t-shirts for their birthdays.

"Oh yes, that was perfect. They put on the new shirts right away after the party."

In a blue gift bag, she placed Honolulu Cookie Company shortbread cookies, SpongeBob pajamas, and a DVD that Cassandra had bought for their son, Tony.

Secretly, she hoped Tony would invite her to cuddle on the couch and watch the SpongeBob DVD with him between the turkey and dessert courses. She couldn't see her nephews today, but *Mermaid Man and Barnacle Boy* would make her Tony's Favorite Aunty, too.

Her mother asked, "Any hot dates this week?"

Cassandra dropped the pajamas in her hands and leaned over to peer at the laptop screen more closely. Her mother's face was serious, not teasing.

"When would I have time for hot dates? What with shoveling acres of snow, working all day, and hiding in my blissfully warm house all night. How would I meet anyone to date?" How did mothers have that sixth sense? Cassandra hadn't once mentioned going out with anyone.

"Don't you sass me, young lady. I can still come over there and smack your head."

Cassandra made a big smile straight into the camera. "Only if you want to waste a 14-hour day traveling."

"Is that the real reason you moved so far away? To avoid my wrath?" her mother teased.

"Oh yeah, Mom. You're a real scary woman. EEK." Cassandra rolled her eyes.

Michiko Sato wasn't 100 pounds soaking wet, and Cassandra was maybe ten pounds heavier. Neither of them would ever be known for their superhuman strength. Although her mom's Stink Eye could stop a grown man in his tracks and make him slink away. That was *her* superpower.

"You get high temperature today of 52, eh? We're expecting 78. We going to the park with Keoni's wife's ohana. Daddy's making the Kahlua Turkey."

Cassandra's mouth watered at the thought of her father's roasted Kahlua Turkey. She couldn't hide the wistful tone in her voice. "I'm gonna miss that most."

Besides the turkey, there'd be trays of sticky white rice, Portuguese sausage stuffing, tako poke, sashimi, Okinawan sweet potatoes, and plenty of pie. At Ala Moana Park, the keiki would play in the beach's waves or snorkel. The adults would throw a Frisbee or play chess on the picnic tables. Keoni would blast music on stereo speakers set on the drinks cooler.

Her mom's brown eyes zeroed in across the miles as clearly as if she could see into her heart. "You gonna be okay, girl. Stop worrying so much and have some fun for a change."

Her eyes welled. "I'm doing great, Mom. Spending today with the O'Briens, then taking the weekend off. It'll be just like home," she fibbed. "Love you! Aloha!" Cassandra waved into the camera as she disconnected.

Closing her eyes, she imagined Oahu's hot sun beating down on her upturned face until it became so hot she had to catch a breath and the sweat beads dripped down her hairline. Had either of them believed her lie? Wiping her forehead, she resolved to make it true. Cassandra Sato wasn't a quitter.

Chapter Ten

Cassandra felt more like an outsider than she had at any other time since moving to Carson. Twenty people huddled around a 60-something inch big screen TV mounted on the wall, intently watching their beloved football team. Surround-sound speakers in the ceiling loudly recounted the game's play-by-play.

Moving here just for the job wasn't enough. She wanted to cultivate authentic friendships. A successful career wasn't based on work relationships only. Cassandra was determined to learn enough names and facts to carry on sports conversations with her coworkers and students.

Watching them all shouting at the TV and each other during the first quarter while the Nebraska Cornhuskers played made Cassandra re-evaluate how well she knew any of them.

Cassandra had worn one of the three Husker t-shirts Meg had given her for Christmas over the years. Wardrobe-wise, she fit in with everyone else at the party who wore player jerseys, Husker t-shirts, or corn joke shirts.

Marcus Fischer had texted her that morning and offered a ride to the party. Fischer, Connor, and Meg sat on tall bar stools behind the couch, drinking beers, and quietly staring at the big screen. Studying Fischer, a longing warmth started in her chest and spread south. Maybe this party would be so fun they'd plan a second date soon. It was probably her turn to ask him.

She noticed both Connor and Marcus sat on the edge of the room, their backs to the wall. Meg had told her about Connor's unpredictable combat flashbacks. Sometimes he broke out in a sweat or left a crowded room because he felt vulnerable. Did that happen to Marcus, too? For two guys who'd only met a month earlier at National Guard weekend training camp, they seemed very similar.

Cassandra stood near Connor, holding a can of Diet Coke, trying to imagine herself camped on those cold metal bleachers for three plus hours surrounded by 90,000 screaming fanatics dressed in Husker Red. "Those players are down the road in Lincoln today, right?" She checked the temperature on her smartwatch (35 degrees). "Is it warmer there?"

Five big guys took up most of the real estate on Cinda Weller's large sectional couch in her basement family room. A ping pong table filled the center of the room, though no one was using it. The house, probably less than 10 years old, would be considered a mansion by Honolulu building standards, but seemed average within the neighborhood's ranch house subdivision.

"They're a little farther South than we are." Connor considered her question seriously. "Maybe a couple degrees warmer . . . why?"

"Hardly any players are wearing sleeves! How can they play with frozen arms and hands? Doesn't it hurt when they catch the football?"

"Good eyes." Connor shrugged. "You'll notice several guys on both teams have dropped easy passes. That ball feels like a frozen rock in these temperatures. But they practice outdoors every day, so it's no big deal. When it gets super cold or windy, teams run the ball instead because it's more reliable."

The University of Hawai'i was well known for its volleyball team, Oahu hosted the Pro Bowl for many years, and local boys' baseball teams had made it to the Little League World Series more times than Cassandra could count. Nothing in her sports experience matched the fervor she saw here.

Cassandra headed towards the little kitchen and wet bar area opposite the TV end of the room. The countertop was completely covered by crock pots filled with football tailgate food: meatballs, pulled pork, layered dips and bags of chips. She filled a small plate with delicious smelling snacks.

Cassandra's phone buzzed with a notification, so she walked towards the large sliding doors that opened onto Cinda's fenced backyard to read the text. The spacious backyard included a large wooden swing set and brick fire pit. It was twice the size of her grandparents' yard back home.

Andy Summers wrote, "Thought you'd want to know Rachel Nagle was released from the hospital this morning."

She hadn't talked to him since he'd taken Rachel's statement.

A collective shout came from the couch after a dropped pass lead to a punt. "Oh my God what is wrong with you! Why can't you just catch the ball?" yelled a guy so large, he looked like he must've played in his college days.

"If insanity is doing the same thing repeatedly but expecting a different result, why does the coach keep calling passing plays?" Connor groaned.

Looking up from her phone, Cassandra felt torn between the party and work. She was basically on call 24 hours. Tucking it under her pillow while she slept, Cassandra always worried she might miss an important message from security or her bosses. If something went bad with a student, Cassandra got notified. Her "weekend" was a blurry illusion.

She typed back to Summers, "Wow. I assumed she went home yesterday. Are you working now? Not watching the Nebraska game?"

Meg yelled, "The ref needs glasses. The guard was clearly holding!"

Cassandra carried her plate to the other side of the room where a few women clustered around high tables and the bar, chatting and half-watching the game.

Cinda hugged her. "Hey Cass, glad you made it."

"Thanks for inviting me. Your house is really nice."

Sports memorabilia covered the gray walls and dark wood trim gave the Man Cave a masculine vibe. "Does your husband collect all of this?"

Cinda pointed towards a Plexiglas case hanging on the wall that housed an autographed white football. "That football belonged to Jacob's father who got it during the Bob Devaney era. There's a big jar over there with a bunch of vintage football tickets that his grandparents started saving in the 1950s when they first bought season tickets. Otherwise, it's your average Husker shrine you'll see in any family room around the state."

A tall, freckle-faced woman with shoulder-length dark hair added, "At least your football room is painted gray. My husband insisted on painting our family room Husker Red. Luckily, I was able to limit him to one wall!" They all laughed.

Cassandra smiled but thought, yikes.

"Did you make the teriyaki wings?" Cinda pointed to Cassandra's plate. "Those smell really good."

"It's my Grandma's recipe. Ono Wings."

"Ono. Is that a seasoning?"

"No, it's the Hawaiian word for good. Seasoned with Aloha."

"Hawai'i's known for volleyball, right?" asked the freckled woman.

"Our football team mascot is the Rainbows, so that doesn't tend to strike fear in our opponents." Cassandra said, "Our volleyball team is excellent. They have four national championships and have been in the NCAA tournament for more than 30 years running."

"At least you get to go to the Pro Bowl every year, right?"

"I've been a couple of times." Cassandra sipped her Diet Coke and noticed that except for one other guy she was the only person without a red plastic cup or a beer in her hand at 3 o'clock in the afternoon. "I surf. And hike."

"I've always wanted to be a surfer. I bet you're badass."

Cassandra laughed. "I didn't say I was good. I just like it." Her brother was good. His wife, Leilani, had been the badass surfer before she'd gotten busy with the kids.

Meg joined them. "You'll have to go to a game with us some time. Until you see the Memorial Stadium Sea of Red with your own eyes, you won't really get it."

One of the couch guys asked Cinda, "Where's the red beer?" She pointed at a fridge around the corner.

"*Red* beer? They make special beer for Husker games?"

"No, it's a local thing. We pour tomato juice into our beer to turn it red."

Cassandra's eye widened. She couldn't even.

The phone next to Cassandra's hand vibrated with another text from Andy. "Of course I'm watching the football game. I'm streaming it in my office. I gave most of my staff the day off."

Cassandra replied to Andy Summers, "You deserve a day off, too. What can't wait until Monday?"

His response came right back. "I get more done when no one else is here and the phone isn't ringing. Can we meet for coffee tomorrow? I've been thinking about the whole situation with Rachel Nagle and the student protestors."

That word protestors again. She winced involuntarily.

Cassandra felt the air behind her shift and saw someone standing to her right. Little neck hairs rising told her it might be Fischer. Looking up from her phone, she met his bemused half-smile.

"Talking to someone from home?"

He'd been watching her? Her cheeks reddened. "What? Oh . . . No. Just Andy Summers telling me about something from work."

His mouth went flat. Like disapproval. Because it was Summers or because she couldn't stop working?

A loud cheer erupted as one red player broke away from the pack and sprinted down the sideline towards the end zone.

"C'mon baby!"

"Run! Run! Run!"

"You can do it!" Meg encouraged.

"Oh, nice block!"

The couch sitters leapt to their feet and pumped their fists in the air, "Yes! Touchdown Nebraska!"

"Gooo Biiiig Red!"

They high-fived each other and bumped chests. The kick was good, and Cinda's husband Jacob stepped over to a bookshelf and flipped a switch on the stereo. The marching band played the fight song while party goers clapped along, ending with a chant: "Go Big Red! Go Big Red! Go Big Red!"

Cassandra's phone buzzed again from Summers. "Would Rachel Nagle have been hurt without the student booth and news articles? They have to be connected."

She grew more detached from the fun by the second. "I encouraged her to talk to the newspaper reporter in the first place. You mean it's my fault she got hurt?"

When he didn't answer right away, Cassandra thought Summers' silence was answer enough. She didn't feel like partying anymore. Dread formed in her stomach. And maybe, she'd eaten too many chips and dip.

She wasn't like these people and not only because she looked different. She'd never care this much about nineteen-year-olds bashing each other around and chasing a leather ball up and down a field. How could she enjoy a weekend off when someone out there had a vendetta against her students? Not only hadn't she prevented it, she'd been directly involved.

Minnesota was on the 20-yard line, second down and 5 yards to go.

"Of course it's not your fault. I just think we should talk about it more." Summers finally responded. "And make sure nothing worse happens."

Cassandra walked over to Meg, Connor, and Fischer. "Excuse me, would you mind dropping me off at home?"

"Now? If Minnesota scores, we'll only be ahead seven points." Fischer tore his eyes away from the TV screen and looked at her.

"I need to do some research for work."

"For Andy Summers?"

He wasn't jealous, was he? Cassandra shook her head. "I just . . . this game is taking a really long time."

"I'll give you a ride," offered Meg.

Fischer's eyes narrowed as he weighed her request. She pictured his desire to watch the end of the game fighting with his instinct to be a gentleman.

"Thanks, that'd be great." The game won.

Fischer said a distracted goodbye and got another beer from the cooler.

Cassandra thanked Cinda and Jacob for inviting her, gathered her empty crock pot, and left with Meg.

Meg tuned the car radio to the football game station.

Cassandra said, "Andy Summers said if it hadn't been for the news article and the class project, Rachel wouldn't have been hurt."

"And since you're the vice prez in charge, you think it's your fault. Am I right? I hate to be the one to tell you this, but you're just not that powerful. Rachel put herself out there. With Dr. Bryant's encouragement. There's enough blame to go around."

Opening the car door in the driveway, Cassandra apologized. "Maybe. But I want to make it right. Sorry for taking you away from the party. Thanks for the ride."

"No worries," said Meg. "Are you okay?"

Cassandra shrugged. "It was an interesting party. I'm not a big football person. There must be another way I can fit in here and make friends."

"You'll get used to us." Meg patted Cassandra's arm.

Cassandra didn't argue. She knew Meg wanted to hurry back and was grateful for the ride.

Chapter Eleven

Cassandra picked at the cardboard sleeve on her large take-out coffee cup and glanced outside the plate glass window onto the Gas & Sweet's parking lot. The bakery and coffee shop end of the gas station/convenience store had a surprising amount of hipster vibe given there were only a handful of wooden tables with industrial style chairs tucked into the corner in front of a massive bakery display case.

A steady trickle of customers stood in line while she waited for Andy Summers. Gazing at the cute Etsy-style handmade gifts on racks separating the bakery from the gas station side, Cassandra marveled at how many functions an enterprising business owner could include within their limited spaces.

Andy's boyish face lit up when he came in and saw her. A faint warning hummed in the back of her head. This wasn't a date, right? They often shared coffee and treats from this exact shop during the week when they arrived at work before the rest of the campus. They'd hit it off since July when he'd keyed open the building on the first real day of her job.

Had she misunderstood his intentions? Since it was Saturday on personal time had she agreed to something more than coffee between coworkers?

"Hey Cassandra!" Setting his heavy canvas coat on the back of a chair, he stood in line behind a young mother and her two toddlers. "You good?"

She nodded.

Dressed in lightly camo colored pants and a fleece zip-up over a button-down shirt, his face was freshly shaved, and a faint clean scent hung in the air around his jacket. The hum in the back of her head turned into a warning beep. Yep. He was here on a date.

Joining her a few minutes later, his hand shook slightly while he took the little wooden stir stick out of the slot in his cup. He set a small white plate holding three plain yeast donuts on the table between them.

"It's freezing out this morning." She had no shortage of weather-related small talk.

"It's early still. It'll warm up this afternoon. I noticed you don't usually eat regular donuts."

Cassandra felt a pang of affection at his friendly eagerness. Which was bad because she thought of Andy like a little brother.

She shook her head. "Not the giant frosted monstrosities I usually see at staff meetings." She held a warm cinnamon donut up to her nose and breathed in a deep sigh of pleasure. "This kind reminds me of Leonard Bakery's Portuguese malasadas my gran bought for me at home. Except real malasadas don't have a hole in the middle."

"Well, then. Here's to a taste of home." He waited while she took a donut, then they chewed in companionable silence for a minute. "And to the lovely queen coming down from the castle to visit the lowly knight."

Playfully touching a finger to his forehead like a salute, Summers said, "What dragon can this knight slay for you today, my lady?" His attempted British accent was horrible but endearing.

She smiled. "If you could find me a time-turner so I could go back and fix this mess with the Deaf Studies advocacy project, I'd make you a baronet."

"I think Rachel Nagle just hit her head hard. She'll probably be fine."

"I really hope so." She nibbled her donut. "But I know some people think Morton failed to inform deaf and hard of hearing students of dangerous weather conditions. If we're looking at lawsuits, I want to have the facts ready. You said yourself that if Rachel hadn't gotten involved with the advocacy project, she wouldn't have been hurt."

"But only if she was really pushed. If she just slipped on the ice, that could've happened to anyone."

"Either way, if Morton is negligent, that's trouble. You think Rachel is wrong about what happened? I was at the hospital too. I believed her."

"I don't know for sure, yet. Why would someone want to hurt her?"

Cassandra had asked herself the exact same question since Wednesday morning. "One of my students said there might be a situation with a frat guy. Or maybe she's had problems with another student. Or even someone from Omaha. It's not that far away."

"The media coverage is killing my security department budget. Extra guys had to work this week around the Student Center."

He pointed at the last donut and raised his eyebrows to ask if she wanted any. When she said no, he scooped it up and demolished it with three bites. Thankfully, he waited to talk again until he'd swallowed. "The TV people and busybodies overflowed the outside trash bins, and a TV truck left huge ruts in the grass behind the building. Yesterday, I got an email that when the board of directors meets in December they want 'extra precautions' taken—whatever that means."

"What normally happens during the board meetings?" Cassandra couldn't remember previous problems when the board had met.

Summers said, "They've never asked for anything before. With only twelve officers and my assistant, we're gonna be working overtime to get it covered."

"Would it help you if I talk to the guy from the fraternity and ask around if other students disliked Rachel?"

"Yeah, that could save me a lot of time."

"Maybe someone doesn't want the advocacy project to succeed." Cassandra said, "I'll have to think about that more. Who wins if the students don't get what they want? They've been turned down several times before. Maybe there's a reason why the administrators don't want a new emergency management system."

Summers brushed crumbs off his sleeve. "Well, I can guess why. I've checked into the disaster and crisis management software before. Where are you getting the money? Aren't we still under budget cuts?"

"I don't know what administrators discussed before I arrived. I'd really like your input on the security aspects. Can your department make a list of how a text based electronic system would impact police work, student and staff safety, etc.?"

"So you're starting with my dream list? Sure, I can do that," he said. "A more modern system might have prevented her accident. Dr. Bergstrom said the sidewalk was slick and dangerous where the student was found. It must have been just barely cold enough to freeze the rain as the sun went down."

Cassandra frowned. "Wait, Bergstrom was there?"

"Dr. Bergstrom found Rachel and called 911," Summers nodded. "He stayed with her even after we arrived and the ambulance came."

Strange. No one had mentioned that before.

"How long had Rachel been there when Dr. Bergstrom saw her?" Cassandra asked.

"No way to know," shrugged Summers. "When I arrived about five or ten minutes later, she was unconscious and breathing but her skin wasn't cold. So I don't think it was long. But I'm not a doctor . . ."

Cassandra made a mental note to ask Bergstrom for more details about the conditions where Rachel was found, and if she said anything before the EMTs drove her to the hospital in Wahoo. If her family ended up suing the college, she'd want to make sure the reports included specifics about weather conditions, the physical space, and how exactly college staff had responded.

Summers set his crumpled napkin on the empty plate. "I can suggest a few emergency management software packages. I've seen exhibit booths at our state conference. Dr. Nielson was pretty old school. He often said, 'Our students pay a premium price to attend Morton, and we're going to give them a premium classroom experience.'" Summers shrugged. "The housing and classrooms have all been upgraded, but the background infrastructure is outdated."

Before they left, Cassandra needed to get one last thing clear. "Uh, Andy? We're..." She slowly moved her hand back and forth above the table between them. "Is this... we're friends, right?"

His light brown eyes held hers for the length of two breaths. "Sure. We're friends." His smile was self-deprecating. "I'm just a lowly knight, remember?"

Oh, God. She wasn't ready to be anyone's queen.

* * *

Cassandra had just finished gassing her Honda for the first time in a month when a short, thin man with a wispy goatee approached. She didn't know many local people yet, so her expression was guarded. "Can I ... help you?" Summers had already driven off and only two other cars sat by the gas pumps.

His face seemed familiar, and she waited for him to introduce himself, but he looked down at his smartphone where the screen was full of text. "I understand Morton College has been accused of being inaccessible to deaf and hard of hearing students?"

Her right eyebrow reflexively raised. Wait. She looked more closely. "The Omaha Daily News, right?" When she'd first met Goatee once about a month ago, he'd worn a baseball cap. But she easily recognized his voice.

"That's right!" Delight crossed his very pale face. "I'm glad you remember me."

"Derek Swanson." His pushy, cub-reporter eagerness was already annoying. "What're you doing in town?" She craned her neck around the side of the gas station to see where he'd come from. "Are you following me?"

They might be the same age, but Swanson dressed like a high school kid in need of a wardrobe upgrade. His skinny black jeans ended an inch above his ankle, exposing a sliver of white athletic socks between his pants and worn black leather shoes. In lieu of a winter coat, he wore two layers of hoodies.

"There's like two places open in Carson on a Saturday morning." He held up a bakery bag. "I'm getting background for my next big story. My headline so far is 'Emboldened by Petition's Success, Morton Students Plan Protests.' Catchy, huh? I'd already begun investigating background on the petitions and the protests when your student ended up in the hospital. Lucky turn of events that was." He seemed almost happy about Rachel's misfortune as he slid his phone into his front pocket. "What is the administration doing to address this situation?"

It sounded less like a newspaper headline than click-bait for a grocery store tabloid. Which was the last place Cassandra wanted her name plastered on a headline.

She needed to distract him from including her in his article. Cassandra released a long, slow yoga breath. "The facilities department has prioritized adding captioning on all media screens in public areas of campus." It was only a slight exaggeration.

"With the upcoming board of directors meeting and the new President, I could see national civil rights groups interested in assisting the Deaf Studies student group's cause." His grin was smug. "Maybe even the ACLU."

The next task on her weekend chore list was buying a rake from the hardware store to tackle the orange leaves covering her yard. The last thing she felt like doing at this moment was giving this dude ammunition for another Morton College exposé. She wanted him to go away and leave her name out of it.

"Morton College is continually improving the learning experience for our students. We are dedicated to providing an excellent, liberal arts education in a safe, enjoyable environment," said Cassandra. "Included in U.S. News and World Reports Top 50 small private Midwest colleges, we welcome suggestions from faculty, staff, and students for ways to keep Morton one of the best higher education institutions in Nebraska."

"That's impressive," nodded Swanson. "Did you memorize that whole blurb from the website?"

Why did he have to be so adversarial? Cassandra's second eyebrow raised up. "Most of the students went home for the weekend." Didn't this clown take a day off? "No one is upset. No protests. Attentive administrators encouraged students to advocate for their needs using formal communication channels."

"That's not what the student newspaper said," said Swanson. "Do you suspect that Rachel Nagle's recent 'injury' was retribution for her involvement in the movement or was there a more personal motive?"

What movement? A chilly breeze swept between the gas pumps reminding Cassandra that she was arguing with this guy in a public place. It wasn't a good look. "If by 'movement,' you're referring to the Deaf Studies student advocacy project, I can't imagine why anyone would feel threatened by Dr. Bryant's students' ideas. Morton is conducting a thorough investigation." She didn't mention her role helping Andy. "We take student safety and concerns very seriously."

"Oh, trust me, I'm going to ask Dr. Bryant for his comments, too," Swanson seemed unhurried. "Doesn't anyone else find it an interesting coincidence that Rachel Nagle's grandmother died here while she was a student? And now Rachel herself has been assaulted."

Technically, it would be assault if Andy Summers could find evidence. But why Swanson cared about Rachel's birth family was baffling. "Mr. Swanson, that happened in the 1970s. I fail to see the connection."

"Oh, don't you worry. If there's any dirt, I'll find it. Who worked here forty-three years ago? There's plenty of gray-haired academics wandering around these ivory towers. Obviously, someone wants Ms. Nagle silenced."

It took all of Cassandra's practiced years of acting more mature than her age to clamp her mouth shut as Swanson strutted away towards the side parking lot. Maybe if Swanson wasted enough time reliving the 70s, it would give her time to implement concrete proposals on the accessibility requests.

Chapter Twelve

Cassandra raised her travel cup to her lips during the Monday morning administrative team meeting, a sharp pain stabbed near her ribs, and her shoulders complained over the micro-movement. Although filling twelve large bags with leaves from her yard had been a satisfying way to spend most of Saturday and Sunday, she paid for it now. Yoga stretches didn't work the same muscles as raking and bending.

Dr. Gregory, the rotating chairman, led the meeting in a large multimedia room in the library. Cassandra anticipated a productive return from Thanksgiving break, starting with her Diversity Council update and helping Andy Summers investigate Rachel's injury.

Another old, bearded academic, Gregory was nearing retirement as the Business Office VP. He rattled through half the agenda in record time, including reiterating Professor Zimmerman's exam reminders as this was the last regular week before Dead Week.

Cassandra noted in her planner to expect student conduct complaints from faculty or staff, though she held high hopes for a quiet, positive ending to the semester.

Fischer had come into the room about ten minutes late and sat in the far opposite corner of the large U-shaped table from her. Which was unusually tardy for him. She tried not to stare in his direction, but the gravitational pull was hard to resist.

His leather flight jacket with a sheepskin collar was unzipped over his button-down flannel shirt. The man had wardrobe independence. Working with the facilities and maintenance staff, he didn't need to impress anyone with a fancy suit and tie. Inhaling, she remembered his woodsy, sporty scent, although he was too far away now to catch it.

Gregory gave a short reminder about keeping building temperatures cool during non-work hours and turning off lights when rooms weren't in use.

Dr. Winters piped in. "I don't like to offer public criticism of my staff, but we're all colleagues here. The Green Initiative is another one of these higher ed buzzwords that people use to make it sound like they're doing something innovative, when all they're really doing is using fancy labels. Being good stewards of Morton campus resources has been an important mission ever since I began working here in the 70s. Turning off lights, keeping rooms efficiently cool or warm, or conserving paper have been historically common ways to manage our limited resources."

Cassandra nearly choked at the mention of efficient heating and cooling. Dr. Winters had apparently never spent time in the Student Affairs office which seemed to have only two settings: freezer or sauna.

Winters wasn't done. "We were the first educational institution in the state to plant a community garden that to this day not only provides fresh vegetables to students and staff, but also sends the leftovers to the Methodist church for distribution to the poor families in town. In 1978!"

Heads nodded. Dr. Gregory smugly crossed his arms. "Now they call it farm-to-table."

Winters pointed to him. "Exactly! You can package it up, design a new logo, and waste time bragging about it on social media, but the fact is you could be using that time to focus on cutting excess somewhere else."

This rant highlighted the desire for transparency in higher ed finances, but Cassandra wondered how it contributed to the current agenda. Gregory must have realized it too, because he cleared his throat and called on Winters for the next item.

"Thank you, Dr. Gregory." Winters solemnly folded her hands on the table in front of her. "Regarding the student who was injured last week. The campus security director informed me that there is no evidence anyone intentionally harmed her. Therefore, we will consult our attorney and ensure we have proper documentation of weather mitigation measures." Winters leaned over and nodded at Fischer.

He said, "I'll send over the paperwork this afternoon," and wrote in his small black leather notebook.

Why did Andy tell Winters the investigation was done when Cassandra hadn't completed her student interviews?

Cassandra's next appointment was with T.J. Baranek to follow up on his relationship with Rachel. Her lips pursed.

A fluttering unease formed in her stomach. Like watching a Twilight Zone episode. She seemed to be the only person taking Rachel's alleged assault seriously. Before she could analyze it, Gregory called on her next.

"Thanks. As you might remember, Dr. Nielson established the Diversity Council to elevate the discussion about making Morton College accessible and inclusive for all students. In the past, a handful of non-white or disabled students, faculty, or staff attended or were employed here. In the future, Nielson envisioned a diverse, international campus community that celebrates the differences of people and promotes opportunities for them to become leaders in today's world. Currently the council is planning our first campus-wide Diversity Day event for the Spring Semester. I'll keep you updated with specific details when they're available."

Cassandra crossed her legs under the table and smiled pleasantly. Heads nodded around the table. That summed it up nicely.

Fischer jumped in. "Dr. Sato and I are also working to address the accessibility concerns raised by the Deaf Studies class advocacy project. We've enabled the captioning on the campus screens and are working to integrate a text-based version of the daily PA announcements."

Cassandra smiled, grateful that he'd added the advocacy project part without being prompted.

Dr. Gregory clarified, "As long as these changes won't affect our budget allocations, they sound reasonable."

Good. Dr. Gregory's support was key. "One item concerns purchasing an updated text-based emergency management software system." Cassandra said, "We don't have enough information yet to make a formal proposal."

"Is a Diversity Council even necessary?" Winters countered, "The Golden Rule has been around for thousands of years. We don't need a fancy council to prescribe twenty new ways to treat others with respect."

Wait, of course the council was necessary! She had to make Winters understand. "A more modern interpretation of the Golden Rule is to treat others how they would choose to be treated, instead of assuming they want exactly the same treatment you want."

Winters' mouth formed a tight, small grimace. She did not appear pleased with Cassandra's assertiveness.

Cassandra was right. She wasn't going to defer to her boss this time.

Winters' gaze returned to the table. "Dr. Sato, before we expend another cent, I'd like you to gather demographic statistics by department. You're following instinct, but you're inexperienced. We need cold facts before we hop on your merry bandwagon. Let's identify true needs and priorities regarding diversity and inclusion." Her index finger touched a spot on her notes. "Dr. Nielson wouldn't want us to shirk the analysis step in this process. Let's hold off on further council meetings until after the next board of directors meeting on December 9th. Your summary will help them prioritize funding proposals this fiscal year."

Cassandra's jaw dropped and her eyes widened. Winters had to know she was setting a near impossible deadline. "But—"

"I'll need that Diversity and Inclusion report by next week. I do understand if that's not enough time, but we can't afford to waste our resources. No point jumping ahead to action steps before we've identified the relevant issues. Keep us posted."

Winters nodded once and didn't even take a breath before moving on to the last agenda item.

Her cheeks filled with heat, Cassandra peeked around the room to see the others' reactions to Winters' request. No one made eye contact with Cassandra to roll their eyes, shrug a shoulder, or nod their head in silent support. Nothing.

They all took Winters' ultimatum at face value. Like Winters was right. Why had no one spoken up to support Cassandra?

Lastly, she looked in the corner at Fischer. To her astonishment, he signed to her in ASL, "You are fine." Then he winked. Like a supportive—you got this—kind of wink. When had Fischer learned ASL? The man had layers like an onion.

* * *

The student seated in Cassandra's office armchair looked about sixteen years old, with a baby soft chin so smooth she couldn't see any dark stubble. His blonde, gelled hair stuck up in tufts from his forehead and his right knee bounced nervously.

He hadn't said a word since Logan had led him into Cassandra's office. His lips formed a timid half-smile while he probably wondered why he'd been called into the Vice President for Student Affairs office.

Cassandra guessed he'd never been in serious trouble his entire life. "Thanks for stopping in today, T.J. I'm sure you have a busy week."

"Sure, Dr. Sato," his voice actually squeaked. "Yeah, I'm working on two group projects."

"I'm going to get right to the point. I'm following up with friends and acquaintances of Rachel Nagle who was hurt last week."

"I thought she fell on the ice when it sleeted?" His eyes shifted uncomfortably. "I heard she's okay now, right?" One hand slid up and through his gelled hair, making it more disheveled than stylish.

"She's back on campus, yes. Can you tell me how you know her?"

Confusion still showed in his eyes, but he seemed used to answering to authority. "Not very well. We went to the Harvest Moon Formal a few weeks ago for my fraternity. She's a friend of my roommate."

"Tell me about the formal, please."

"Umm . . . it was about three Fridays ago?" He looked down at the backpack resting against his knee, which still bounced. "And we ate dinner at the American Legion hall. There was a DJ playing music."

"Can you tell me about why Rachel left early without you and came home with her friends?"

His face reddened and his eyes watered as he probably realized Cassandra knew a lot more about the evening than he expected. "Look, I don't know what she told you, but I tried to tell her I was sorry."

Actually, Cassandra had heard Rachel's version of events from Haley and Logan, but she wanted to know his side of it. So far, everything was second-hand news anyway.

"I never dated anyone in high school except senior prom." T.J. looked down and spoke to the front of Cassandra's desk. "My roommate set me up with Rachel, and the other guys told me if I had a couple of drinks first, I wouldn't be such a goon."

She nodded, encouraging him to continue.

"I've seen *Pitch Perfect* a few times, and I thought girls wanted guys to try to um . . . ah, ya know." His Adam's apple bobbed up and down convulsively. "I might've had too many drinks at the party. There was a big trash can full of punch. Rachel's so pretty and nice and I didn't want her to think I wasn't good enough to go out with her. She has her choice of guys who want her. So, I kissed her a few times and then when we danced, I . . ."

He pantomimed moving his hands all over her while they danced but couldn't seem to say the words out loud. Was he really that shy and inexperienced? "I remember she kind of shoved me away and said, knock it off. We danced some more, and I tried again. I heard sometimes girls say no the first time."

Cassandra's eyebrows both flew up of their own volition.

He put his palms up in front of him. "But now I know that's not right. She called me a jerk and left the party. My friend Haley told me later that what I did was not cool. And I get it. I do."

So far, his story pretty much aligned with what Haley had told Cassandra.

"I texted her the next day to apologize but she didn't answer me." Tears dribbled down his cheek and he swiped them away. "I invited her to coffee a few days later but again, nothing. Look, I get that it was a jerk thing to do, but I'm trying to show her that's not the real me. I wanted another chance to make a better impression. I sent flowers to the hospital."

As much as she wanted to dislike this kid for getting handsy with Rachel, it was painfully clear to Cassandra that, although he was guilty of trying too hard, he probably wasn't a spurned lover seeking revenge. "T.J., where were you last Monday, November 23rd in the afternoon?"

He sat up straight. "Am I in trouble?"

"We have to follow up on incidents whenever students get hurt on campus. Where were you?"

"Studying in the library?"

"Did anyone see you there?"

His voice cracked. "See me? Studying? Uh, I was by myself... no wait. I tried printing my paper but it was broken. They called an I.T. guy who fixed it for me." He stabbed the air in front of him to emphasize his innocence.

Cassandra wrote a note in her journal and folded her hands on the desktop. "Thanks for your cooperation, T.J. We'll let you know if we have more questions later."

Before she'd even finished the statement, he was already standing near the door wearing his backpack. "Is this going in my files?"

"I can't say for sure yet, but I do appreciate your time answering my questions."

She'd check his story, although Cassandra's instincts said T.J. wasn't the person who shoved Rachel.

Chapter Thirteen

If Cassandra hurried, she might catch Meg for a quick lunch. Grabbing the keys from her office, she hustled out her door, colliding with Meg who was coming inside. "Yeesh—" Cassandra squeaked. "A little warning, eh?"

"Hey, you crashed into me. I was just bringing you lunch, 'cause I figured you'd be too busy to take time for a break," said Meg.

An intoxicating scent of yeasty bread and fries radiated from the white Runza takeout bag Meg raised to eye level. "Your ability to read my mind is borderline creepy, but right now I'm grateful for your superpower."

Cassandra ushered Meg inside and closed the door, grabbed her water bottle, and cleared off the coffee table. Meg turned around one of the student armchairs to face Cassandra on the couch. She passed Cassandra a steaming pile of fries and onion rings.

Cassandra sunk her teeth into a hot onion ring and savored the greasy crunch. It was so foreign to the sautéed veggies and rice that comprised 90% of her daily diet.

"You gotta have the French Onion dip, too." Cassandra made a little groan of delight when she dipped a crinkly French fry into the creamy dip.

Meg said, "You seem in more of a tizzy than usual."

"Cuz Dr. Winters hates me."

"Did she call you a diva again?"

"Not exactly." Cassandra shrugged. "Also, I'm checking into who pushed Rachel Nagle and why."

Meg's lips pursed like they always did when she tried to find a nice way to say something direct. She usually failed. "Isn't that a job for Security and Andy Summers? Or the Facilities department and Fischer? How is that *your* job?"

Cassandra raised an eyebrow. "Because I care when a student gets assaulted on campus. I don't need your negativity here."

Meg rolled her eyes. "Someone has to keep you in line."

Cassandra licked salt from her fingertips. "Mmmm . . . How did I never think of Frings before I moved to Nebraska? I love onion rings. I love fries. Those Runza geniuses know just how to make a bad day disappear."

"Never say I don't treat you right." Meg pushed her long, curly red hair off her shoulders, passed a warm paper wrapped bundle to Cassandra, then raised her Runza sandwich in a little salute.

"Did you get me a Swiss mushroom Runza?" Cassandra preferred the melty cheese version of the beef and cabbage stuffed in a yeast bread crust that locals considered fine cuisine—so much so that an entire restaurant chain placed them as the centerpiece of their menu.

Meg said, "Summers filed an incident report, right? If he doesn't follow up, you could try the sheriff's office."

"After we finish eating, I'm going to call him again. During our team meeting this morning Dr. Winters put the Diversity Council meetings on hold."

"I didn't realize Winters had that authority," said Meg. "It was established only two months ago. Can she really stop it without board or Faculty Senate approval?"

"She got wind of the disagreement during the first meeting. I'm supposed to research diversity demographics by department and submit a report at next week's board of directors meeting. She wants me to compare Omaha and Lincoln institutions too, and see what programs, services, and technology they use."

"That's not much time, but you thrive on deadlines," said Meg. "You wrote your dissertation in six months. Maybe Winters wants a more complete, top-down approach than the grassroots council Nielson envisioned."

"Oh please. Winters is stalling." Cassandra's eyes blazed. "This is not simply a 'report' that I crank out in three hours, put on a shelf, and never use again. My name will be front and center on the cover page. It will explore the current campus environment and compare our college with similar institutions. It serves as a master blueprint to move Morton College from one of the more backwards institutions in the area to the most inclusive, innovative campus in the region. If I do this well, it will lead to conference posters, collaborative papers with like-minded colleagues, and positions on national professional organizations. It's gonna be a work of art!"

Meg stared at her like a pineapple had just sprouted from the top of her head. Now if only Cassandra could channel some of that passion while she wrote the darned report.

"Well... alrighty then. Point taken. But I'm with the students and Dr. Bryant on this one. It's time for Morton to invest in making campus accessible for all students. How can the board deny the costs if other campuses our size have similar technology?"

"I'm supposed to include how many deaf students attend Morton and their demographic data," said Cassandra. "Winters seemed concerned that the cost of expensive new communication systems would only benefit a few students."

"You're kidding me." Meg put her food down and sat up straighter. "So now we ignore deaf and hard of hearing students' needs because there aren't *enough* of them? There's what—20 baseball players on the Morton team, but they got upgraded locker rooms and a new smoothie machine. Isn't emergency notification a higher priority than the right fielder's protein shake?"

"What if donors pay for the protein shakes?" Cassandra asked.

"My peeve is when people argue that providing access for a small group like deaf people costs too much money per person." Meg's normally freckled pale face reddened. "Once you start text-based systems and visual alert systems, you'll find that it benefits everyone. Even people who can hear like to receive text updates warning them about weather, maintenance issues, or—God forbid—violent attacks. What's nice is you can read a text message while you're away from work and still know what's going on there. Like maybe when it's safer to stay away, too."

"Winters is postponing the issue until she finds a way to quietly end the council," said Cassandra. "And now she's appointed me to give the report so that if anything goes awry or there are complaints, my name will be in the headlines instead of hers."

"You gotta admire her strategy," said Meg. "I can definitely level up my manipulative skills by watching Winters."

"So . . . here's my theory. When the AP spread the story nationally and Rachel became the poster child for the advocacy project, suddenly she became the face of the movement. Winters had to stop her," said Cassandra. "To save Morton."

Meg rolled her eyes. "You can hear how lame this is, right?"

Cassandra said, "Winters' dog scratched my leg and I have the scar to prove it. Rachel said she heard a dog bark before she was pushed. Maybe Winters' dog got loose and scared Rachel."

"Isn't he a little white floor-mop sized thing? You don't seriously think Winters trained him to attack?"

"She's trying to eliminate the Diversity Council. What else is she willing to sabotage for the sake of Morton's reputation?"

"So your theory is that Winters pushed Rachel because she wanted to prevent her from ruining Morton's good name?" Meg summarized. "Oh, and her dog is ferocious. That's what you've got?"

When Meg said it like that, her theory sounded silly. But so far it was the only thing that made sense. Cassandra shrugged. "It's a work in progress."

"Don't let Winters get to you." Meg finished off her Runza. "Hey, when's your next date with Fischer?"

"Nice diversion." Cassandra's lips tightened to a flat line. "I was going to call him tonight when I get home and see if he's free Saturday."

"Are you ever gonna tell me what went wrong the first time?"

It was too complicated to go into detail, but basically Fischer wasn't Paul, her former fiancé. Cassandra stalled by finishing her drink.

Meg didn't give up that easily. "Oh c'mon. Marcus is smart, kind, and good looking. How bad could it have been?"

Cassandra blew out a sigh. "He surprised me with a hobby he enjoys so I could learn more about him outside of work."

Meg nodded, her big grin anticipating a good story.

"Only problem was he didn't give me any details beforehand. So, I wore nice clothes and shoes, but he took me to a state recreation park area, and we fished at a pond. Actually he fished, and I sat on a fleece picnic blanket trying not to touch slimy earthworm or fish stuff."

One hand covered Meg's mouth while she tried and failed to stifle a laugh. "He figured you'd show up in jeans and a sweater like every other Nebraska girl he's dated. I can totally picture you perched on that blanket, thinking the whole time how bad your Macy's ensemble would stink when you got home."

She broke out into full peals of laughter.

Cassandra did one stink eye as a warning.

"Did you burn the shoes and outfit or toss them?" Meg asked.

"Tossed them," Cassandra confirmed. "I held the fishing rod thingy while he set up our picnic dinner. The date wasn't completely horrible. I smiled and chatted while he reeled in a big splashy one, so maybe he didn't notice fishing's not my jam."

Meg shook her head. "Uh . . . Trust me, he noticed. Well, the good news is your second date pretty much has to be an improvement, eh?"

"Yeah, no pressure," said Cassandra.

"I'll text you my no-fail romantic suggestions later."

Cassandra had no time for a snarky reply because Meg stood and gathered her things. "Look I gotta run to class. See you later."

Cassandra brushed crumbs into her hand before throwing the trash in the waste bin. "Mahalo for the ono grub."

* * *

As soon as Meg left, Cassandra called Andy Summers. He said, "I'm mostly finished with the incident report. I talked to Dr. Bergstrom after the ambulance left the scene. I talked to her roommate Sarah. Plus, we got Rachel's statement at the hospital after she woke up."

"At our team meeting this morning, Dr. Winters said you're treating the incident like an accident. But I believed Rachel. She seemed convinced she was pushed."

"I'm just looking at evidence, Cassandra. There isn't any that proves her allegation."

"But isn't it too early to give up? I can follow up with more teachers."

"It's a waste of time. She couldn't even say if what hit her was human. I'm sure you have more important things to do than looking for an imaginary psycho."

Okay. So she was on her own in believing Rachel.

"One more thing," said Andy. "There's some group calling themselves the Deaf Rights Now Coalition who emailed me asking if they needed a permit to assemble before the board meeting next week. Have you ever heard of them?"

A permit to assemble? That sounded like a code word for protests. Exactly what she'd been trying to avoid for weeks. "I haven't, but I can ask Meg what she knows."

"I'm not taking any chances. I've arranged for extra security before the meeting. We're closing the south and east entrances so that everyone who wants to come on campus has to go through our security checkpoint and sign in. We've had enough accidents lately. I'm making sure nothing happens this time."

Cassandra heard a howl that was more like a growl. It started low and cut off abruptly. Cassandra assumed one of the students in the main office was watching a YouTube video with the volume turned up too loud.

Irritated, she glanced out the open doorway of her office, then returned to Andy. "Should we ask the sheriff's office to help your investigation? I mean assault is a crime, right?"

Summers said, "Technically, it would be assault if we had someone to press charges against. But right now, I'm done. I doubt this would be a high enough priority within the entire county to merit a full sheriff's investigation. If we identified an actual suspect, we could ask them for help."

Cassandra said, "I talked to T.J. Baranek this morning about Rachel and he claimed that he was in the library when Rachel was hurt. It all checked out. He told me the truth about where he was last Monday. Also, I think he likes her too much to hurt her."

"I appreciate your help following up with the students because this board meeting logistical stuff is keeping me busy. Even if T.J. didn't hurt her, he'd better leave Rachel alone."

"I think he's gotten that message loud and clear," Cassandra said. "This is all so frustrating. I still have a lot of questions, and no one seems to know the answers."

He chuckled, "Welcome to my life, Cassandra. Those words will probably be on my tombstone someday."

The second time, the howl sounded like someone had slammed a finger shut hard in one of the office's snack cabinet doors. A cross between a moan and a cry of pain, it made chicken skin crawl up her arms and the back of her neck.

Loud footsteps ran through the outer office and a male voice yelled, "There it went!"

"I'd better go, Andy. The main office is having a crisis. Talk to you later." Cassandra poked the disconnect button on her phone.

When she rushed into the outer office, she nearly plowed into Bridget who was coming from her right, duck-walking and bent over with outstretched arms. A golden-brown medium-sized dog reared onto Cassandra's shoulders, knocking her off balance.

"Oh!" Cassandra exclaimed, then fell backwards onto her butt.

The mutt woofed a few times and streaked out the front door into the hallway.

Cassandra shook her head. She was not clumsy. However, since moving to Nebraska, Cassandra seemed to embarrass herself weekly over silly mishaps. No photos of her sprawled on the floor of her office had better end up online.

Logan followed him calling, "Stop that dog!"

Bridget paused long enough to offer Cassandra a hand and pull her up. Then, she ran after Logan leaving Cassandra in the office alone. George Hansen, the Assistant Director of Student Affairs, poked his bald head out the door of his office.

Cassandra shrugged, "Runaway dog?"

George muttered, "Damn kids." Then his age-spotted face disappeared back into his office and his door closed loudly.

Cassandra had been here three months and still wasn't completely sure what George did all day. She suspected he was laid out on his burgundy leather couch napping most of the time. He rarely decided student conduct cases and didn't mentor any thesis or doctoral students. No one had mentioned his age, but Cassandra guessed it was minimum ten years past retirement.

Several minutes passed before Logan and Bridget returned to their posts in the office.

"I chased him to the first floor, but he got away," said Logan, his chest rising and falling rapidly while he caught his breath.

"He bit my finger!" Bridget frowned at her right index finger.

Cassandra peered closely but there was no broken skin.

"I told you not to pet him," Logan said. "Hence, the sign down on the main door? 'Do not let the stray dogs inside.'"

Bridget laughed, "Wait 'til you see the video I posted of you trying to grab him! You missed by a mile."

Just what Cassandra's office needed right now, more social media. She breathed in deep and imagined calming waves. "How many stray dogs have you seen on campus? Are they all that big?"

Logan said, "I've seen a couple other strays and one big retriever that I think one of the groundskeepers owns as a pet but brings to work. The one we chased out was maybe a Boxer-Retriever mix?"

A Retriever mix could be heavy enough to push someone down.

"I see a few dogs out behind the library when I walk by, but they aren't very tame," said Bridget.

Cassandra noted in her journal to find out who fed and cared for stray dogs. Maybe Fischer knew. She was disappointed that Andy was too busy to investigate the someone or something who pushed Rachel. Cassandra was on her own.

* * *

Seeking advice on tying together all the threads Cassandra was pursuing, she stopped by Dr. Bergstrom's office in Bryan Hall on her way home Monday afternoon. He might not tell her exactly what to do next, but she always felt better after a short chat with her fatherly mentor.

After accepting a cup of hot tea, Cassandra sank into Bergstrom's low couch. Dust puffed out where she set her tote bag on the ancient couch cushion, and she was pretty sure the thing poking her back was a worn metal spring. "Why didn't you tell me you were the one who found Rachel Nagle by the football stadium? She's lucky you came along. It was cold outside last week."

Whether Rachel was hurt from the ice or a person, Cassandra still needed to get a full picture of everything Morton personnel did at the scene. If this ever went to court, she wanted the notes to reflect helpful competence.

"I was walking to my car." Bergstrom lifted a shoulder. "There was nothing heroic about calling 911 and waiting for help to arrive. Anyone would have done the same." His rolling desk chair faced Cassandra, and he sipped from a delicate china teacup that looked like a toy in his sausage-sized fingers.

"Still, with her concussion, getting immediate medical care was key." Cassandra said, "Hopefully she'll be able to catch up on her missed classwork."

"I'm sure her professors will understand if she needs to withdraw or transfer," he said kindly. "There are plenty of schools she can attend in Omaha. She was pretty banged up."

Rachel had only missed three days of classes and a test. Why had Dr. Bergstrom mentioned transferring or withdrawing? Cassandra slowly brought her cup to her lips and sipped, hiding her confusion at his overreaction.

She said, "When she woke up in the hospital, Rachel said someone pushed her. She didn't fall from the ice. I'm helping Andy Summers figure out who could have hurt her and why. Did you notice anyone nearby when you found her?"

"It was nearly dark. I didn't see anyone else. I assumed she'd slipped on one of the icy patches."

"Did you notice any salt or sand on the sidewalks? There've been whisperings of a lawsuit from the parents."

"It wasn't a complete sheet of ice. Just a few slick spots." Bergstrom set down his cup. "Morton wasn't negligent. It was just an accident."

Great. She'd write those exact words in her notes for Andy. "This investigation seems important, but so does my work getting new initiatives off the ground. I'm torn between supporting the students' needs and satisfying the whims of the president or the board. Just when I think I know which direction to head, a random news story pops up and I have to chase another disaster."

"It's the nature of higher education. Always has been." Bergstrom began packing his briefcase with papers to bring home. "You can focus on improving the institution, but at the end of the day the students are customers and without them the college has no reason to exist."

"That reminds me. I had a weird encounter Saturday with that newspaper reporter from Omaha. He's investigating Rachel Nagle's birth family and their background. Were you at Morton in the 70s? Do you remember Susan Peters, the young woman who died?"

"Not to sound callous, but we lose students every year, Cassandra. Some suicide, some overdoses. A few car accidents. I don't remember them all."

"And you worked with Dr. Winters when she was at Morton, right?"

"We were colleagues here for quite some time before she left for another job."

"She doesn't value the diversity and inclusion initiatives I was hired to implement. She can be unpredictable." Cassandra was being generous. "I need her to understand the importance of serving all the students, not just the majority. I'm afraid she'll dismantle everything I've begun."

"Back when she was department chair, people called it the Reign of Error."

Cassandra had gone out on a limb. She thought no one else had noticed. "Oh, you understand what I mean? It's like being in the movie *50 First Dates*, but without the romance."

Bergstrom laughed so hard his eyes watered. "Dr. Winters is an expert in the Music Composition field, but that woman would try a saint. Sometimes instead of head-on you have to attack a problem from another angle."

"Well for now I have to compile a diversity and inclusion report before next week's board meeting. Do you mind if I attend your next department meeting and take notes on their status and needs?

"If it'll help, of course you're welcome." He tapped his temple then pointed at her. "Oh, I meant to ask you earlier. Liz and I are having a Sunday Salon gathering at our house this Friday. You should join us."

"*Friday,* sir? For a Sunday Salon?"

Now who was confused?

"Back in the dark ages, there was a group of us who took turns hosting the salon weekly, on Sundays." Bergstrom said. "My wife Liz loves to cook, and it gave her an excuse to make a bunch of food. Nowadays, we only do it once a semester. We kept the name."

"Um, nowadays most colleges discourage faculty and staff from hosting events in private homes," said Cassandra. "There's too much opportunity for liability. Especially if under-age drinking is involved."

All it would take was another embarrassing social media photograph and she'd be laughed out of the state and back home to Hawai'i. That was not the way Cassandra planned to return home.

"We haven't served alcohol for many years," he said somberly. "We do our best to keep today's students' attention and impact the next generation's intellectual development. That is, if I can pry their eyes from those ridiculous phones they carry around all day long."

"I can come. I guess you can't fit the whole college at your house. How do you decide who gets invited?"

"Besides the regular faculty group, I ask student leaders and let them each bring a friend or two. The numbers seem to work out."

"Thanks for including me. I look forward to it." It might be a good opportunity to talk to faculty and students for background on her report.

Chapter Fourteen

From the moment Cassandra had bumped into Omaha reporter Derek Swanson, it had only been a matter of time until his sensational story hit the web. Sure enough, Tuesday morning over Spam and a fried egg, Cassandra saw his feature article about Morton College in the *Omaha Daily News.*

First Swanson summarized Rachel's injuries, hospitalization, and recovery. To his credit, he had interviewed Andy Summers and quoted the Security Director directly, "We're following up on all credible leads for Ms. Nagle's injuries, but at this time we have no suspects."

Later, Swanson implied a relationship between Rachel's work in the advocacy project and her so-called accident. It seemed Swanson believed it wasn't an accident either. He and Cassandra were both looking for reasons why she was pushed.

Swanson included a list of the deaf and hard of hearing students' requests for campus improvements. Who had given him that list?

The next paragraph quoted Dr. Bryant. "We want to collaborate with the current administration at Morton, but we also know that costly suggestions tend to be the first items on the budget chopping block during economic crises."

This point was rebutted by Board Chairman Hershey. "Morton College's annual budget is over 50 million dollars, and the board prides itself on being a good steward of the student's tuition dollars as well as the generous donations we receive from alumnae. Student safety is a high priority at Morton College. I'm unaware of these specific improvements you've asked about, but I can assure you the board will get to the bottom of this issue during our December meeting."

Dr. Winters hadn't passed along the students' accessibility requests to Hershey. Maybe she was waiting for Cassandra's diversity and inclusion report so the board members could consider their requests in light of current demographics.

Swanson had contacted multiple sources; even Dr. Winters was included. "My highest priority is giving an excellent education at affordable prices to all students attending Morton. Morton College is proud of our 80-year tradition and thousands of successful alumnae. I will not stand idle for unsubstantiated criticisms of this great institution. We treat everyone equally and respectfully. We appreciate the same in return."

After focusing on the Deaf Studies advocacy project, Swanson's article turned personal. "The Nagle family's misfortunes at Morton College didn't begin with Rachel.

Archived college records indicate her birth grandmother, Susan Peters, returned to college after giving her baby up for adoption in the mid-1970s. Her untimely death occurred in a one-car accident during a snowstorm in December of 1976 when Patty Nagle was only an infant."

When interviewed, Patty said, "I feel fortunate I was adopted, because who knows what would have happened after my birth mother's accident."

Earlier Mrs. Nagle had been upset when Rachel had spilled the beans about their family history. Cassandra's eyebrows raised. Now, Patty was answering newspaper interview questions.

Alongside the article, a grainy black and white Morton *Maple Leaf* photo showed students wearing bell-bottomed jeans and flowered tops who held Vietnam protest signs that said, "Free the Prisoners," and "Send them tractors not tanks." The caption mentioned that although Nixon had ended the draft, U.S. troops remained in Vietnam. A blonde-haired student with her mouth open wide was identified as Susan Peters, but the photo quality was poor.

Rachel said she and her mother planned to find out more about their family's medical history. "It's a strange coincidence that I'm attending the same college as my biological grandmother. I wish we knew my grandfather's name, but it wasn't listed on the birth certificate."

Now Rachel was telling people she was here by coincidence. She'd admitted to Cassandra weeks ago that she'd chosen Morton with the intention of doing family history research.

Swanson's last juicy tidbit was a second photo. In a grainy, lo-fi shot, a young woman wearing a loose, white peasant top and patched bell-bottom jeans sat on an outdoor bench with a man who had a bushy, dark mustache wearing a polyester button-down shirt with a wide collar. Her eyes were closed, and her head tilted back, laughing heartily. Their legs touched, her hand rested on his thigh. Behind them sat the old library building before it had been torn down in 1985 to make way for the current modern Learning and Media Center. Swanson's caption identified the couple as Susan Peters and then doctoral student Alec Kovar who later became a Political Science Professor.

The personal history stuff came off like sordid gossip. None of this would help Morton avoid a lawsuit or answer Cassandra's questions.

A short passage towards the end of the article went even further. "The accident report filed on the night of Susan Peters' crash details how the car veered off the road less than half a mile out of Carson, drove through a ditch, and struck a large tree. The report noted that tire tracks in the road showed her car had swerved several times before leaving the road. Although the front-end damage most likely caused Ms. Peters' death, additional dents in the rear driver's side bumper and paint scratches were noted. At the time, the investigation concluded that the accident's cause was bad weather."

Again, this read more like a grocery store tabloid than an investigative report into current issues on campus.

The article ended, "Rachel Nagle's dream of attending the same college as her grandmother and discovering her genetic probability for future visual impairments seems worth revisiting. Attempts to contact Ms. Peters' elderly parents, who still reside in Columbus, Nebraska, were unsuccessful."

Even Rachel's mother hadn't known that Rachel had chosen Morton College in order to find out more about her grandmother. Cassandra frowned. How had Swanson found that out? Had Rachel given him background information?

Regardless, Cassandra's takeaways from the lengthy story were that Summers was done investigating, Chairman Hershey needed her diversity and inclusion report before the board could make informed decisions, and Dr. Winters was in denial about any controversies that might tarnish Morton's good name. And it wasn't even 7 o'clock in the morning.

* * *

Cassandra put her dirty dishes in the sink and filled her travel mug with hot coffee. Slipping on her heavy winter coat, warm ankle boots, and a knit hat, Cassandra grabbed her bag, and headed out the door. Her phone's weather app had predicted "unseasonably mild temperatures" with a high of 55 degrees. Cassandra had laughed at the word *mild*. Born in the year of the Ox, Cassandra's stubborn nature meant she'd committed to walk the two blocks to work while the sidewalks were dry.

Cassandra's cheeks quickly chilled, but the *Omaha Daily News* article gave her plenty to think about besides the temperature. The students' advocacy project had gotten a lot of media attention before Thanksgiving. Who stood to gain if their cause was silenced?

Her thoughts were jolted into her immediate surroundings when Cassandra heard a loud bark very close to her left foot. Turning her head to find the dog, she let out a short scream. Ten feet away along the edge of her driveway, Dr. Winters stood dressed for work and holding a large bundle of mail.

She smiled kindly at Cassandra. "I don't know why I bother to check the mailbox. It's always filled with cruise advertisements or credit card offers."

Holding her hand over her rapidly beating heart, Cassandra smiled back. "Yes, ma'am. I know what you mean, but occasionally someone sends a card or letter, and then I'm glad I looked."

Cassandra studied Winters' face a few moments, looking for clues to whether she was driven enough to hurt a student if it meant saving the reputation of the college she loved. "I read the Omaha news story this morning. You gave the reporter an interview."

"Talking to reporters is what good leaders do. We may not agree with what they write, but it's in our best interest to play the game." Murphy sat quietly at Winters' feet, looking up at his owner. "Let them ask the questions. Let them form their conclusions. The real trick is controlling who else is feeding them the facts. It's a calculated risk, but it's paid off for me over four decades. I know what I'm talking about, dear."

Normally, Cassandra would bristle at being called "dear," but her mother's recent admonishment to respect her elders made Cassandra less judgmental. "That reporter, Derek Swanson, wrote a balanced article last month about our biology lab's cancer research. I don't completely trust him though."

"Oh, I followed that whole debacle while I was in Arizona. Dr. Nielson was smart to high tail it out of here after he mishandled the cancer research story. Charlie told me I'd better get up here and see what I could do to fix it."

One eyebrow raised, Cassandra repeated, "Charlie told you..."

Wasn't he Winters' dead husband?

"Before I moved, Charlie and I had a good long chat and he convinced me that the college needed me."

"Like, in your head, right?" Cassandra clarified.

"Of course not." Winters chuckled, "Charlie often visits me before I fall asleep. I enjoy a glass of Chardonnay and tell him about my day. People you love can visit you when they've crossed over to the other side. We only need to welcome them."

Winters believed her dead husband sat up at night chatting with her.

"Just between you and me, I think Charlie's better looking now," she winked. "Not thin or sickly. Kind of perpetually forty years old. Anyhoo, now that I'm back in Carson, I'm committed to doing a better job than Dr. Nielson did of steering the ship." Winters waved the packet of mail she held in her hand to emphasize her point.

Cassandra was open to meditating to both visible and invisible spirits according to Buddhist tradition. But Winters' belief that the spirits were answering back made

Cassandra wonder about Winters' grasp of reality. "There's a limit to what we as administrators can do to quell the negative publicity, right? We can't arbitrarily restrict unflattering free speech or hurt the people who criticize us."

Cassandra paused to see if Winters would admit she'd tried to stop the Deaf Studies advocacy project by immobilizing one of its leaders. "We women in leadership positions in higher education, need to work together, Dr. Winters. Show that we're more willing than our male counterparts to embrace today's issues and make positive changes for our students. Would you like to be the guest speaker at our next Women of Tomorrow meeting in January?"

Perhaps this moment standing in Winters' driveway was an odd time to press her case, but it felt like a good opportunity to speak privately.

Winters didn't answer right away. "I've been where you are." Her eyes darkened to grey and her jaw tightened. "You can't just waltz in here and act like you deserve to be in charge. Everyone sees through your act anyway."

How had Winters known Cassandra wasn't as confident in herself as she acted? No one had called her out on that before, even when she'd been much younger. Cassandra's eyebrows both shot up, but she had no comeback.

"We aren't a team just because you're a woman. I earned every bit of power and authority I've had during my career. I scrapped for it. If you're smart, you'll stay out of my way." Winters nodded once, snapped her fingers at the dog, and both of them trotted up the driveway to the house leaving Cassandra alone near the mailbox.

A shiver went down her back. That glimpse of ruthless calculation made Cassandra believe it was entirely possible that Winters had decided Rachel and the advocacy project would damage Morton College. She didn't want Winters to be that unbalanced, but she had to prevent any more students from getting hurt. Cassandra had a mortgage and her own stubborn streak. She wasn't going anywhere.

* * *

Between appointments, Cassandra was pleasantly surprised when Rachel and Lance came into her office even though neither of them were scheduled to work. Cassandra hadn't seen Rachel since the hospital.

Rachel had braided a front piece of her long blonde hair so it framed her forehead like a headband that covered the shaved portion over her ear, and pulled the rest back in a loose, low ponytail. Her skin color was healthy, and her face looked rested. The only sign of her injury was the black walking boot on her right leg.

"Rachel! Great to see you back." She greeted them and closed the door while they sat in the armchairs facing her desk. "I have a little bit before my next appointment. How are you doing?"

She spoke and signed, "I can't work this week for sure. Probably not Dead Week either. I'm pretty far behind in my Chemistry Lab and the History prof said he won't give me an extension on my final paper."

"I'll find someone else to cover your shifts. What else?"

Rachel eyed her walking boot. "Takes me forever to limp to classes."

"We followed up on the leads we had from the day you were hurt. Until you remember more details, your case is kind of on hold. We're satisfied that Morton took proper precautions to make the area safe." Cassandra had her own theory but now wasn't the time.

"Yeah, I haven't remembered any more about that day. It's just... blank. Other than my memory, I'm okay, I guess. Except for this." She held up her phone screen showing Derek Swanson's news story. "What have I started? My mom's gonna kill me when she sees these photos. She was mad when I told the newspaper my grandmother's name. I had no idea it would go this far." Her hands came up to cover her face while her elbows rested on the tabletop.

Lance softly patted Rachel's arm until she looked at him. He signed, "Not your fault."

But they participated in Swanson's story. "Didn't the reporter contact you and ask you and your mother questions for his article?"

"Yes, but I didn't know he had photos. Or that he'd found my grandfather! Where'd he get them?" Rachel said, "I wanna contact Susan's parents. They're alive and living in Columbus. Do you think they'd meet me? I don't want to tell my mom until I know for sure they say yes. What if I got her hopes up for nothing?"

Rachel's anxiety came spilling out in one long barrage. Cassandra wanted to help her filter out what was real and necessary right now. She didn't know signs for everything, so she did ASL about every fourth spoken English word.

Lance didn't complain. "Rachel. Breathe. Can we agree that you have a very full plate? You're busy healing, catching up on the classes you missed, and studying. What would you say is your number one priority today and tomorrow?"

Rachel didn't hesitate. "Finding out more about Alec Kovar. The black and white photo of him and Susan Peters was blurry. All I could find online was that in the 70s Kovar was a grad student teaching Intro to Political Science to freshmen. Maybe Susan's mother knows more about their relationship. I bet he's my grandfather!"

Even before Rachel stopped talking, Cassandra's head was already shaking back and forth. "School is your priority, Rachel. There's only two weeks left until final exams and you're behind. You have winter break and the rest of your life to find out more about your grandparents."

"This is about my family and my health. I thought you'd help me. You just don't understand how it feels to miss family."

Lance's torso leaned away like he was ready to bolt before an explosion.

She didn't understand. Cassandra gasped as though Rachel had punched her in the chest. "Rachel, my job is to care for the well-being of Morton students. While I recognize that your personal life has become a large distraction, I'm most concerned about your ability to pass your classes this semester." Cassandra crossed her arms over her chest. "If you think your mother is upset by the extra attention because of your injury and family situation, just imagine what she'd say when you fail your classes."

Rachel took a big breath like she was preparing for an angry retort.

Again, Lance tapped Rachel's arm to get her attention. He pointed at Cassandra. "Wait. She wants to help you. You can't fail your classes."

Cassandra was impressed that Lance had understood the gist of their conversation even though she couldn't sign most of the words fluently.

"Okay fine." Rachel heaved a dramatic sigh. "I can wait a few weeks. It'll probably take that long for my Mom to chill once she sees all this."

"Let me know if you need help talking to your professors. They're supposed to be flexible with students who have extended medical absences."

Cassandra eyed Lance's hand on Rachel's arm, guessing that they wouldn't remain in the friend zone for long. Maybe Rachel and Lance weren't aware of the undercurrent of budding feelings between them, but it seemed obvious to Cassandra.

They stood up to leave. "I will. Thanks."

Cassandra's breath eased out as they left her office. She'd promised to have Rachel's back. Sometimes that meant telling the unwelcome truth.

* * *

Several hours later, Cassandra had scheduled the last two Housing Director campus visits, answered all her emails, and pored over departmental census numbers. She opened her office door looking for fresh air and personal interaction with actual people. Her neck cracked when she did a quick stretch, and her lower back throbbed from sitting too long in one place. Even the most expensive office chair wasn't designed for three hours of immobility.

A quick glance at the outer office showed Logan and Haley working on respective laptops. Leftover Halloween fun-size candy bar wrappers were piled on the desk between them.

Carrying her water cup, Cassandra walked down to the restrooms and water fountain. On the way back in, she passed behind the reception desk where one laptop screen showed the same *Daily News* article Cassandra had read first thing in the morning.

The air hung heavy with the acrid smell of burnt popcorn.

Haley stood in the snack station corner at the pre-historic industrial-sized microwave, carefully monitoring what was cooking inside. "I don't think the auto popcorn timer is working. We already ruined one bag. I'm always worried my lunch will spontaneously explode."

Cassandra made a mental note to request a new model. Surely there was room in the budget for a $60 microwave?

Haley said, "We read the article about Susan Peter's car accident. Logan and I tried looking up who taught in the 70s. I mean, my psych professor is ancient. Wouldn't it be cool if he remembered Rachel's grandma?"

Cassandra couldn't think of anyone who was over 65 years old. Besides Winters and Bergstrom, maybe. Nielson was pretty close to that age.

Logan said, "I bet there's old yearbooks in the library. We could check photos for who taught here then."

"Shouldn't that stuff be online?" Haley asked.

"Not everything from back then was scanned and digitally archived," said Cassandra.

Shortly after Logan and Haley left, Bridget came in for her shift. After she settled in and got a snack, Bridget said, "Dr. Sato? Haley texted me that the yearbooks aren't in the library."

Cassandra was in her office but could hear Bridget through the open doorway. "Oh. They were talking about Rachel's family before you came. I guess Logan and Haley went to the library to find copies of the Morton yearbooks during the time Susan Peters was a student."

A few minutes later Bridget said, "She said 1973-1976 are missing, but the other years are on the shelf."

Cassandra barely heard Bridget because she'd pulled up the *Omaha Daily News* article and scrolled through the comments. Her eyes widened and her heart skipped. Things had gotten worse.

The one that caught Cassandra's eye first challenged Dr. Winters personally. "Interesting that the Morton administration maintains radio silence about this professor-student relationship from the 70s. Does Dr. Winters condone such behavior?"

Winters had actually answered the post herself! Cassandra hadn't expected her to be so internet savvy. "Morton College does not respond to innuendo about events from more than forty years ago. It may be difficult for current students to understand the historical lens of the 70s decade in proper perspective. Applying today's morals to past behavior is troublesome. Without commenting on this specific photo, anyone who was working in higher education during that time knows that relationships occasionally occurred between students and faculty members. Morton does not get involved in relationships between consenting adults on campus. We do not tolerate any harassment whatsoever, whether among students, faculty, or staff of any ranking. We urge victims to come forward and report incidents either past or present. However, it's highly likely that due to the historical societal pressures of the times, this student voluntarily protected the father's identity. The difficulty is in determining the truth when it's a case of he said/ she said."

Following Winters' response was a number of other comments:

"The faculty senate takes offense from Dr. Winters' insensitivity regarding the alleged relationship between a former student and faculty member."

"Did he force Susan Peters to have sex with him for grades? How many other students experienced the same harassment? If it happened once, it happened more often."

Cassandra sipped her water, the wheels in her brain spinning. Dr. Winters had spent two weeks protecting Morton's reputation, but with one post she'd invited the entire internet to comment on the state of higher education in the #MeToo Era.

Someone from a completely different college added, "Happens more than you know. My lab TA told me the only way I'd pass was by meeting him in the storage room for a quickie after class."

"Morton's 'don't ask, don't tell' policy allows predators free reign of impressionable young adults."

The most recent commenter said, "Rachel's mother's DNA should be compared to the DNA of Dr. Kovar's other children to determine if they share the same genes from their father."

Shaking her head, she wanted to throttle Winters. Recalling their driveway conversation hours ago about enjoying a glass of wine and talking to her dead husband Charlie, Cassandra laughed. She would've relished the chance to regale Paul with tales of her long day.

Cassandra had finally convinced Rachel to put aside her concern about her family's health and history and focus on school. Not likely now.

Chapter Fifteen

Wednesday morning, Cassandra hoped she didn't run into anyone on her way to the Media Center to meet with the Deaf Studies advocacy stakeholders when she slipped out of the Osborne Building and checked the temperature on her smartwatch. Forty degrees with a predicted high of fifty later in the afternoon.

The stakeholder meeting wasn't exactly a secret, but Cassandra had invited a few key people to triage the Diversity and Inclusion report and prevent further damage. In two weeks, everyone would leave campus and very little work would take place until the new term in January.

Recognizing Fischer looking at his phone coming down the path towards her, she readied a non-committed greeting.

In return, he flashed his full-wattage face transforming smile that dimmed a few notches when she hesitated. "Hey Cass, heading to our meeting?"

His free hand was shoved inside the pocket of his thick leather flight jacket. No hat or gloves. He was immune to the cold, as though he had an internal furnace.

"Yeah, thanks for coming at the last minute. And for Monday at the administrators' team meeting. I didn't know you knew ASL."

Fischer laughed, "Like five signs and a few cuss words, that's all."

"Oh, well thanks anyway," she said. "I called a few directors and VPs after Monday's meeting to request their continuing support for the Diversity Council. I'm not giving up without a fight."

Three beats of silence passed while they stood there awkwardly.

"Listen—" they both started at the same time.

"You first—" he said.

"No, you can go—" she said at the same time.

They both stopped and smiled, waiting for the other to start.

"I'm sorry about the football party Friday afternoon," he said. "My Husker fanaticism may have gotten a little out of hand . . ."

"I just had a lot of work to do. It was nothing personal," she said. "I'm glad you had a good time."

"Until the last quarter when the Huskers lost. It was a cheap call by the official, but that's in the past." His mouth formed a slight smile. "Are we still on for Saturday night?"

"Didn't I see snow in the forecast?"

"There's a thirty percent chance of snow or freezing rain," said Fischer.

Right. Maybe they needed an alternate plan. "Should we check in on Saturday afternoon in case we need to cancel?"

Fischer's warm laughter curled her toes inside her furry boots. "Nah, a thirty percent chance is practically nothing. Locals don't even pay attention until it's at least 80%."

"Ok then. It'll be fun." Cassandra had already searched at least five possible date locations in Carson and nearby towns, none of them a hotbed of excitement.

"I'm looking forward to it."

Yeep. No pressure.

They moved inside the Media Center and made their way to the meeting. Cassandra waved hello to Dr. Bryant and Meg, seated across from each other. Meg looked a little tired, but there wasn't time to talk now. Lance was there representing the students. Cassandra had texted Rachel and Cinda, but they were busy with class or a meeting.

"I really appreciate your making time to talk today. So much has happened since the last time we met. I'm hoping we can come to agreement about the items on the Deaf Studies student advocacy project list."

Dr. Bryant rocked back a little in his chair. He signed and Meg spoke, "Just approve the whole thing and we can all go home."

He laughed at his joke, but Cassandra just stared at him. After a couple of seconds, she said, "Can we start again at square one and talk about the requested items?"

Lance slid a document towards Cassandra. It didn't look much different than when he had first typed out the list on his phone nearly two weeks earlier.

Public TVs and announcements not captioned, no emergency alert or 9-1-1 text system. Non-voting student representation on the Diversity Council and board of directors.

"The Americans with Disabilities Act was passed in 1990. Before I was born." Lance signed while Meg interpreted. "Yet deaf people are still discriminated against every day. Some of my profs show videos that don't have captions. I'm supposed to watch them using my interpreter and then pass a quiz on the content."

Cassandra pointed to the list. "I'm sorry, Lance. I didn't know. The Facilities department has been checking into how to provide text-based updates to accommodate your suggestions. They've added captions to the flat screens around campus any time a video or TV feed is posted. We're working to integrate the morning and afternoon spoken announcements that are made on the building PA systems with the flat screens to show a running list with the same announcements."

Fischer had unzipped his jacket but left it on. "We've already received positive feedback from students who are in classes during the public address announcement times. They like being able to read the updates on the screens when they can't hear the announcements or when they're outside and miss them."

Cassandra caught the look that passed between Lance and Dr. Bryant. If she had to put words to it, she'd guess it meant, "duh."

Lance signed, "That's the thing most people don't understand. Updates that are visual and text-based benefit everyone, not just people who have a hard time hearing the spoken announcements."

"Another reason why a text-based 9-1-1 dispatcher and emergency notification system is a necessity not a luxury," said Bryant.

"Student safety is a high priority for sure. I'd feel awful if a student got hurt because they didn't receive notifications. That said, those systems and software are very pricey for a small college." Cassandra pulled out a few pages that Andy Summers had given her with the estimates. "We might have to consider phasing the costs over several budget cycles instead of all at once. And I feel like I have to warn you that some of the board members are traditionalists who won't spend money on something they feel only benefits a small group of people."

Bryant said, "Unless that small group included themselves, of course."

Touché. Meg's hands rested on her stomach. Cassandra looked to Fischer for help.

"In the two weeks since the Deaf Studies project went public, we've already made some upgrades," Fischer said.

"What if we applied for grants to help pay for some of this technology?" Cassandra said, "Over winter break I could see if we'd qualify for federal telecommunications grants or other funds."

"Matching funds..." Bryant sat up straighter in his seat. "Maybe students in one of my classes could take their information booth project to the next level. Like create a video and enter it into some Shark Tank-style competitions. That might be a good hands-on type of activity for them to tackle for starters."

"Great idea!" Little excited tingles spread out from Cassandra's spine while she made notes on her papers. "I could present these options to the board next week as part of my Diversity and Inclusion report." With him onboard, there'd be nothing to protest.

She closed her leather portfolio and said, "Morton would really appreciate it if you and your students could use your influence to put out positive social media messages about what we're doing to address the issues."

Bryant smiled, "Are you asking me to impinge on the academic freedom of my students, Dr. Sato?"

Her mouth dropped open a little bit. Was he really dragging academic freedom into the debate? "Of course not, Dr. Bryant. But you have a lot of influence. If you were to post that progress is being made, it would help our image."

Bryant stood and put on his jacket. "I said the new emergency texting system would be a good *start*, Dr. Sato. I need more Deaf faculty in my department, the video conference room needs upgrades, and a new cappuccino machine in the faculty lounge would be much appreciated."

He was joking, right?

She said, "Oh, before I forget, do you know of a group called the Deaf Rights Now Coalition?"

His dark brows met over the deep frown in his forehead. "They're a new outfit out of Virginia. I've seen their booth at professional conferences I've attended."

"Well, they might be coming to Morton next week to watch the board meeting."

Bryant laughed. "If the Coalition comes to Morton, the students' social media posts will be the least of your problems. Their Deaf Rights advocacy group has a big following."

He was very good at having the last word in a conversation. Cassandra found it maddening.

Fischer left the opposite way out of the building.

"This job gets better every day." Telling someone they looked tired was always a tricky thing. "You okay, Meg?"

"I need a nap." Meg shrugged and waved goodbye.

* * *

A short while later, Cassandra returned to the Osborne building and stopped at the presidential suite. Keeping an eye on the closed inner door to Dr. Winters' office, Cassandra approached Julie, her assistant. "Hey Julie, how're you?" Cassandra stepped closer to the desk to keep her voice quiet.

Always calm and unflappable, the perfect assistant for such a stressful position, Julie's skin was puffed into bags under her eyes and her makeup seemed washed out as though she'd rushed out of the house this morning and forgotten to apply color. "Oh you know, living the dream! The reporters have stopped calling so that's one positive thing. My grandson's birthday party is tomorrow night, and he wants Grandma to bake him a Lego cake."

Her mahogany executive-sized desk was parked in front of the door to Winters' office like a sentry, its surface covered in a large computer monitor and neatly stacked papers arranged in low piles.

Cassandra said, "I might have mixed up a few dates in my calendar and thought maybe you could tell me the right timeline."

Before Cassandra had even finished her sentence, Julie already had her calendar program pulled up on her computer. She'd give her right arm for a professional assistant. "I can check for you. What meeting were you questioning?"

"I was trying to remember the exact day when Dr. Winters started at Morton? Like when she first came into the office."

Fine gemstone rings adorned every one of Julie's fingers, ending in long pointed fingernails with a nail salon manicure and fancy artistic swirls. Cassandra didn't know what Julie's husband did for a living, but they must've done pretty well to afford that much bling. Her short fingers tapped on the keyboard briefly.

"Her first day was November 18th."

"I just had an idea I wanted to run by you, Julie. Even though Dr. Winters worked here before, she'd been away for five years. Do you think a Welcome Coffee would be appropriate or has too much time passed since she started? I thought the new staff who weren't here during her first tenure might like to meet Dr. Winters and get to know her better."

"I'm not sure Dr. Winters would want that, but I can gently ask her. Maybe just a two-hour open-house type event where people stop by her office and say hello might be nice. The redecorating just finished last week. So no I don't think too much time has passed."

"That's what I thought," confirmed Cassandra. "Do you know when she interviewed for the position? It seemed very fast between when Dr. Nielson resigned and she started."

Julie hesitated.

Cassandra assumed she had a natural inclination to protect the boss's privacy. "I'm sorry, I don't mean to overstep. Dr. Nielson welcomed me to campus on my first day, and it occurred to me that I was so busy with my own duties when Dr. Winters first started that I didn't really chat with her before all of the controversy began with the students."

"Yes, it has been a busy couple of weeks for sure." Julie smiled. "It all happened quickly once Dr. Winters let the board know she was interested in coming back to Morton."

"How is Dr. Winters with the internet? Like reading articles online?"

She'd gone too far. The edges of Julie's smile drooped, and her eyes shrewdly focused on Cassandra's. "Okay, spill. You didn't come in here to plan a Welcome Coffee or ask about my weekend plans. Why do you need to know about Winters' reading habits?"

Her chest tightened. She'd been caught and didn't have a ready reply. The truth sounded ridiculous. *Oh, just wondering if your boss attacks people she deems a threat to her alma mater.*

If Cassandra said it aloud, she'd be laughed out of the office.

Cassandra's leg leaned against the front corner of Julie's desk to avoid squirming. "Here's the truth. I'm working on a Diversity and Inclusion report with a very tight deadline. I'm curious how she reads these types of reports. Like, suppose I were to submit the first 30 pages on time, while continuing to work on the last 10 pages. Would she notice if the last part arrived a couple of days later? If I send an online attachment, she'd know I switched them by the time stamp."

Cassandra did her winning 100-watt smile. "If Dr. Winters reads paper documents, then her trusty assistant could slip in the last few pages and appendix when I finish them?"

Julie visibly relaxed and chuckled. "Dr. Winters' computer wasn't even hooked up until last week. She has a smartphone, but she mostly uses it to make calls or send text messages. She's pretty good with devices but prefers paper documents. We kill a lot of trees in this office."

"Thanks so much, Julie. That's all I needed to know. I'll take it from here." Cassandra pulled out her phone and looked at the calendar. "Let's pencil in next Friday for a Welcome Coffee. I'll talk to the other administrators and you can double check with Dr. Winters that it's okay with her."

"That should fit in her schedule."

Cassandra slowly followed the hallways back to the Student Affairs wing. Looking down at her calendar again, she realized that Meg had been right all along. Without a computer or internet in her office until Thanksgiving, the odds were slim-to-none that Dr. Winters had master-minded an attack against Rachel Nagle.

There simply hadn't been enough time for Winters to accept the job, unpack her new house, read the news articles, and form a diabolical plan to take out a student leader all in one weekend.

Cassandra's number one suspect was a pain in the neck, but she wasn't the bad guy.

Chapter Sixteen

During Cassandra's Oahu State College days, she was often awakened in the middle of the night by someone from work reporting break-ins, or kids who were too drunk to stumble back to their dorm rooms, and one memorable night when a Greek housemother had hit the gas pedal instead of the brake and rammed her Jeep through the plate glass window of the campus pizza place.

Since the move to Carson, Cassandra's ability to wake up instantly ready for the emergency at hand had diminished to the point where she was both surprised and foggy to feel her phone vibrating under her pillow late Tuesday night. Sitting up, Cassandra squinted at the clock on her phone—11:30.

Was it morning? There wasn't any light slivered around the outside of her curtains. No, it must still be nighttime, although she felt well-rested. Which was impossible since she'd been asleep for less than two hours. "Hello?"

A familiar male voice brought her fully awake. "Hey, it's Connor. Sorry Cass, but can you come over? Now. I'm taking Meg to the hospital. We need you to stay here with Tony."

Cassandra was out of bed and pulling on sweatpants as soon as she heard the word hospital. "Of course, Connor. I'll be there as fast as I can. Is it the baby?"

She heard a mechanical sound in the background and imagined him standing in their kitchen making a cup of coffee.

"Yeah. She's cramping and there's a little blood. I'd call her mom, but they're out of town this week."

"It's fine. Really. I'm on my way."

Less than five minutes later, Cassandra pulled out of her driveway and pointed her car East. The O'Briens' acreage in Gretna was normally half an hour away, but traffic on the two-lane highway was minimal.

It was so pitch-black dark that Cassandra drove with her bright headlights on the whole way until she got closer to town, worried she might hit a deer or other animal. She searched her memory for details of Derek Swanson's article. Where had Susan Peter's car been damaged? Could she have swerved to miss an animal on the road? Something to consider.

Pulling in front of the house thirty minutes later, Cassandra hadn't reached the door when Connor backed his pickup out of the garage. He disappeared inside the house for a minute then returned supporting Meg's arm as they walked out together. He boosted Meg into the front seat before going around to the driver's side. Cassandra stood in the open car door next to her friend. Slightly bent over, Meg cradled the bottom of her baby bump.

"We'll be okay. It's just a little cramping. Connor's being cautious." Meg's smile was strained.

The truck was so high, Cassandra couldn't reach in for a full hug. Channeling every positive spirit and feeling she could imagine, Cassandra gently squeezed Meg's thigh. "He's right. The doctors will make sure, ya?"

Cassandra's pregnancy and childbirth knowledge would fit in a thimble. She knew Meg's previous miscarriages amplified concern over every ache and pain.

Meg's eyes teared up as Cassandra stepped back and closed the door. Cassandra shivered in the still night, watching the red lights on the back of the truck make their way down the long gravel driveway towards the main highway. Looking up at the bright stars overhead, she could see a glow from the East where the city lights of Omaha blotted out the twinkly canvas.

She whispered, "Namo Amida Butsu, Namo Amida Butsu, Namo Amida Butsu."

Once inside the house, Cassandra closed the garage door and turned off the lights in the kitchen and hallway. Grabbing a throw blanket, she nestled herself into their couch and rested her head.

Too wired to sleep, she had plenty to think about. If Dr. Winters wasn't responsible for Rachel's assault, who stood to gain by messing up the advocacy project? Was it remotely possible that Dr. Bryant would arrange a publicity stunt that went wrong?

The next thing Cassandra was aware of was a weird shifting in the air nearby. She must've dozed off. Quiet breathing came from her right, and as her eyes adjusted to the dark, she saw Tony standing inches from the couch holding the stuffed SpongeBob she'd given him for Christmas when he was a toddler.

"Where's my mom and dad?" His eyes were wide and scared.

"They wen see the doctor. They asked me to stay with you."

Maybe it was the late hour, or the quiet house, but Cassandra slipped into her local Hawaiian speech patterns instead of the haole formal way she usually talked at work. She scooted aside to make room for him and reached both arms out to invite him to join her.

"Huh." Looking younger than his ten years, he climbed up next to her and tucked his feet under the blanket, letting his head fall onto the arm of the couch.

"You want me to walk you back down the hall to your bed?"

"Nah, aunty. I stay with you."

"Okay, brah." She rested a hand on his side and waited.

"Is my Mom going to lose the baby again?" His voice was so low, she leaned her head closer to hear him.

She shouldn't have been surprised that he'd worked out why his parents would make an emergency trip to the doctor in the middle of the night. Tony had been in the house with his mom the last time she'd had a miscarriage while Connor had been out of town on National Guard training weekend.

She wouldn't lie to him. "I don't know, sweetie. Your mom didn't feel good so they wen took her to one doctor.

Dey try take good care of your baby bruddha or sistah. Same like you."

He nodded, and satisfied with her answer, closed his eyes. Within ten minutes his breath became regular, and his leg twitched indicating he'd fallen asleep.

Cassandra looked at the fireplace and chair opposite the couch. The wall was filled with framed photos of their family, mostly Tony at different ages. The large window to the left of the fireplace showed the dark shadows of evergreen trees in their back yard and Cassandra could make out the outline of their huge wooden playset. A pleasant linen smell blanketed the room. Tony's limp weight pressed warmly into her side, and she slowly petted his dense, curly hair. Red like his mother's.

As a girl, Cassandra had always imagined that by thirty-four she'd have at least one, if not two keiki running around her island home. Her engagement to Paul had happened right on time, just like everything else she'd carefully scheduled. Like it was fated. Her plan had completely flipped eight years ago upon his death. Now she lived alone, more concerned about her students and her job than with filling a home with laughing children.

Was it time to give up on that plan? Her biological clock hadn't even budged when colleagues brought their new babies to work, or she spied a newborn in a car seat at the food market. Besides her nephews and Tony, she hadn't often played with little keiki and didn't really miss it. The solitude of her house well-suited her schedule. Becoming a college president with a family would be a big challenge.

Sure, women with high-powered jobs had children, but that balancing act came with trade-offs.

And what prospects did she have for a man to fill the empty slot in her dream family photo? For so long that photo had included Paul. She was too proud to settle. Her parents' long and happy marriage was too strong of an example. She didn't want to be a single mother. She didn't want a busy corporate type who would see her as the successful prize for his hard work. She wanted love.

Cassandra had proven the past eight years that she didn't need a man to be happy. But did she want one anyway? She'd seen the way guys looked at her at meetings and national conferences. She recognized the unspoken longing in Andy Summers' eyes when he thought she didn't notice. So far she'd chosen to ignore it and enjoy their easy friendship.

In all this time, Marcus Fischer had been the only person to spark even an ember of fire in her heart. Their first date had been a dud. They'd mostly talked about work. Maybe they had too little in common. She couldn't force something that wasn't meant to be.

Edging her nose closer to Tony's hair, she stealthily inhaled his little boy scent of shampoo, dried sweat, and warm sweetness. She loved the comfort of his slightly sticky hand resting on her arm. The way he trusted her, unquestioning.

Dr. Bergstrom had told her not long ago that things worth having required work. She'd accomplished so much already in her career. Falling in love shouldn't be hard work, too. Thinking about her date with Fischer, and being totally honest, had she passively expected him to do the wooing while she soaked it up effortlessly? Might things go better if Cassandra tried making *him* welcome or happy?

Her love language had always been Gifts, because Cassandra knew that the more she gave of herself to others, in return she received far better gifts because they were intangible. Maybe instead of thinking what feelings Fischer stirred within her, she should think about what she could do for him?

* * *

Cassandra's phone vibrated under her shoulder and she felt between the couch cushions until her fingers grasped the case. The display showed Connor's name. Sliding out from behind Tony, she tip-toed into the kitchen.

"How is she?" Cassandra whispered.

"Better. They gave her medicine to stop the cramping. She's resting. The bleeding stopped."

A big sigh emptied her lungs. "Thank God." Standing in front of the sink, Cassandra looked out the window to the softly lightening sky that glowed purple behind the trees. "Tony woke up once, but he fell back asleep. What time should I drive him to school?"

Cassandra didn't exactly know where Tony's school was, but surely he could tell her the name and her maps app would take it from there.

"He rides the school bus. Can you wait with him at the bus stop until 7:30?"

"Got it. Anything else?"

After getting a few morning routine details from Connor, they hung up.

Cassandra peeked in the refrigerator to see what she might cook Tony for breakfast. How hard could it be to make pancakes shaped like SpongeBob and Patrick?

Twenty minutes later, she flipped the first two cooked pancakes onto a plate and placed it in the oven to keep warm.

Tony appeared rumpled and crusty-eyed, standing next to the refrigerator. Only half-awake, he was so adorable her arms itched to hug him.

Spreading his arms open wide he said, "Good morning world and all who inhabit it!"

Recognizing the SpongeBob reference immediately, Cassandra opened the fridge and lifted a small jug of orange juice out of the door. She danced over to the cabinet and pulled out a glass, singing, "The most important meal of the day, serving it up Gary's way—pop!"

She poured a tall measure of juice in the glass and handed it to Tony. "Enjoy, buddy."

The smile he flashed her was bright enough to make her eyes fill.

Being a mom might be a lot of fun. She'd have to think some more about the husband and keiki situation.

Chapter Seventeen

Cassandra had made it back to Carson, showered, and was toweling off her hair when she got a text from Andy Summers.

"Are you okay?"

Wrapping the towel around her head, she replied, "Yes, fine. What's wrong?"

He texted, "I stopped by your office, but you weren't there."

She smiled a little. Her head ached and no matter how many times she brushed her teeth, Cassandra couldn't shake the hungover feeling that came with such a short night of interrupted sleep.

"No stalkers or vandals here. Just coming in late to work. Thanks for checking on me." Not only did she have friends who needed her, she had other friends who cared enough to worry about her absence.

Cassandra had already called her office and left a voice-mail about being late, so she decided to follow her normal yoga routine and eat a full breakfast before going in to work.

* * *

One benefit to arriving late was that she didn't get immediately swept away by whatever drama occurred in the office. George her officemate had to pick up her slack for a change instead of the other way around.

Now that Dr. Winters was off her naughty list, Cassandra was out of ideas for how Rachel got hurt.

She sent an email to Ibrahim Kouri, the facilities guy who kept track of the stray animals asking what kind of vet services they received, how they were fed, and whether any prior complaints had been filed. She hadn't heard of anyone being bitten. But since the one thing Rachel had remembered was a barking dog, it was worth double checking.

Derek Swanson's article had morphed into another news cycle of criticism. Cassandra called Cinda to get the short version instead of chasing down individual social media rabbit holes.

"Hey girlfriend! I was just thinking about you. I got you a present."

A photo appeared on Cassandra's phone screen. What did she need an oven mitt with a sharp edge thingy at the end for? "It's not my birthday. You shouldn't have." Cassandra zoomed in on the photo. Squinting, she gave up after a few seconds. "No, really. You shouldn't have."

A siren sounded faintly in the distance.

"It's for your car. You scrape ice off your car windshield, but your hand stays toasty warm inside." Cinda sounded very pleased with herself. "Just tuck it under your front seat. Trust me, you'll need it. Did you see the forecast?"

"Thanks. Snow on Saturday, right? Hey, I called to ask what people are saying online about Dr. Winters' comment to the Swanson article. I haven't seen any more news stories. Is there anything else I need to worry about?"

"I've only read the main threads on Facebook and Twitter where the article was shared. Some well-wishers wanted permission to set up crowdfunded donations to cover Rachel's medical expenses. Several crackpots said they'd fathered Patty Nagle and were willing to give a sperm sample. *Ewwww.* One couple claiming to be former Morton students remembered Susan Peters and offered to contribute to a memorial scholarship in her honor. I'll send you their names."

The sound of the fire engine got louder.

"One thing you might want to follow up on." Cassandra waited while Cinda's keyboard clicked in the background. "A few specific rumors about sexual harassment by current faculty. I can copy those posts if you want to look them up."

No one else seemed concerned about the college's exposure if a #MeToo incident surfaced. "Yes, please send me screenshots of anything you think we should take seriously. Do you hear that siren?"

They'd focused on a lawsuit for negligence with the weather conditions, but sexual harassment lawsuits would be just as damaging. "I really appreciate your following all this, Cinda. I feel like we need someone tracking these things all the time." Cassandra noted that in her bullet journal. "I wonder which department that would fall under?"

"Office of Student Stalking?" Cinda laughed. "Yeah that siren sounds very close. Now what?"

And then abruptly, it stopped.

Cassandra stood and did a visual sweep out her window, but didn't see anything amiss.

"I don't know but I'd better get going."

"Me too. Talk later."

Maybe five minutes passed before Cassandra's watch alerted her to an incoming call from Andy. "Hey. We've got a situation at the library. You'd better come look at this."

"Sure—"

Summers hung up as soon as she got the word out.

Cassandra took an extra minute to switch out her dressy heels to plain black flats. Grabbing her coat from the rack behind her door, she looked down and noticed her black dress pants were now pooled on the floor because she'd had the pants hemmed to wear with heels. She threw the flats back in her bottom desk drawer and pulled on the sheep-skin-lined boots she'd purchased for snowy days. Tucking the extra inches of pant legs inside the boots, she zipped up her coat and stopped in the reception area where Haley was sitting at the front desk.

Haley took in Cassandra's parka, boots, and gloves. "Going to the Arctic for lunch?"

Cassandra ignored her smirk. "I'll be at the library if you need me."

"Was that where the fire truck went?"

"I'll let you know," she said halfway through the door.

Before Cassandra opened the front library doors, the blaring alarm and flashing red light overwhelmed her senses. Arriving in the main lobby, Cassandra was about to text Summers for directions where she should meet him when she saw two uniformed staff members heading towards the back corner carrying buckets and a large broom and wearing medical face masks like you see in cities with heavy smog. She followed them down a hallway and turned at the end of the bookshelves.

The first thing that hit her was the smell. Sweet and woodsy. But also acrid like burned paper. A hazy, white smoke filled the area and slowly dissipated out the open windows. A firefighter in full regalia and gas mask opened the window closest to her.

Stepping closer, she saw Summers huddled with two librarians at the far end of the stacks. Along the whole long wall there were alternating setups of two bookshelves and a two-person study carrell where the people faced each other with a wooden partition between them. The adjacent wall held a couch and seating area. A few students gathered to the side of the study area among the bookshelves.

As Cassandra neared the corner, the smell intensified until the mixture of sweet and acrid burned the back of her throat. After a few more steps, she saw the source: a wet bowl of burned twigs and leaves had dumped over on the coffee table. The nearby couch was discolored by a wet spot and smoldering charred area. The study table nearby had a backpack and laptop on it, but the chair lay on its side.

Summers broke away from the library staff and stared at Cassandra's dress pants and boots as she approached. When he opened his mouth, she expected a snarky remark about her outfit, but he clamped it closed again. Wise man.

When Cassandra was close enough to hear, he said, "Someone started these leaves on fire on the table next to a student seated here." He pointed to the abandoned study desk. "Student didn't notice at first until the smoke really got going. Says she threw her water bottle at the bowl to stop the smoldering but the whole thing tipped over onto the couch. The couch started burning. Then the fire alarm went off."

Cassandra took in the whole corner, from the study desk with the partition wall to the large clay bowl, spilled ashes, two rolled up bundles of herbs and the burned couch.

"Did anyone see who started it?" she asked.

Summers said, "Student reported that she was studying with headphones in and not paying attention to people walking by. Lunch time probably made this a nice, quiet spot."

"Are end of semester pranks a Morton tradition?" She made a slow 360 turn to look at the handful of students and staff who remained.

Summers held up a hand to the guys with the buckets. "Let's leave it here for now. I've called the sheriff's office to come and fingerprint the bowl and the area."

"Fingerprints? Yeah." Cassandra nodded. "Setting off fire alarms in the library will end in disciplinary action if we ever catch who started this. How's the student who was studying at this desk feeling now?"

When Summers didn't respond right away, Cassandra turned her head and locked eyes with him. "It was Rachel Nagle. She was coughing quite a bit and her eyes were irritated. The head librarian took her to the urgent care clinic."

Why hadn't he opened with that? Cassandra gasped. Quickly, she scanned for clues to why someone had targeted Rachel. Again.

The desk looked like Rachel had jumped up, knocking the chair over when she realized the bowl with leaves and herbs was on fire next to her. She'd dumped water on the fire, but when it spread, she ran away.

Cassandra noticed a white sheet of paper on the coffee table near the burned leaves and mess. Looking closer, the paper was held down by a white crystal bar about six inches long. In large, bold computer-printed letters the paper said, "You're not welcome here. Stay Away Forever."

That sounded more like a bullying kind of thing than life-threatening arson. Maybe someone just didn't like Rachel or her student activism.

Summers walked over to take statements from the remaining students and staff.

Cassandra squinted at the whole mess, her nose wrinkling from the smell. She stared a few extra seconds at the white crystal, then joined Summers in the stacks. "I'll go check on Rachel at the clinic."

Summers nodded an acknowledgment that he'd heard her.

Zipping her parka, Cassandra walked through the library lobby and saw Dr. Bergstrom coming out of the bathroom holding his briefcase.

What was he doing here? She measured her steps to catch up to him. "Dr. Bergstrom?"

His beard looked scruffier than usual and a chunk of hair on his head was askew, although he smiled at her like always. "Hello Dr. Sato, what are you doing here?"

Why didn't he ask about the fire truck or the smoke? "I was just leaving." An instinct nudged her to confirm something about Rachel. "Actually, I'm glad I bumped into you. I wanted to ask you something about Rachel Nagle. The student you found on the sidewalk. Well, there's a chance that she knows who her biological grandfather was. A former professor here at Morton. Maybe you knew him too . . . Alec Kovar? Taught Political Science."

"Yes . . . I knew Dr. Kovar for many years." The hand holding the briefcase twitched making the case hit his leg repeatedly. He seemed unaware. "What makes Rachel think he's her grandfather? That's outrageous."

"There's a photo online of Susan Peters and Dr. Kovar in an intimate setting. If they weren't a couple, they seemed very close."

Bergstrom stopped walking and closed his eyes. "The man is dead. Can't he rest in peace?" His head bowed towards his chest a moment before he raised it and met her eyes. "Does everyone know?"

When Cassandra nodded, he sighed, "Susan Peters and Kovar did have a brief relationship while he worked on his PhD and she was an undergrad. It ended before her death and that's all I'm going to say about it."

The first time she'd asked Bergstrom about Susan Peters he had acted like he didn't know her. Maybe the news stories had jogged his memory. "The whole truth is going to come out, sir."

Several beats of silence passed. His voice changed the way it always did when he was about to deliver a wise quote. "Listen to me, 'when a man comes to me, I accept him at his best, not at his worst.'"

He'd chosen the wrong philosopher if he thought that would stump her. She laughed. "True, Dr. Bergstrom. But Confucius also said, 'Study the past if you would divine the future.'"

His look of surprise was a great reward for besting him at his own game. "See you tomorrow at the Philosophy focus group, sir." She turned quickly and exited through the side door towards the urgent care clinic.

During the ten-minute walk, Cassandra texted Connor O'Brien for an update on Meg.

Immediately he replied, "She's resting at home. All good now. Mahalo. You da best."

She sent back, "Whew. So glad for you. Talk later."

Cassandra arrived in the lobby and waited. After a while, Patty Nagle stepped through the sliding glass doors appearing more like Rachel's sister than her mother wearing yoga pants and lined boots like Cassandra's with a fleece pullover jacket. Her hair was pulled back in a ponytail and designer sunglasses rested on top of her head.

"My Rachel has been back on campus for like three days, and you people can't keep her safe!" Her index finger stabbed the air between her and Cassandra. "I want bodyguards assigned to her 24/7."

Cassandra stepped back and put her hands up defensively. "Hello, Mrs. Nagle. I'm just waiting for Rachel. The front desk person called the doctor to ask if it's okay for me to go back there. "

Mrs. Nagle looked left and right. She looked like she'd bust through the lobby if no one stopped her. "Rachel texted me on her way over." She walked towards the front desk and spoke loudly as though someone down the hall would overhear her. "It's okay for me to go back there. That's my daughter who's hurt."

Gee, Mrs. Nagle must have floored it to get here so quickly. Cassandra smiled at the harried student wearing a Morton polo and a name tag that said, Molly at the front desk. "I'm sure it will just take a few minutes to sort out, ma'am."

After a five-minute stare down, a technician in cheery superhero scrubs came down the hallway. "Mrs. Nagle, she's just finishing up. Your daughter will be out in a few minutes."

Cassandra let out a big breath. It must not be too bad if they treated her and let her go.

Mrs. Nagle did a *huff* but didn't make a scene.

Shortly, the same technician led Rachel into the lobby. Rachel did not look happy. "Mom! I texted you to let you know that I was fine. I told you not to drive here. Geesh!"

The bruises and swelling on Rachel's cheek from her fall on the ice were completely gone now. A purple stocking cap covered the shaved part of her hair. Looking more closely, Cassandra noticed red irritation around Rachel's eyes and nose.

Her mother touched Rachel's cheek. "Look at you! How much of those toxins did you inhale?"

"It was just some smoky leaves and herbs, Mom. It was a prank. If I hadn't knocked the bowl over, nothing would've caught fire. I put it out before any real damage was done." She pleaded, "Please go home before my friends all see you. They already think I'm high maintenance."

Mrs. Nagle seemed reassured by her daughter's feistiness. "You tell that security guy that we are pressing charges. What kind of idiot pulls a prank like that?"

Pressing charges. Again with the lawsuits. Cassandra's chest tightened. If she got her hands on whoever started the fire, she'd definitely pursue disciplinary measures. And a giant Stink Eye.

Rachel slowly limped with her broken booted foot. Mrs. Nagle joined Rachel in heading for the door. "I'll pull the car around front honey and drop you off at the dorm."

"We have to stop at the library first so I can run in and pick up my backpack."

Once her mother had left, Rachel turned to Cassandra. "I stopped in your office this morning, but you weren't there."

"I was helping a friend and came in late. What did you need?"

Rachel's voice was raspy, like smoke had gotten into her throat and lungs. "It's okay. That other guy already helped me."

Cassandra frowned. "The other guy... oh you mean Dr. Hansen." George had actually surfaced out of his lair long enough to be helpful. Now if she could pawn off more appointments on him, maybe she wouldn't feel so overwhelmed.

She'd tried delegating to him the first two weeks on the job, but George had smiled and nodded and then done absolutely none of what she'd asked. Eventually, she'd quit asking for his help. He saw a few students a day, but she honestly had no idea what else he did or who he answered to. It sure as heck wasn't her.

"Yeah, he signed an accommodation form for one of my classes so I could turn in a late paper with permission. He told me I reminded him of his old student, Susan Peters."

Cassandra still hadn't seen a clear photo of Susan but was becoming more curious. Many young women here had long, straight hair in shades of blonde and brown, but maybe she resembled Susan more than usual.

Rachel eyed the doorway for her mother's car, then clutched Cassandra's arm, "Hey, did you see the sign on the table at the library?"

"Rachel, that wasn't a prank. The whole library could've burned down."

"I know it wasn't a prank, but don't tell my mom! I feel like the library thing wouldn't have happened if I hadn't spoken out so much about the Deaf Studies project." She smacked her forehead. "I can't believe I'm saying this, but maybe my mother was right. I should've kept my story more private." Mrs. Nagle's car stopped in front of the clinic and Rachel implored Cassandra. "I don't care who wants me to leave, Dr. Sato. I need to pass my classes. You think I want to go through all this crap and then retake them next semester? That's a big fat no."

"I'll talk to the security director and let you know what he says." This couldn't be a coincidence. "Maybe someone will escort you to class and make sure you're not alone for a few days. Until we find the person who did this."

"Maybe I could ask Lance to walk with me." Her sly smile confirmed Cassandra's instinct that there were more feelings between them than simple friendship. "Someday this could all be a funny story we tell our grandchildren about how we met in college and got together."

Cassandra just hoped their story had a happy ending.

Chapter Eighteen

Exhausted from the week, Cassandra decided to make another late entrance to work on Friday. Well, 7:30 a.m. was late for *her* anyway. She also planned on leaving early to go home and change clothes before Dr. Bergstrom's Sunday Salon house party. Two weeks before the end of the semester, and she'd become an official slacker.

"HA!" She laughed out loud in her quiet office. "If my friends at Oahu State could see me now..." Still the first person to arrive, the outer office lights were off, the dawn pinking the sky behind the chapel across the quad.

A steady stream of students filled her morning either pleading with her to convince a professor to give them the benefit of the doubt when final grades were posted (not her role) or telling enormous whoppers about how they needed an extension due to an unlikely family illness or death.

One tragic junior called from a funeral home where he'd been helping his family plan his mother's burial services. The woman succumbed to complications of breast cancer and pneumonia. Cassandra had been so touched by his story that she'd contacted his professors, referred him to Cinda's office, and sent flowers to the family.

The Philosophy focus group meeting at Bryan Hall had finished mid-afternoon. Balancing her laptop bag, travel cup, and oversized poster pages, Cassandra followed Dr. Bergstrom up two flights of stairs to his office. He set the remaining supplies they'd used while facilitating the meeting on the floor in front of his office while he unlocked it. Opening the door, he stood aside and let Cassandra through. Searching in vain for a clean surface to put her armload down, she carefully set the cup on a small side table in the corner and sunk down onto his dilapidated couch. She rolled the large note pages into a long tube, so they'd be easier to carry back to her office, let out a sigh of relief, then stuffed her empty travel cup into the bag's side pocket."Your department had some great ideas," Cassandra said. "I can use their examples in my report next week. I really appreciate your time and support getting this off the ground."

"The President isn't the only decision maker on campus. When you do a great job on the report and presentation next week, the board will recognize you for it."

He added the box of markers and pens to a teetering stack of books on the floor next to his desk. It didn't matter how many times she came to his office, Cassandra always felt a twitchy discomfort at not being able to clean it all up and organize his junk. How old were the papers on the bottom of the 15-inch high stack of folders to the left of his clunky millennial-era desktop computer monitor? The students who had handed in those papers likely had long since graduated and moved away, working at their careers, oblivious to the fact that once Bergstrom had entered the semester grade the papers lived in his pile indefinitely.

"Thanks. After last month, I still feel like I need to redeem myself in their eyes." She'd been caught off guard when her reputation had been shredded virtually overnight based on flimsy hearsay and unfounded accusations. Luckily, once they saw how she'd protected the students by putting her own safety on the line, she'd recovered their goodwill.

"I won't allow Winters to take the credit for your contributions."

"Being able to mention specific examples like starting an international student support group and training for how to have civil discourse with people who share different viewpoints are good starting points. I need to communicate better about how the Diversity Council will benefit the whole college, not only faculty and students of minority groups."

Fighting her pride, Cassandra acknowledged that one benefit of this Diversity and Inclusion report was that she had met more than half the faculty members. She practiced mindfully listening to complaints from individuals and groups who didn't feel included in the college dialogue. She'd opened a whole new planning document in her files with a list of Morton's future needs and goals.

Cassandra might not be in the running for President this go-around, but she wanted to be ready the next time they conducted a search. Many of Morton's needs were also present at similar-sized colleges. She was beefing up her portfolio, so she'd be ready when it was her turn to accept complete responsibility for a similar institution.

Two sharp knocks sounded on the closed office door. Bergstrom yelled, "Come in!"

An undergrad wearing nose and eyebrow rings opened the door. His loud voice said, "Excuse me, sir, that overseas conference call you were expecting is waiting for you in the main faculty office."

Not only was Bergstrom so old school he used the land lines, he also walked down the hall to the main office because he couldn't figure out how to transfer a call to his own desk phone.

Bergstrom said, "Sorry Cassandra, this person has tried to contact me several times with a question about my research. I need to take this call. Please make yourself comfortable. I'll just be a few minutes."

Cassandra debated returning to her office and catching up with him later. Instead her desire for a quick break won out and she slid a vanilla latte coffee pod into his Keurig— the one shiny modern convenience in his office. Biting into a British caramel biscuit Bergstrom kept in a plaid tin next to his coffeemaker, Cassandra savored the sugar and caffeine. The protein energy bar she'd eaten hours ago wasn't nearly as tasty.

Relaxing into the lumpy, flowered couch, she inhaled the lingering aroma of brewing coffee mixed with the tobacco smoke that had seeped into the ceiling and walls. Her father's pipe growing up had the same musky, sweet scent. Smoking on campus had probably been banned in the nineties, but that smell would never go away without replacing the drywall.

The window over his desk was coated by a dingy layer of residual nicotine that dimmed the light emitted by the overhead ceiling fixture. Cassandra's favorite parts of the office were Bergstrom's framed philosophy prints that quoted Aristotle and Batman.

Frowning, Cassandra stopped short mid-chew and leaned forward towards the bookshelf several feet away. Next to the vertical volumes that Bergstrom used as references when teaching his Philosophy of Batman class was a horizontal stack of DC comic books. On top of that were four slim hardbound books, the bottommost one's spine said, "Maple Memories 1973."

A cookie chunk lodged in her windpipe when Cassandra sucked in a startled breath. She coughed twice hard to clear it from her throat, and sipped coffee from the dainty china cup. Tears ran down her cheek while she cleared her throat a few more times until her breathing returned to normal. Glancing at the closed office door, she reached out to open the top book from 1976. The title page carried an embossed stamp pronouncing the yearbook as part of the Morton College Library collection.

Footsteps sounded in the hallway, and Cassandra shut the book and tossed it back on the pile as though it was hot lava. While the door remained closed for several seconds, she examined the rest of the books on his bookcase more closely. The top shelf contained ornate, leather-bound volumes of a collection that looked like it had been purchased as a set. Towards the right side were commemorative boxed sets of the Harry Potter, Lord of the Rings, and Narnia series next to a dog-eared copy of Nietzsche's *Beyond Good and Evil.*

Cassandra had never asked Dr. Bergstrom his exact age, but she'd assumed he was between 65 and 70 years old. Shouldn't he have more yearbooks stashed in nooks and crannies throughout his office? A quick visual scan of his piles and clutter found no other memory books besides those four.

Weren't those the exact years the students couldn't find in the library? Why did he need them? How weird was that?

By the time she'd finished her coffee and the cookie, she again heard footsteps approaching. Without conscious thought for why, Cassandra reached up in one smooth motion and snatched the four yearbooks off the shelf, sliding them into her laptop case.

The doorknob turned and Dr. Bergstrom stepped inside, smiling. "Thanks for . . . uh, waiting?" He sniffed and smiled again. "You helped yourself. Excellent. Did you get a biscuit, too? They're so thin, surely there's no calories in them." He chuckled and winked at her.

Looking down, Cassandra noticed that one of the blue books hadn't fit in the bag and stuck out several inches. If Bergstrom looked near her feet, he'd clearly be able to see the spine of the book, "Maple Memories 1975."

Leaning way over to cover her bag, Cassandra stretched across the couch to the corner end table and placed her empty china cup on the stained surface. Meanwhile, her unseen hand groped around until she felt the book's edge. Pressing it fully into the bag, she smiled back at Dr.

Bergstrom. "Yes, actually I had such a busy morning I'm counting the cookie as late lunch."

Cassandra didn't know where to put her hands. She wanted to hold one casually near her ankles, over the open laptop bag. But moving her hands now would draw attention to them. She forced herself to sit still.

Holding the poster paper tube, she said, "Again, thank you Dr. Bergstrom for recruiting your department to participate in the focus group meeting. One of my student workers will transcribe the notes from these. I'll send the draft for your review before I include the recommendations in the final report."

Bergstrom plunked his robust frame into his creaky desk chair. "Remember that no task is unworthy. *You* are worthy, therefore your time is not wasted, provided you do your best."

More sage advice. She assumed they were playing his game again. "Which philosopher said that?"

He laughed from the bottom of his belly. "I just did."

Cassandra had purposefully hidden something from her mentor. Guilt rose up her throat like bile. What instinct had made her take those yearbooks?

Bergstrom gazed directly at her. Did he recognize her indecision?

Waving goodbye, she left his office before she changed her mind. Something was off. Without being able to articulate the reasons, she'd felt it was important to view the yearbooks in private. Bergstrom might be wise in philosophy and history, but Cassandra had enough life experience behind her to trust her gut.

For the time being, that was reason enough.

* * *

Back in the Student Affairs office, Cassandra rubbed her hands along her arms to warm herself up from walking between buildings. Something Rachel had said at the urgent care clinic the day before had jarred loose an idea. Before she forgot, she wanted to follow up.

At the front desk she asked Devon, "Does Dr. Hansen have anyone in his office?"

Devon laughed. "He sees maybe three people a day, right? Nah. He's probably sleeping."

Cassandra wondered again how Hansen flew under the administrative radar so well.

"You might want to knock first though. One time, I opened the door when he was on the couch, but he'd taken off his pants and shoes. Snoozing in his boxers." Devon did a big shrug.

Cassandra's jaw dropped. "Gross!" Why didn't George retire so he could nap on his own couch at home? Yikes.

Stepping up to his closed door, she rapped three times and waited. Only a few folks remained at Morton from the days of Susan Peter's death.

He called, "Enter!" in a loud enough voice that it seemed like he was already awake.

She opened the door and stuck her top half inside. "Thanks, Dr. Hansen for covering for me yesterday while I was out of the office. I heard you helped Rachel, one of our student workers with some paperwork." Encouraged that he hadn't barked something rude at her, she added, "There's something I want to ask you about . . ." then stepped inside and closed the door behind her.

George had been here during the old days, too. Maybe he remembered something she hadn't heard yet. "Do you remember the former professor Dr. Kovar?"

"Of course I knew Kovar. He worked here forever. Died some years back. Cancer. Nasty business." Hansen's fleshy cheeks quivered when he spoke.

"There's recently been a photo posted online of him with a former student, Susan Peters. Do you remember her too?"

"The one who died? Yeah. Weirdest thing happened. I swear her ghost was in here yesterday asking me to sign a paper."

She'd heard Rachel resembled her grandmother, but Cassandra had yet to see a clear photo of the former student. "Do you know if Dr. Kovar had a relationship with Susan Peters?"

"A *relationship*? Like, was he doing her? Wouldn't surprise me. That idiot never could keep his pants on. What do I care about that crap though? The last time I had sex, G.W. was President. Are we done here?"

Cassandra's eyeballs burned even imagining Hansen having sex with anyone. Alrighty then. Check Dr. Hansen off the helpful eyewitness list.

* * *

Before leaving for the day, Cassandra crunched the numbers for her diversity and inclusion report. Since Monday, Cassandra had done an unofficial census throughout forty-two academic majors.

When she dug deeper into demographics for deaf and hard of hearing students, Cassandra counted ten students and three faculty who considered themselves Deaf and used ASL. Another ten hard of hearing students were included because they requested accommodations like captioning or notetakers in classes.

Spending thousands of dollars for an emergency management system that would be used by twenty-three out of four thousand people still seemed like a big hurdle.

She called Meg. "Howzit. Are you home resting?"

"I worked my class last night. I'd sat on my butt for 19 hours. I needed to move even if it was only for two hours."

Cassandra frowned. "Connor gave you his blessing?"

"Let's just say he understands me. I had to promise to park right next to the building and take it easy."

"Are you coming to Dr. Bergstrom's Salon party tonight?"

"After sitting home all day again today, you bet I am."

Meg was one of those people who hardly sat still. She was probably ready to climb the walls. "Good, I'll see you there. But now I need your help."

"I live to serve," Meg said.

"How do I know if someone is deaf or hard of hearing if they don't ask for special services or accommodations on campus?"

"You don't. Unless you see them wear technology like a hearing aid or cochlear implant."

"I only came up with twenty-three students and staff for my report." Cassandra frowned at her notes. "Shouldn't that be higher?"

"About 20% of people over sixty have hearing loss. Look at how many faculty and staff are that age and use that number."

"Ohhh that helps for sure." She penciled in another 100 in that column. "See you later!"

Next thing she knew it was time to head home. Dressed in coat, hat and gloves, she locked her office. Cassandra was exhausted from the week of worrying about assault, Meg's baby, arson, and a dangerous oddball on the loose. Tonight, she'd keep an eye out for students or faculty who had a grudge against the Deaf Studies group. These attacks felt personal, but she had no answers for why anyone wanted to hurt Rachel Nagle.

Chapter Nineteen

Standing next to Meg, Cassandra held a glass coffee mug and stared open-mouthed at Dr. Winters.

Several students huddled around Winters in Dr. Bergstrom's home. Only two blocks from campus, Bergstrom's neoclassical house perfectly suited the party's vibe. The high-ceilinged room's couches had been pushed against the walls and a small coffee bar was set up in the corner, complete with a bowtie wearing barista. The dining room table covered with delicious food was pushed against a wall of windows looking out onto the back patio and yard.

Cassandra had soaked in every architectural detail, from the crown molding to the formal paintings hanging from picture rails high on the wall. This was a *parlor*! She was actually attending a 1900s era European-style salon like the ones she'd read about in history books.

Even more astonishing, Cassandra had discovered that President Winters was charming. Wearing a simple cream-colored suit, her hair in soft waves around her face, Winters' cheeks shone from the chandelier and candlelight.

Winters laughed, "...Old rat-face Cunningham, the Provost, hauled Bergstrom, Kovar and Gregory into his office at 2:00 a.m. and berated them for so long Gregory fell asleep! The others dragged him back to the graduate dorm."

Nearby, Bergstrom finished her story. "Only you escaped punishment, Deborah, because we'd dropped you off at the women's dorm first. We got caught stumbling across the quad past curfew."

Winters laughed so hard she had to wipe her wet eyes. "It was totally worth the monster hangover I had the next day. God, we had fun at that Husker football game."

Cassandra exchanged bewildered stares with Meg. Not once had she previously gotten the impression that Bergstrom and Winters were friends. Since neither of them had mentioned anything in common besides their age, Cassandra had assumed their connection was superficial. Tonight, they told road trip stories like old buddies.

Bergstrom's big smile was so relaxed, Cassandra was struck by the contrast with his recently gloomy expression. His infectious personality had seemed dimmed these past few weeks, like there was light inside him that wanted to come out, but something blocked him from letting his full emotions show.

Winters said, "Charlie loves that story. I'll remind him of it when I get home tonight."

Cassandra's hand jerked a little when Winters mentioned her dead husband. In the present tense. Cassandra thought of Paul and their memories together often. But talking to him like he was in the room with her? Winters legit seemed to believe Charlie was waiting at home for her.

Bergstrom's head tilted to the side and he stopped smiling, but he didn't correct her.

Winters saw people looking at her curiously and said, "Oh that's right. Charlie's gone. I knew that."

Bergstrom said, "I spent twenty minutes last night searching for my reading glasses all over the house. I found them. In my shirt pocket." He laughed, "Getting old is rough."

Meg whispered into Cassandra's ear, "Winters is a few French fries short of a Happy Meal."

Cassandra did a grimace and slowly turned around estimating crowd size. Whenever she attended these types of social gatherings, she planned ahead for which important people she needed to chat with and whom she should impress or avoid. Tonight, she was also on the lookout for how people acted around any deaf students.

In each room groups of three to five students, grad students and faculty stood chatting, eating, and drinking punch or steaming coffees from crystal cups with handles. Across the two-story entryway and on the other side of a twisting staircase was a door that opened into a beautiful wood-paneled library. The shelves reached all the way to the ceiling, and a large couch was tucked into a bay window.

Lance Erickson and Rachel Nagle sat next to each other signing. No one else from their advocacy group was with them. People walked past and didn't pay much attention to them. Again, Cassandra thought they made a cute couple, even if they didn't know it yet.

Cassandra and Meg faced them. "Good to see you here. This is a great house," Cassandra said. "What do you think of the party?"

Rachel signed and spoke at the same time. "I feel like I should've studied for this. I hope none of these professors are going to ask me what I've learned so far in class."

Two professors walked past their couch group arguing heatedly. "I tell you that Medicare-for-all is not Socialism."

"Maybe not, but it's a slippery slope. Once you go down that road, eventually you get Communism. And Stalin."

"Yikes. I should've studied, too," Cassandra laughed. "Okay if we aren't arguing about political theories, what should we talk about?"

Rachel said, "I can't wait 'til the semester is over. I'd better pass my classes. I gotta catch up on quizzes and class." She stood up and tugged on Lance's arm. "Let's check out the desserts. You can have our seats."

Cassandra perched on the edge of the couch, and balanced her cup and cookie on her lap. "Can't sit here long. I gotta mingle, you know."

"Sure," Meg said around a mouthful of snack mix. "Just stay with me a few minutes before you do your VP schmoozing thing."

Dr. Harris entered the library with five female students trailing him. Dressed in a simple navy button down with the sleeves rolled up and khakis, he still stood out among the other faculty. He walked slowly and confidently, knowing that people would hang on his words, whether they were about the latest superhero movie or Ancient Rome.

Thinking of handsome professors, Cassandra asked Meg, "Dr. Bryant isn't here?"

"Nah. I don't think this would be his thing."

"Is anyone acting suspicious around Rachel? I don't even know what to look for."

Meg rolled her eyes. She didn't seem to take Cassandra's spying objective very seriously. Meg whispered, "Maybe the Sunday Salon is a front for recruiting students into a secret Greek society?"

"Morton College isn't the Ivy League." Cassandra nudged her elbow into Meg's arm. "My investigation isn't a joke. I thought this casual setting might be a good place to spot someone acting funny or out of place."

"Who said I'm joking? I've always wanted to wear dark robes and join one of those secret societies!" Meg's eyes sparkled with excitement. "The kind where we traipse around campus in the middle of the night, meet in caves with flashlights, and recite poetry."

Professor Bergstrom walked through the library with his arm around a tall woman Cassandra assumed was his wife, Liz. She held a small wooden mallet and tapped a hollow metal instrument that produced a low gonging sound. "Join us in the parlor, please."

They followed the small crowd into the main room. Meg smiled like she was at a costume party. "Is this the part where we all stand on the desks?"

Cassandra kept her lips together, but the corners turned up.

Meg stood at attention, her shoulders back. "Oh Captain, my Captain!" she whispered before scooting away to interpret.

Cassandra giggled. No one pictured Robin Williams in *Dead Poets Society* without giggling.

In the parlor, Professor Bergstrom and his wife waited for everyone to quiet. "First of all, welcome to all of our new guests," Bergstrom had exchanged his normal tweed jacket with elbow patches for a dark dinner jacket and slacks. "Raise your hand if this is your first time here."Cassandra held her palm up to shoulder height, along with about ten others.

"Excellent. And to those who have made a habit of eating and drinking us out of house and home, welcome back!"

A low rumble of laughter went through the group.

"As you know, the point of these get togethers is for you to meet people you might not normally talk to during your regular days on campus."

"My beautiful co-host has prepared a couple of ice breaker questions for you. Liz . . . "

Liz had to be near seventy years old, but her tan skin and spunky personality reminded Cassandra of someone who spent a lot of time outdoors. Liz smiled, "Your assignment, should you play along, is to find someone you've never met and ask them the following two questions: What are you most grateful for? Secondly, what was the best gift you ever received and why was it your favorite? And, go!"

Immediately after Liz had stopped talking, people looked around for someone to pair up with and began chatting. Soon the room was filled with laughter and animated conversation. Meg scooted over to stand by Lance and interpret. Cassandra didn't see anyone else without a partner.

Liz herself moved to Cassandra and bent over to speak closer. "You must be Cassandra! I've heard only good things about you from Mike. Please excuse me for not saying hello when you first came in. I'm so happy you were able to join us tonight."

"It's nice to meet you. Dr. Bergstrom told me you folks have hosted these since he was in graduate school? You must really enjoy entertaining."

"Back in the day, we took turns hosting at our houses or apartments. None of us had family nearby, so we formed our own little group of friends. Of course, professors need victims willing to listen to them lecture for hours, so eventually we started inviting students." Liz looked around the bustling room. "We never had children of our own. Some of our friends have passed away. Getting to know these undergrads keeps me feeling young. You only have to answer the icebreakers if you get stuck on conversation. I feel it's just a good way to get people started."

Several steps to their left stood a quiet woman about the same age as the Bergstroms. Tall and thin, her cropped dark hair was in need of volumizing hair products to fluff it up.

Liz turned and included her in the conversation with Cassandra. "Connie, did your boys come home for Thanksgiving?"

The woman answered, "No, their families both live in Des Moines. I went there this year. Their wives and I woke up early to go shopping on Black Friday."

Liz said, "Dr. Sato, I'd like you to meet my dear friend Connie Kovar. Her husband taught at Morton for many years before he passed away. Eight—"

"Ten years ago," Mrs. Kovar corrected her.

Yikes! Her husband had the *alleged* affair with Rachel Nagle's grandmother. Cassandra hadn't seen this coming. "Nice to meet you, Mrs. Kovar. I'm sorry about your husband."

Mrs. Kovar nodded.

Liz waved at someone across the room and touched Mrs. Kovar's arm. "Excuse me. I'll be back." She set off towards the entryway.

Cassandra smiled at Mrs. Kovar, unsure of how to start a conversation. "So, you and the Bergstroms have been friends since grad school?"

Mrs. Kovar nodded. She had the deeply wrinkled face of a long-time smoker, but also the graceful poise of an experienced dancer.

"How do you keep busy nowadays?" Cassandra asked. "Do you work?"

Mrs. Kovar's smile didn't reach her eyes. "I know who you are and don't pull that polite act on me. You may have the Bergstroms hoodwinked but not me."

This woman gave her chicken skin. Cassandra went still. "Excuse me?"

Mrs. Kovar's face remained pleasant and she looked out towards the middle of the room where students in pairs were animatedly chattering about Christmas gifts. "You're the one encouraging these newspaper articles with their crackpot theories. You wouldn't believe the lunatics calling my home phone." Her voice lowered. "I'm warning you. Stop dredging up the past." Her eyes landed on Rachel Nagle and Lance Erickson choosing cookies from the snack table on the other side of the parlor.

"Ma'am, I'm so sorry." Cassandra cleared her throat. "This can't be easy for you. I think Rachel's just trying to find closure for her family."

"Who does she think she is? Digging up dirt from 40 years ago. What's the point of dragging my husband's memory through the mud? He made a mistake. A very long time ago. There's no benefit to rehashing it."

Cassandra kept her tone neutral. "From what I've seen, Rachel's as much a victim of circumstance as anyone right now. Someone has hurt her. Twice."

"Enough." Mrs. Kovar turned to face Cassandra directly. "Here's my advice for that Rachel girl and you too. Keep the past in the past. Leave my husband's name out of this whole sordid story."

Cassandra's intention to respect her elders was falling apart. "Yes, Mrs. Kovar. Sorry to have upset you." A hasty retreat was her best defense. Cassandra headed towards the parlor doorway thinking she had a new name for her list of people who might have a grudge against Rachel.

Passing through the front entryway, she glanced left and saw Bergstrom standing alone holding a can of Dr. Pepper. She asked, "Are you all right?" Thinking back, she realized she'd never seen him drink alcohol at any of the college events, even when others had taken advantage of the free bar. "You know, I've never seen you drink anything stronger than Dr. Pepper, Professor."

He stared blankly at the front door. "Why do we fall? So that we can learn to pick ourselves up."

That was cryptic. She raised an eyebrow.

"Alfred the butler. Batman Begins." She laughed but had no comeback. Bergstrom considered a moment. "Some people don't have to completely hit rock bottom to figure out that something is bad for them. When I was a much younger man, I drank. Sometimes too much, as young men are prone to doing. It didn't take long to realize that I liked my job and my wife too much to lose them."

"You seem . . . sad sometimes."

"Not sad so much. More of a deep understanding of our reality. Sometimes I wonder why I'm still here."

"Doesn't everyone have to answer that question at some point in their life? I'm here because I want to help students. I believe education gives people opportunities to make the world better."

"And one day you catch yourself wishing the person you loved never existed so you'd be spared your pain."

What the heck was he talking about? It was as though he recited the lines from memory, not like normal conversation. Then he turned to her intently. "What you really fear is inside yourself."

That hit close to home. She laughed uncomfortably and sipped her coffee. "Inside me, sir?"

"More Batman." His shoulders rose and fell. He snapped out of his weird musing. "Just the ramblings of a man who's read too many comic books."

He was sure in a strange mood. She said, "Maybe we need smart friends like Alfred to help pick ourselves up."

Was she paranoid, or did everyone who worked at Morton crack up eventually? Dr. Nielson was AWOL. Dr. Winters had drinks with her dead husband every night. Her officemate Dr. Hansen was a professional napper. And Dr. Bergstrom thought he was a senior citizen superhero. Maybe five years at this place would be enough.

"Dr. Bergstrom, you worry me sometimes." She laid a hand on his forearm, but he didn't say anymore.Cassandra left Dr. Bergstrom and recognized Professor Zimmerman by the food table. She'd seen him at the Faculty Senate meeting, but they hadn't spoken privately since October and her first ill-fated trip to a cattle farm. About 5'7" tall, his male-patterned bald head, combined with dark washed skinny jeans and an untucked plaid flannel shirt made him look more like a telecommuting dad than a tenured professor.

"Hello, Dr. Sato! Good to see you. I hope you're doing well and completely recovered from our field trip last month." He chuckled a little when he said the word recovered.

"Nothing that a vat of shower gel and a garbage can couldn't fix." Cassandra's face reddened at the memory of her ruined outfit and shoes from when she took a huge tumble into a cowpie right in front of Dr. Zimmerman and Fischer. "What's it worth to you never to mention it again?"

"Sorry, I didn't mean to embarrass you." His light-brown scruffy goatee was thin enough she could see two deep dimples in his cheeks, further emphasizing his boyish looks. "That fall was quite spectacular, and I'm just glad you weren't injured."

"Only my dignity."

Zimmerman said, "That whole business last month was disappointing. And now, what did I hear about someone trying to burn down the library?"

Another reminder that word got around quickly. "We're still checking into who was behind it. One student ended up in the medical clinic, but she's better now. If you hear of any students or strangers on campus acting suspiciously, I'd appreciate a heads up."

"Sure, I'll keep my eyes open." Professor Zimmerman said, "I'll be glad when this semester is over, and we can all take a nice long winter break."

"I'm ready to find out what boring feels like," she agreed.

Once again in the parlor, Cassandra saw Bergstrom's wife, Liz, standing by the window, her eyes scanning the room. Judging by her flushed cheeks, the highball glass in her hand probably contained something stronger than punch.

Cassandra joined her. "Your house is lovely, Mrs. Bergstrom. I could spend days in that library."

When she smiled, deep parenthetic creases reached from her nose to the saggy part of her chin. "Mike has collected those volumes for more than forty years. They're his pride and joy." Her words slid out a little sloppy, and her eyeballs flicked back and forth like she was trying to keep her balance.

Cassandra gently moved her hand under Liz's elbow. "Would you like to sit with me over there?"

When she nodded, Cassandra led her slowly to an empty love seat a few feet away.

Liz sat steadier than she'd been standing, but her words were still slurred. "Mike promised five years ago he'd retire and take me on one of those European river cruises. Every finals week, he says, 'Maybe one more semester.' I swear the man is going to die in that hellhole office of his. You know, after he stepped down from the president's job, he actually tried to retire. After three summer months home, he returned to the philosophy department as a hobby." She tried to make air quotes on the word 'hobby,' but splashed her drink instead. Dark droplets spattered the front of her floral blouse.

Bergstrom's wife hadn't given up the booze with her husband.

"I saw that young blonde-haired girl earlier. Looks exactly like her grandmother."

Cassandra said, "I've heard several people say that!"

"Can I be honest with you? We've known the Kovars for years. That whole baby ordeal affected so many lives." She laid a hand on Cassandra's arm and confided, "Tragic. I always thought there was more to that story."

An electric spark zinged up Cassandra's spine. Obviously, she needed to pay more attention to Susan Peters' relationship with Dr. Kovar. "I didn't realize folks knew about the affair or the baby."

"Men think their wives don't know," Liz laughed. Her glass swayed so close Cassandra leaned away, afraid she'd be the next person to get splashed. "A group of us ate lunch every week at the country club."

Carson had a country club? That was news to Cassandra. How did a town with two bars, four fast food restaurants, and two gas stations support a country club?

"Trust me, the wives know. Now... I don't think my Mike strayed. Not like Alec anyway." A sour look passed her face. "Alec Kovar flirted with *everyone*. Back then, we didn't have all this Face Chat social media garbage. We wives stuck together."

Dr. Winters walked through the room and into the entryway carrying her coat over her arm. She looked tired. And softer than she usually seemed at work.

Liz's chin jutted out towards the empty doorway. "Except her. She was a wild one."

She'd heard a taste of that from the story Dr. Winters had told earlier. Cassandra raised an eyebrow. "Deborah Winters?"

"Before she met Charlie, she was a complete party girl. After Charlie, she did a one-eighty. Became the driven woman you see today."

Cassandra wondered what kind of guy had the power to change a woman like Dr. Winters. Maybe she'd ask her someday. The salon had been one revelation after another. For such a small town, there were plenty of secrets here.

Chapter Twenty

Michiko Sato would not approve of the messy state of Cassandra's kitchen counters. A bag of premixed salad greens rested next to a large plastic bowl. Leftover rice warmed in the microwave. Breakfast dishes were stacked next to the sink. Two Mahimahi filets defrosted on a baking sheet. Worst of all, the mail and Cassandra's large tote bag occupied her two-person dining table right where she'd dropped them the night before as she'd raced into the house from work.

Luckily, Mrs. Sato lived nearly four thousand miles away and would be blissfully unaware of her daughter's shame if Meg were to show up on time for lunch and see the mess.

When bright sunlight had streamed through her window Saturday morning across her face, Cassandra had startled awake. How had she so quickly become one of those lazy slugs who couldn't drag herself out of bed in the morning?

She'd nearly forgotten that she'd agreed to attend the Saturday morning Fine Arts Exhibition until Meg texted her to confirm their lunch plans. What was happening to her? The exhibition for upper class and graduate students showcased their semester projects, and she was one of the judges.

Cassandra had planned to come home early, change clothes, tidy the kitchen, and turn on soothing music before Meg's arrival. Instead, the organizers hadn't paid attention to time, making the awards ceremony late. By the time she'd raced home, Cassandra was seriously off schedule.

Standing in her bedroom in her underwear, Cassandra heard the back door bang shut. "Rats!" She pulled black sweatpants and an oversized University of Hawai'i hoodie on and slid her feet into sheepskin mule slippers.

Hurrying through the living room, Cassandra heard Meg call into the kitchen, "Aloha!"

Cassandra took a big breath while Meg hung up her coat in the little stairwell landing off the back door and walked up the three steps into the small 1950's era galley kitchen, a simple room about 8 feet wide with a sink and cabinets lining the one long wall. The opposite wall held a stove, refrigerator, and small pantry. Warm sunlight glowed through the lone window highlighting the dated floral wallpaper. Maybe over winter break she'd have time to strip that off and paint it a color from this century.

Pouring Meg a tall glass of water, Cassandra said, "Please ignore the mess. Looks like a hurricane came through."

"I promise not to tell Aunty Michiko that her daughter works eleven-hour days and weekends and isn't perfect."

"That's okay, she wouldn't believe you anyway. I am her favorite child." Cassandra poured water for herself.

"I thought that title belonged to your sister Kathy now that she's engaged?"

Squinting her eyes at Meg, Cassandra used one of her favorite phrases from home. "You get one mean." She seasoned the fish with lemon pepper and placed sliced onions on top before sliding the baking sheet into the oven.

"Just keeping it real, sistah." Meg seated herself at the small gate leg table pushed up against the far wall. "You play your cards right and you'll make your sister wish she'd held out longer. Fischer looked as dreamy as a Hemsworth at Cinda's Husker football party last week. Those snug, dark-wash Levi's. The No-shave November beard."

Cassandra mixed the salad ingredients together. "You aren't supposed to be looking at his Levi's."

"I'm married, not dead." Meg slouched against the wall behind her chair. "I saw photos of Connor in Baghdad with a long beard, but he shaved it off before he landed stateside, thank God. Prickly kisses are ticklish."

Cassandra cleared the mail off the table and moved it with her bag into the former dining room that she'd converted into an office. "Beards are kinda hot. The rugged, masculine look. Like Clooney and Morgan Freeman." Returning to the kitchen, she set the table with her blue Noritake china and black chopsticks. "My Mom loves Tom Selleck's mustache."

"Within limits. I'd make Connor shave if he started looking like he's headed for the World Series."

"What about Dumbledore?" Cassandra asked.

"Of course, Dumbledore has different rules. And Aragorn." Meg raised her glass in a toast. "Aragorn can have whatever facial hair he wants; I would still have his children."

"To Aragorn!" They clinked glasses.

"Actually . . . Fischer and I are going out tonight. I found a winery not too far away. I thought maybe a wine tasting would give us something to talk about."

"Solid plan!" Meg set down her glass. "Just remember the point is to have fun. Relax. Enjoy the moment. Don't talk about work. Imagine him doing your laundry, mowing your lawn, and forgetting to hang up his wet towel. Imagine those Levi's and the guy attached to them actually in your life."

Cassandra held up one hand. "Stop! Sheesh. I've dated before. I know what I'm doing."

"Do you really?" Meg held up one hand. "You gotta make something happen. Ya know, God can't steer a parked car."

Maybe not, but could He at least give her a road map first? Cassandra's eyebrows flew up in a warning that Meg dismissed with a Ppfft. "I watch *New Girl*. College dating is way different than grown up dating."

"Says the girl who married her high school sweetheart." It was time to change the subject. "Okay, tell me the truth. How are you *really* feeling?"

"The medicine they gave me seemed to work. No more cramping or spotting. I'm laying low the rest of today and tomorrow."

Good. Meg had quit bugging her about Fischer. "Last night's party was too crowded to talk. So much happened while you were out of the office." While they ate their salad and fish, Cassandra told Meg about the smoke alarm going off in the library.

"Does Summers still think the first time near the football stadium was an accident? Could Rachel's luck really be so bad that she's in the wrong place at the wrong time again?"

"The library wasn't an accident. Someone left a sign with big block letters saying, 'Stay away forever.'"

"That's disturbing." Meg nodded. "On so many levels. It's like someone is bullying her."

"I'm worried her family will accuse Morton of negligence. We knew about the other incident but didn't prevent more damage. I wonder if that Deaf advocacy coalition is still following our accessibility discussion."

"I looked online while I was home resting." Meg said, "Most of the social media has died down. I haven't heard anything more about planned protests. But I was out of the office for two days."

"I didn't say anything to Summers, but the library incident Thursday looked like a smudging gone wrong."

Meg's face crinkled into a questioning frown.

"Don't even Google it, it's a thing," Cassandra swirled her fingers between them like smoke. "Smudging is a mystical ritual that people do to get rid of unwanted spirits or energy."

"Smudging like how the priest draws a cross on my forehead on Ash Wednesday?"

"Uh, no. Burning white sage, cedar or grasses makes ritual cleansing smoke."

Understanding blossomed on Meg's face. "Like Catholic incense on holy days?"

"Kinda like that." Cassandra picked up their dishes and ran the hot water to wash them in the sink. "Buddhists and other religions have done smudging for centuries. The New Age folks made it more popular."

"What about the kid who likes Rachel?" Meg shrugged. "Maybe he doesn't know how to take no for an answer."

"Nah, I talked to him myself," said Cassandra. "He's guilty of being inexperienced and awkward, but T.J. likes Rachel too much to hurt her."

Meg said, "I overhear guys in class talking about getting so wasted they trip over the curb and fall flat. Girls puking in garbage cans. I remember drinking when I was in college, but I must have blocked out all of that stuff."

"We built bonfires at the beach. We sat around 'til all hours playing ukuleles and singing or dancing. I don't remember puking anywhere though."

"Tony's never going to college. He'll live at home with us until he's 35. Then maybe if he meets a nice girl, he can marry her. He's never going to do stupid things like we did when we were young."

Cassandra laughed. "And how will he support this nice girl without any marketable skills except playing Xbox?"

"Well, maybe he'll be one of those child protégés who has his master's degree at 20 years old. Although, I gotta admit, he's not starting out as a rocket scientist. His mid-term report card came home yesterday and he's pretty much a middle of the road B-student."

"Tony's the cutest, smartest 4th grade B-student I know. He can come here to college and his Aunty Cassandra will keep an eye on him."

She snapped her fingers, "You just reminded me! You'll never guess what I found yesterday." Cassandra ran into the office and pulled the yearbooks out of her bag. "I've heard several people say Rachel looks just like Susan Peters." She handed one to Meg. "I'm not gonna lie. I'm curious what Rachel's grandmother did at Morton before she died."

For several minutes, the only sounds were pages turning as they both flipped through the yearbooks looking at the formal individual photos and in the indexes for team or club photos.

Meg held up the 1974 volume. "Jesus, Mary, and Joseph! You've got to see this one of Dr. Bergstrom." Meg passed over the annual and pointed at Bergstrom's face. His dark hair flowed long and straight, well past his shoulders. A bushy handlebar mustache hid his entire top lip, but the twinkly eyes and pronounced nose were the same. He gave an old-fashioned lecture at a podium next to a chart resting on an easel and held a long wooden stick for pointing. "He's a baby! A hippie baby!"

The opposite page held a smaller photo whose face Cassandra barely recognized. What jumped out at Cassandra was the caption: Deborah Winters, School of Education. This shapely, young woman with long, straight hair parted down the middle wore a polyester pant suit but looked nothing like the Dr. Winters who currently gave orders. The photographer had caught her mid-laugh, her whole face lit up by happiness. Winters still smiled a lot, but usually Cassandra felt it was manipulative instead of joyful.

Cassandra found the 1975 individual photos, turned to the P's, and her jaw dropped. Reaching out, she grabbed Meg's wrist and passed the open yearbook across. "Look!"

Meg's eyes bugged out and her mouth formed an O. "Wow! Rachel looks exactly like her grandmother! Not just a little bit. Like *exactly*!"

Finally seeing a clear photo definitely satisfied her curiosity. "How cool is that?"

"Okay, what does it mean for Rachel now?" Meg asked. "Any chance she did the library smudging thing herself to chase away the bad energy that's followed her around? Maybe she was too embarrassed to admit it when the fire alarm went off and it made a mess?" They paged through the other yearbooks, but no other names stood out.

"I wondered that before, but it seems unlikely. I've always thought it had something to do with the attention on Rachel when the Deaf Studies project started." Cassandra stacked the books. "You should've seen Mrs. Nagle Thursday at the urgent care clinic with Rachel."

"She really drove all that way just to make sure she wasn't hurt?"

"I tried to put myself in her shoes. I mean it was scary last time when she ended up in the hospital. But Rachel is a young adult. And she was not happy to see her mother show up ready to blow a gasket."

Meg looked at her smartwatch and shifted uncomfortably.

Cassandra raised an eyebrow. "What?

"Well ... Tony's teacher at school gave him a bad test grade. He didn't fill out the back page, and she deducted a bunch of points." Meg leaned forward, suddenly intense. "He brought it home for us to sign that we had seen the 'D'. Tony told me he knew the answer, but he didn't see the back side of the paper. I told him to go to school and ask if he could redo that part to get partial credit back. He came home the next night, and said the teacher told him no."

"Happens to all of us, right?" Cassandra nodded.

"But he's only in fourth grade! He should have known to look on the back side, sure. I just don't get how that's testing his knowledge of the material. He knew the material. He just didn't see the back side. I'm going to the school and talk to the teacher."

"I bet he will never again forget to look at the back side of the test page for the rest of his school career."

"You agree with his teacher?"

"I see her point. She's teaching him a life lesson."

"But Tony's trying to get a good Social Studies grade. He'll learn the life lesson anyway, even if he fixes the test. Even partial credit would be better than a zero on those questions."

"True. Bottom line it's her classroom and her rules. If you go in there and convince her to give your baby special exceptions today, then what will it be tomorrow? What if he doesn't make the basketball team? Will you go talk to the coach to ask him why? Will you become the mom who whips out the tape measure during the college orientation tour to size up your son's dorm room bed and closet? When does it end, Meg?"

"Advocating for my child's best interests in fourth grade is not going to turn me into Momzilla! I coached him on what to say. He went in and talked to his teacher, but it didn't work. Maybe he didn't explain his side well enough. He's still learning."

"Listen. I know I don't have kids of my own, but I see these students every day. I see the ones whose parents let them fail. Who let them fight their own battles even when it doesn't work. You can Mother Cub him as much as you want, but at some point, you have to let him have the last word. You shouldn't step in to fight a battle he can fight himself."

"That's a lot easier said than done." Meg admitted.

"You've often told me mothers are badasses."

"Amen to that." Meg got up to leave, picking her coat off the rack behind the door.

"Are you saying I'd better prepare for the worst with the Nagle family?"

"I know the rage I feel when someone hurts my son. If anything else happens to Rachel or another student because of bullying or the Deaf Studies project, her mom is going to go full Apache Helicopter. God help you."

Chapter Twenty-One

Cassandra swirled the white wine in her tasting glass and held it to her nose while inhaling a slow breath. It smelled sweet, like apples. "I'm so relieved you were right about the weather forecast. It didn't snow like they predicted."

Or was it woody, like a tree? Who was she kidding. She was no fancy wine connoisseur. Slowly she lowered the glass to the table so he wouldn't see her shaky hand. She fidgeted with the top button on her intricately embroidered mandarin-collared tunic. Looking at the quiet man seated opposite her at the rustic wooden table, she told herself to act normal. Whatever that meant.

"Yeah, pretty much you have to assume that all winter long-term plans are temporary until the day of." He sipped from his glass. "You have to be flexible until you know for sure whether you'll be able to leave the house. What's your tire situation?"

Nebraska conversations could be so odd. She nearly laughed out loud. "When my father found out I was moving here, he researched online and bought me special winter tires. I'm supposed to get my regular ones switched soon."

She'd saved a twice per year calendar reminder on her phone especially for the new habit.

"For someone who's never driven in snow before, that's a smart way to go." Fischer's light blue eyes caught hers and he smiled. "Is that one sweeter than the first glass you tried?"

Normally at home, a box of cheap wine sat in the fridge for weeks and Cassandra measured out a glass when she was in the mood. At the Sandy Creek Winery, she made a show of paying attention to the differences in each variety.

Allowing the wine to sit on her tongue long enough to taste whatever it was she was supposed to taste, she hesitated. Her nose wrinkled a little. "Not really sweeter, but it has a bite to it at the end. Like those sweet tart candies."

When they'd arrived at 7:30, the only empty table was by a large stone fireplace. In the airy tasting room, floor-to-ceiling windows lining two of the walls reflected twinkly white lights and holiday greenery covering the outdoor landscaping.

After scouting out nearby possibilities, this seemed the best non-wildlife date option without driving more than twenty minutes away or meeting for dinner at the Home Team Bar. She wanted to get to know the real Marcus instead of just Fischer, the capable coworker.

Fischer read his tasting menu. Cassandra took advantage of his distraction to study his face more closely. She could imagine waking up to breakfast every morning sitting across a table from those eyes and smile. He'd probably be one of those disciplined men who got better looking with age. She couldn't imagine him with dad bod at forty-five.

Cassandra bit into a thin herbed cracker from the charcuterie board they'd ordered. Tonight, Fischer dressed like he did at work: light brown jeans and flannel shirt under a forest green quarter zip sweater. The fingers of his right hand stroked his trim black beard.

Though technically an extrovert who could talk to anyone about nearly anything for at least thirty minutes, Cassandra found herself wondering what to say next.

"Did you see those fires in California? That looked very serious."

His eyes left the menu and squinted at her in concern. "Do you have family there?"

"No, I just felt bad for the people who lost their homes," said Cassandra. "My cousin's house burned in the volcano fire on the Big Island and is now forever buried under 5 feet of hard lava. He had to move their family of five into his in-law's house."

She'd assumed during their fishing misadventure that her aversion to slimy worms and being seriously overdressed had contributed to the stilted conversation. At work, they always had friendly chit-chat before and after meetings. This shouldn't be so hard.

"I lived in my parents' basement for a few months when I moved back to Nebraska last year," Fischer said. "But I couldn't handle that as a long-term solution."

Not long ago, Fischer had spent the night sitting guard at her house in her big leather armchair during the horrible week she'd been stalked by a creepy thug. Everything between them had seemed so comfortable and intimate that night.

One big difference: Cassandra had been under the influence of relaxing pharmaceuticals that Fischer had provided for her out of a zipper bag he happened to carry in his jeans' front pocket. She'd yet to ask him about those yellow pills he had dispensed. Now didn't seem the right time either.

Finally, the wine kicked in sending a pleasant easing from her chest outwards towards her shoulders and spine. "I bet your parents were glad to have you back home safely. Where do they live?"

"Near Rising City. It's about half an hour straight west of here."

Their conversation felt more like a legal deposition than flirtatious banter. Her previous breakfast table fantasy lost its luster. Would they have nothing to say and ignore each other by reading the news instead of talking? She'd prefer living alone forever to boring conversation. "So . . . before you got the housing job at Morton, you were in the military, right?"

"Army. Infantry. Iraq War," he said. "Four years active, six years reserves. Did some construction work through college. I switched to the Nebraska National Guard when I moved back."

Cassandra remembered admiring that quality about him during department meetings when she'd first started working at Morton. He was the only department director who showed up consistently with a brief summary of what his people had accomplished and one or two items they would address next. Most other directors liked to hear themselves speak and would drone on twice as long as needed with less pertinent information than Fischer. She had guessed that was a key reason he'd been recommended as a ready replacement when his boss retired last month.

"How do you like being Housing and Facilities VP? Is it much different than what you were doing before?" She'd planned to avoid work talk, but his new job was a personal accomplishment, too.

Fischer made the first genuine smile she'd seen since they'd sat down. It took her breath away. "I never realized how much of Dave Gonzales' job I was already doing before he retired." For the first time she noticed slight dimples in both of his cheeks. "Not much has changed in my daily routine. Looking forward to my first paycheck, though."

Cassandra waited for him to add more, but instead his eyes scanned the mostly full room, taking in the large moms' night out group near them, and the young couple to their right who sat legs touching on the same side of the table, heads together in serious conversation. Several musical instruments and stools were arranged in one corner and a spotlight shone on the empty space where a band was scheduled to start playing any minute.

Musical distraction would be welcome. Subtly covering her mouth with her hand, Cassandra smothered a yawn.

Maybe this had been a mistake. She hadn't dated in eight years. She was out of practice. Saturday nights usually found an exhausted Cassandra in her yoga pants and thick sweatshirt eating popcorn and M&Ms for dinner while watching a Netflix series.

Fischer was interested enough to ask her out, but not enough to ask about her life before Morton? It didn't make sense. She longed for the days with Paul when she knew all his family and friends. Their playful banter. His odd love of 80s hair band music.

Tonight, she was trying to hold up her end of the conversation and Fischer . . . wasn't.

"You seem quiet." She couldn't be more direct without coming right out and telling him he was boring her to death. "What's on your mind?" She was five minutes from slipping out to the bathroom and texting her sister to call with an emergency from home.

"Dating's not really my thing. Before I usually just hung out with a group and met women who were friends of friends." Fischer laid the menu on the table and leaned forward. "I've never had a personal relationship with anyone from work before. Well, for one thing, most of my army coworkers were dudes."

"Neither have I. Dated anyone from work. I've seen it go bad for other people."

"So what are we doing, then?" He had a way of getting right to the point. "Are we just friends?"

The little stab of disappointment in her stomach said just friends was the wrong answer. "To be honest, I haven't dated anyone since Paul died. Eight years ago." For all her smarts, she didn't know how to salvage this night or this connection. "Before him, the last date I had was sophomore year of college."

"You must've had offers."

"I was busy with school and work. At home, my family and friends get together a lot. I traveled." She shrugged. "I thought the right guy would come along." She knew from the little electric sparks down her spine whenever he held her gaze or stood close by her that they had chemistry.

Fischer listened attentively, like he was analyzing everything she said. "How long are you staying at Morton?"

What did that have to do with tonight? She sipped from her glass to buy a few more seconds. "Well, I bought my house. So I plan to be here for a few years at least."

"Right. And then where to next? A bigger city probably." Instead of a deposition, their romantic night had turned into a job interview.

One eyebrow went up. "Um, . . . that depends where jobs open up when I have the experience. I'll want somewhere that's a good fit." She touched the initial necklace at her throat. "Maybe a warmer climate. What about you? Is Morton College your end goal?"

"If not Morton, then somewhere close to my family. Where I can settle down with my wife and kids and a dog. Coach t-ball. Go fishing with my buddies."

Cassandra held a bundle of grapes, plucked them off one at a time, and popped them into her mouth. Chewed slowly.

Fischer laid a slice of cheese over sausage and stacked them on a cracker. "You want a big career and don't have time for a husband or kids. I'm 34 and ready to settle down." He bit into the cracker.

He'd summed up their entire hour in two sentences. She finished off her glass and escaped to the serving counter to get the next one on her tasting menu. If she had known the night would be this rocky, she'd have ordered one glass instead of the 5-pour taster.

On the way back to the table, she passed him going to get his next glass. By the time he settled back into his chair, the music had started, and it was too loud to talk. She tried to enjoy the lead singer's clear, beautiful voice and the accompanying guitar. His clinical dismissal of their conflicting life goals stung. Deeply.

After a while, the singing duo took a break and switched the speakers to softer background music. Cassandra tried to articulate her career dreams in a way he'd understand. "Can't women have successful careers and a family, too?"

"Sure, they can. My oldest sister is a radiologist with two kids and a nanny. From what I've seen since I met you, I thought you think of the students like your family." She took in a deep breath to protest, but he shook his head. "I'm not judging. I just mean you care about them."

Cassandra couldn't stop herself from tensing defensively. "I do feel somewhat . . . protective. I've gotten to know my office workers and doctoral students better. Like Lance, for example. I mean, his roommate died, and he dealt with it by becoming a campus leader. He has so much potential; I'm trying to mentor him." She shrugged one shoulder sheepishly. "And Rachel. Someone is targeting her, but no one knows who or why. I can't stand by while terrible things happen to people I care about."

"Who do you still suspect?" He leaned forward, interested.

"It's a pretty short list," she answered. "There was a questionable frat guy. But we found out he was busy when the football stadium thing happened. Then for a while, I thought Dr. Winters was someone who'd do anything to preserve Morton's untarnished reputation in the press."

Fischer laughed. "Really? Dr. Winters as a criminal mastermind?"

"I know. It's a stupid idea, but it seemed plausible at the time. After them, the motives get more vague. Like Dr. Bryant, for seeking attention for his causes. Or I met Rachel's birth grandfather's wife last night, and she seems bitter about all the publicity." Her shoulders relaxed and she laughed, "Honestly at this point, I just want to make it through the board meeting next week. There's a national advocacy group who might try to use our campus to gain notoriety."

"Yeah. I'm on Andy Summers' email chain for the board meeting preparations. Let's hope it's just rumors."

A few crackers, sausage and grapes remained on the wooden board between them. Fischer finished off his glass and offered to get their final pours. Watching him walk away, she followed his weaving progress between tables to the serving bar. The smooth, athletic way he moved. When he said something that made the tattooed young woman behind the bar laugh, Cassandra felt a tinge of jealousy. Could chemistry alone bring two people together?

Returning with their glasses, he said, "Is it just me, or is tonight . . . kind of a struggle?"

She'd never get used to his directness. So far, tonight hadn't yielded much in the way of details about Marcus Fischer. He'd lived in his parents' basement and fought in the war. And wanted to be a husband and dad. Sooner than later. She blinked. "Why can't we talk about non-work things, eh?"

"Because our dating skills are rusty. Because we have time consuming jobs." His eyes actually twinkled with mischief. "Because you're not high on Valium?"

When the stalker had broken into her house last month, she'd freaked out. Her cheeks reddened. "Yeah, about those little yellow pills..."

She held her breath while his face closed a bit. Maybe he didn't want to go there. Fischer answered in a flat voice. "My Humvee was on patrol passing through a crowded outdoor market, when insurgents jumped from behind the fruit stands. One antitank grenade landed under our vehicle. The blast didn't pierce its metal, but the force drove my knee through the door."

Even though Oahu crawled with military families, she'd never really heard a firsthand story this close. She stared at his knee half-hidden by the table.

"Usually, I can deal with the pain." He looked away and took a big breath. "Sometimes, in large groups of people I just get a pressing feeling. Being too close. Like something bad is about to happen. My doc says it's anxiety." He shrugged. "So, no. I'm not selling opioids to undergrads for my side hustle."

"I never thought—" Cassandra said, her hands raised in protest.

"It's fine. I'm glad you asked. Now you know."

Her heart ached for that scared young man who'd survived a grenade blast under his vehicle. Impulsively, she laid a hand on his knee. Like by her touch alone, she could absorb the pain. "I had no idea you still suffered."

"One of the weirdest things about civilian life is how jarringly different it is. Not being constantly on alert. Sometimes I still open my car's glovebox and feel surprised to see an umbrella and sunglasses in there instead of two grenades."

She gasped lightly. "Hasn't it been more than ten years since the war?"

"Some days, it feels like I never left." Looking down at his knee, he seemed to notice her hand for the first time and covered it with his own, squeezing gently. "I'm fine. Really."

Softly, over a lump in her throat, she said, "We're really different, but I want to know you better."

The music started again, a soulful holiday tune that enveloped the air around them. Leaning over, his mouth nearly touched her ear. "May I have this dance?" His hand held hers as he led her to the tiny wooden dance floor.

Chapter Twenty-Two

Cassandra approached the Osborne Administration building's darkened entrance so early in the morning, the whole place seemed deserted. Cassandra had heeded the Sunday weather forecast warning people to bundle up all week because the temperatures would be below normal with possible snowfall predicted. Too early and dark to walk this morning, she'd driven her car to work.

Removing a glove, she unlocked the glass door and pulled the handle, hitting a solid object. She let go of the handle and removed her other glove. Her breaths made steam cloud the air around her head. Cassandra bent over to get a closer look at the dark lump blocking the door when suddenly it barked twice.

Cassandra screamed and jumped back, her heart pounding. He scrambled up to his full height but didn't attack. She peered through the hazy yellow light coming from the sconce next to the door. He might be the same dog who'd run through their office last week. Maybe forty pounds of wiry hair, his front paws were apart in an aggressive pose like he was ready to fight or flee depending on her next move.

Only she didn't have a next move. Their family had never owned a pet. Unless you counted the beta fish Keoni had had in one of those round fishbowls for a month who went belly up when her brother forgot it needed to eat every single day.

In fact, the only dog she'd ever liked was Meg and Connor's dog, Bert, who was much larger than this stray. Using her singsong teacher's voice, Cassandra squatted down as best she could in her bulky, long winter coat and held out a hand far enough away that she could snatch it back if Fido decided to lunge for her. "Hey sweetie. What are you doing? Did you sleep here?"

After a few seconds, his matted tail raised and slowly wagged. He stepped closer and sniffed at her hand. Cassandra backed up downwind of the musty, rotting smell coming from him. His skeletal body shivered in the cold. She fished her phone out of her coat pocket and called Andy Summers.

He answered, "I have emergency donuts, and I can be at your office in five minutes."

"I wasn't calling for donuts, thanks. But can you bring over a leash and some blankets? There's a cold dog outside the Osborne building and we need to get him to a shelter."

"On my way." The line clicked off.

* * *

Several hours later between appointments, Cassandra showed Bridget and Devon her photos of the dog that Summers and she had rescued. Although he was probably a stray, Cassandra had snapped the photos as evidence in case the dog bit anyone or they located an owner. Wrapped in an old blue towel, the mutt's brown and white head peeked out from the bundle like a hairy baby.

"Look at him," Bridget cooed. "Poor thing, he's so cute! I just want to take him home."

"My mom would kill me if I showed up with a dog. She's allergic," said Devon.

Looking at the photo again, Cassandra's eyes shifted from the pathetic, huge brown puppy eyes to Summers. When Summers had arrived with the leash and the towel, he'd spoken softly, and the dog went right to him without hesitation.

He'd cradled the dog gently. "Good thing you called me. You're right; he's shivering pretty badly. I bet it dipped into the twenties last night outside."

Her eyes widened and her stomach clenched at the thought of sleeping outside in the cold. "Will he make it?"

Little lines crinkled around the corners of Summers' eyes and he smiled up at her. "Finders keepers?" Her heart skipped a beat at the kindness she saw in them.

When he didn't say anything more for a few seconds, Cassandra said, "Wait, oh you mean me? Oh no. I don't want a dog. I've never had a pet. I don't like dogs. They don't like me. I don't have time for a dog."

He buried his nose behind the dog's filthy head and whispered soothing murmurs into his ears.

"Last week I emailed the facilities guy, Ibrahim Kouri, who's in charge of the stray animals but never heard anything back from him." Cassandra said.

"Kouri sets out food, I think." The dog seemed to relax and know he was safe in Andy's arms. "But I don't know the schedule or what he does during the winter."

"I'll follow up with him."

"Reminds me, I wanted to tell you. About the smoke alarm in the library?" Andy said, "I checked the video feed and that corner was outside of the coverage area for the floor. Can't see anything that happened before the fire alarm went off."

"Rats. I was hoping to get some evidence this time. We keep striking out."

Summers had taken the dog away and left her with a small, brown bakery bag with a warm cinnamon donut inside.

Ignoring Devon and Bridget nearby, Cassandra stared at Summers' hands in the photo and felt a tug of longing. How good would it feel to have Andy hold *her* confidently and gently? To relax into his safe embrace.

Wait, where had that thought come from? She'd just had a semi-successful date with Fischer on Saturday. Had he crumbled some wall inside her that had held repressed lust in check all those years after Paul? She'd better not start looking at every man who crossed her path as a potential—

Devon said, "Hey, remember Rachel said a dog chased her when she was down by the football field? It couldn't be this one, could it?"

Cassandra blinked twice to bring herself back to the present conversation and shook her shoulders to brush off the sentimental spiral that had overcome her. "That's a good question, Devon. I wonder if Rachel could recognize which dog she saw. Maybe she'd remember more about what happened to her."

The three of them oohhed over the last photo Summers had sent her two hours later of a transformed animal. He must have taken the mutt home and bathed him. In the photo, the clean, fluffy dog was curled up on a pile of old towels next to a heating vent in a corner of Summers' security office. The photo caption said, "Every office needs a mascot."

"I'd like one of those." Bridget pointed at Cassandra's phone screen.

Cassandra looked at her, confused. "A dog?"

"No, silly." Bridget laughed. "A down-home country boy who's good with animals."

Cassandra's mouth clamped together. Oh, that.

Bridget handed her a few pink slips of paper. "You got some calls during your last appointment. And one referral from Cinda Weller."

In her office, Cassandra flipped through the messages and returned calls. The last one was from Cinda telling her to call Lillian Peters. A zip of excitement sparked when she recognized the last name.

An old lady voice answered the phone. "Mrs. Peters? This is Cassandra Sato from Morton College returning your call."

"Oh, yes. You've got our great-granddaughter there at the college, don't you?"

Cassandra's heart did one big thump. Her guess had been correct. "What's your great-granddaughter's name?" Reaching for her blank legal pad, she wrote Lillian Peters' name and phone number. "How can I help you?"

"The one in them newspaper articles. Rachel Nagle. My husband Merlin don't want me to call, but I told him she's family, and we're too old to hold onto grudges."

"Yes, ma'am Rachel Nagle is a student here."

"That one what with the blonde hair."

Eighty percent of the young women on campus had blonde hair, so that wasn't exactly a distinguishing characteristic. Cassandra closed her eyes and told herself to be as patient as when she talked to her own Gran.

"She's the spitting image of my Susan." Her frail voice shook. The woman must be in her eighties. "It's like the time clock spun backwards and she's alive again." The woman's whisper was ripe with hope. "Can we meet her?"

A lump in Cassandra's throat blocked her ability to reply for a few seconds. "I can pass along your name and phone number, ma'am. I can't make any promises."

"Merlin is sick. I thought if he saw Susan's granddaughter it might . . . help him." The energy seemed to drain out of Mrs. Peter's voice. "He never believed it was an accident."

Cassandra understood the urge to bring someone you've lost back to life. Surprising herself she asked, "Why didn't Mr. Peters believe the police investigation? Wasn't there bad weather?"

"Susan had drove on the farm since she could reach the pedals. The police just filled out them papers and had done with it. But what about them other skid marks on the road or the car's dented bumper? The facts didn't add up. Merlin even hired a private investigator to prove it wasn't our baby's fault. Waste of money, if you ask me. He didn't do no better than the police."

Cassandra wanted to bring these people closure. She couldn't imagine living with the pain for forty years of believing your daughter's death wasn't an accident. "I'm so sorry for your loss and your husband's illness. I'll give Rachel your number, ma'am."

"Tell her to ask for me when she calls. Merlin don't need to know yet. Sometimes the Holy Spirit brings a body back into your life for a reason. Maybe that girl needs us. She's as beautiful as our Susan."

Cassandra replaced the handset on her office phone and waited a minute for her eyes to dry.

Standing up, she consulted her bullet journal to see what to do during her time between appointments. From somewhere in the building below her office, she heard a muffled yell. Her head raised. Was there an emergency siren she'd missed? Or a fire alarm? Two silent seconds passed, then another loud shout that sent chicken skin running up her arms.

Stepping to her window, she slid the glass open and realized the yelling came from all four buildings surrounding the campus green space. Two or three students gathered in windows on various floors screaming like crazed banshees. Her heart pounded and she looked to the gray sky to see if the low clouds were spinning. Maybe a tornado had been spotted and she'd missed it.

From the window next to hers, she heard an ear-splitting screech followed by laughter. Cassandra ran into the front office. Bridget and Devon had been joined by another student standing in front of their open window. Cold air blew into the room and Cassandra shivered.

Devon said, "One, two, three. Go!" And all three of them screamed again.

When they stopped, Cassandra raised her voice, "What the heck are you doing? Is something wrong?"

"It's 10:00 a.m.!" Bridget laughed.

Cassandra peeked at her watch to confirm it, but still didn't know what she'd missed. She did a palms-up. "And?"

"It's Dead Week. It's a Morton tradition dating way back. The Primal Scream," explained Devon.

"The Primal Scream." She felt like an empty-headed parrot.

"Technically, back in olden times they did it at midnight on Sunday of Dead Week, but years ago they changed it to Monday morning so that kids living off-campus could be involved. Plus, I think the neighbors complained."

Bridget and the other girl gave one last scream and closed the window.

"Is Dead Week that stressful around here? I read a policy that student organizations aren't allowed to meet, and professors can't give tests." To her recollection, screaming had not been covered in Dr. Zimmerman's All-staff policy memo. "All you have to do is study for final exams.

Aren't there 23/7 mandatory quiet hours in the student dorms, too?"

Devon nodded, "Lots of shenanigans during the Rowdy Hour."

Cassandra raised an eyebrow. Then she did the math. Oh. Probably Devon meant the one hour each day that wasn't a mandatory quiet hour.

"Last spring during Dead Week, someone let a greased pig loose on the quad during the 4:00 p.m. Rowdy Hour." Bridget said, "Everyone ran out of the buildings and chased it down, but that thing was fast."

"Yeah, he could move for how fat he was. Finally, one of the farm boys got a rope and caught him. I probably have video of it on my phone." Devon pulled out his phone and started scrolling back in his photos.

"No that's fine. I don't need to see it," Cassandra held up both hands. "Any other bizarre traditions I need to know?"

The students looked at each other for a few beats. Bridget said, "The seniors may or may not run naked through the fountain over by the Arts Center on Friday afternoon."

Devon said, "And if you have a craving for free donuts and energy drinks, go to the library at midnight, right before the Silent Dance Party."

Now that her heart had stopped its fight-or-flight response, Cassandra sincerely hoped the seniors wouldn't streak anywhere in this cold weather. *Nobody* wanted to see that. "The Silent Dance Party?" That stupid parrot again.

"There's a students-only, private Twitter group and someone posts a Finals Week playlist. At the designated time, everyone studying at the library puts on their headphones and dances to the playlist."

She'd give them bonus points for creativity. Cassandra's eyes lit up. "Putting the 'silent' in the Silent Dance Party! That's so smart."

"If you aren't in the group chat, it probably looks funny to see everyone dancing but there's no sound. The staff just thinks we've lost it."

Still smiling, she stepped back into her office and closed the window. Rubbing her hands along her arms, she moved her office thermostat a couple of degrees higher to warm up the office again.

* * *

Checking her to-do list again, Cassandra steeled herself to make an uncomfortable phone call. Adulting meant calling people you disliked. She wanted more information about Susan Peters and starting with the reporter who'd researched the long story made sense. Even if she'd rather eat Minute Rice than talk to him.

Derek Swanson picked up after the first ring. "Aloha, Dr. Sato! Howzit?"

She pulled the phone away from her face and made a big frown at the screen. How did Swanson know local words like howzit? She spoke in standard English. "I'm doing well. How are you?"

"Sorry, the only other Hawaiian words I learned on my one trip to Maui were 'pau hana,' 'mahalo' and 'pakalolo.'"

He chuckled like he'd made a great joke and they were now buddies.

Cassandra ground her back teeth together. "The reason I'm calling is to follow up on your research about Rachel Nagle's family and ask whether you've spoken to Susan Peter's parents?"

"Nah. I left a few messages on their answering machine, but they haven't returned my calls."

Good. He didn't know what she knew about Merlin Peter's suspicions and hiring a private investigator. "What else did you find out about Ms. Peter's time at Morton?"

"Not many people that age still live around Carson, but the photo that accompanied the story got several social media comments saying that Professor Kovar was a perv who liked dating his students. No one with an actual name that I could verify and print though."

Good. Without substantiated #MeToo accusations, she could look forward to the end of that discussion. "Your article last week spawned controversy about faculty-student relations and the Deaf Studies advocacy project. I don't understand why you didn't limit your account to the current issues at hand without dredging up the irrelevant Nagle family history. I can't imagine that Rachel's family appreciated the intrusion."

"That's an understatement." His snickery laugh creeped her out. "I've gotten two voicemails from Rachel's mother and one from their family's attorney. This is exactly the kind of story readers want to know more about. Maybe I can help the Nagle family find closure. Someone who read my article is bound to remember Susan Peters. Like an old classmate who never came forward back then."

No good. He was using sordid details to gain attention to his article, no matter who got pulled into the fray. She hoped the Nagle family sued him and the newspaper. "But Susan Peter's accident has nothing to do with Morton College being accessible to deaf and hard of hearing students."

"When readers know the background of a human-interest story, they more fully understand the ramifications of how the past influences what happens today."

She couldn't understand how a forty-year-old accident had any relevance to today. "You said Susan swerved around before going off the road. Why did you mention the stuff in your article about her car having dents on it if the police ruled it an accident?"

"Because what are the odds that the same family has multiple catastrophes forty years apart at the same school? If you assume Peters had an affair with Kovar in '75, had his baby in the Spring of '76, and gave it up for adoption, wouldn't there be some drama around that kind of situation?"

Meh. She wouldn't call a smoke alarm in the library on the same level of catastrophe as a secret baby. "Can you send me a copy of the police report?" Maybe Swanson had cherry-picked the facts he included in his article to fit the scenario he wanted to emphasize.

"I'll send it, but I wrote the most pertinent points. It was a snowy December night. She attended a house party. The police chose weather as the obvious cause. Or maybe

Peters went off the road and hit the tree on purpose. With one-car accident investigations back then, they didn't have GPS and cell phone data."

"Listen, is there anything that will bring some closure on this issue?"

"Not unless we uncover new information." Swanson's voice changed to a more condescending tone. "Hey . . . lucky you called me. I've been researching text-based emergency management systems. Do you want to compare numbers? I heard you're in charge of writing the report for the board of directors meeting."

Also, not good. Cassandra didn't want to be the subject of his next investigative report. "You and me? . . . Compare numbers?"

"I've called my contacts at colleges nearby to ask which systems they use and how much they cost. Frankly, I'm surprised Morton is still using such an antiquated public address system."

Holding the desk phone's handset away from her ear, Cassandra sent a Stink Eye so strong it should have burst into flames. She did a big cleansing breath and then brought the phone back to her face. "I have everything I need to produce the report without your help. In fact, it's time we get off the phone right now. Goodbye!"

"Always a pleasure. Mahalo, Dr. Sato."

Kiss up. She rolled her eyes even though he couldn't see her. Their conversation raised no new ideas for who hurt Rachel. But now Cassandra had two sources who thought Susan Peter's car accident was suspicious.

Chapter Twenty-Three

The protests began with four folks who looked a few years older than an average college-aged student. Cassandra noticed them Monday after lunch when she was walking back from the Student Center to get a pre-packaged chicken Caesar salad. The weather forecast called for a mild day, but sleet and snow later in the week.

The four strangers wore matching black coats with a logo over the chest and assembled near a white van in the visitor parking area next to the main front entrance. At first, Cassandra had thought a catering vendor was setting up for a special Dead Week lunch, but later they gathered on the edge of the brown grass quad in the campus' center. One large red sign's slogan was "Deaf Rights = Human Rights" with a graphic of a fist held high. Gazing out her office window, Cassandra spotted the black coats intercepting students on their way to classes. Last month, that area had been settled by a traveling street preacher who'd occasionally ranted about the evils of fornication, but in general had been polite and nonthreatening. Cassandra already missed her. This group would make things more difficult.

Cassandra turned when she heard a knock on her open office door. Lance stood holding his phone, his eyes filled with excitement.

He gestured asking if he could enter her office, and Cassandra waved him inside. Lance brought his phone to her and showed her the screen where a social media post proclaimed, "Deaf Rights group demands response from Morton College."

The post had already been liked and shared. What the heck? Cassandra made a palms up gesture and mouthed, "Why today?"

Hadn't anyone told these people it was Dead Week? Were they completely acting on their own or with the cooperation of local campus organizers?

Lance shrugged and signed, "I don't know. We didn't invite them here. They came to help us." That excited look was still on his face. He wanted to be in the middle of an important social justice moment.

Cassandra was a huge supporter of social justice too, but she also had a job to do. She pulled out her own phone, typed into the Notes app and held it up for him to read. "Can you tell them it's Dead Week? We have 23/7 quiet hours."

His glaring eyes held hers for several seconds. "*Quiet* hours. 23/7 quiet hours. Ha. Ha." Then Lance laughed out loud.

Yes. Ha, ha. Deaf people can sign quietly all day every day. She might be slow, but she got the joke. "Seriously. Tell me how to contact their leader. People are studying. This isn't a good week."

Whose bright idea was it to schedule a controversial board meeting during the quiet hours of Dead Week? She needed to find out what Dr. Winters thought of the protestors and Cassandra's role in keeping the campus a safe space for all the students to study for final exams.

"I can try," Lance signed. "But... look at these comments." Scrolling down the page, already opponents to replacing the emergency management system were complaining about potential tuition increases. She hadn't even presented her proposal to the board and already it was blowing up online.

* * *

After lunch, while Cassandra was proofreading minutes from the previous week's focus group meetings, Cinda texted Cassandra. "Do you feel something heavy on your back? Dr. Winters just threw you under the bus."

"WHAT? Where?" Cassandra texted.

Cinda sent a screenshot from Twitter where Dr. Winters had announced, "Students who skip classes to join uninvited meddlers sowing discord and disorder at Morton College will be referred to Student Affairs VP Dr. Cassandra Sato for disciplinary action. Our administration does not tolerate outside groups circumventing policy revision processes."

Winters' post was less than an hour old, but Cassandra was mortified that her name was publicly attached to something without her input. She replied, "I had nothing to do with this. I don't have time to duck falling busses right now."

Swept along in the process, she felt unable to counter these messages. "I'm doing *actual* work on the diversity and inclusion report." Cassandra's thumbs tapped her phone screen. She backspaced several times because her hands shook while she replied to Cinda's text. "Unlike useless Tweets by someone else who shall remain nameless." She added a few eye roll emojis for good measure.

Looking out the window, Cassandra wondered where the protesters had gone. Maybe they were on a break. Good. Next time she saw them, she'd try to find a Coalition leader and reason with them.

She kept going over what she knew and didn't know about Rachel, the deaf advocacy project, and Susan Peters. Swanson had said they needed new information, but Cassandra was out of options to find it. One question surfaced, and she knew someone she could call for an answer. Leaving a voicemail, she went back to work on her report and PowerPoint.

* * *

When her phone rang for the fourth time in thirty minutes, Cassandra closed her laptop's lid and gave up productively slaving at her desk for the moment. Cassandra had left messages and emailed Dr. Winters trying to confirm the protest group had followed proper procedures. Ironic that the woman had time for social media posts and responding to comments, but not a conversation with one of her own advisors.

Grabbing her cell off the desk, Cassandra slid "open" to answer Fischer's call.

"You've seen the Deaf Rights group out by the quad, right?" Fischer asked.

One glance out the window showed the four organizers had been joined by a handful of students. Mostly they stood around in semi-circles signing to each other or saying hello to students passing on the sidewalks.

"Yes, I saw them too." Cassandra decided to do a lap around the inside of the building and waved at Lance as she walked through the reception area. "I'm assuming they got permission through Dr. Winters' office. They haven't trespassed or done anything wrong so we can kick them off campus." If she started on the top far corner and made her way down and up the stairs a couple of times, maybe she could work off the tension building inside her. "I only wish I knew how to prevent people from posting exaggerated information online. Morton isn't opposed to the students' requests; we're discussing them rationally." Reaching the stairwell, she slowly circled around to the basement level and turned around heading back up to the fourth floor. "They act like people are getting hurt left and right because we aren't accessible, when that's just not the case."

"The more positive messages Morton puts out, unfortunately we invite uninformed strangers to add their two cents. Half of the comments aren't even about Morton. They brought up problems with other schools, but it gets tagged onto our whole controversy."

"I can't believe Dr. Winters is posting on social media. Where is she anyway? Shouldn't she be busy ensuring student safety? Rachel Nagle has been targeted twice already. Maybe I should ask Andy Summers to check on her."

"They don't seem aggressive. So far, they're taking photos and mingling with students. You might want to worry about the Morton Parent group who's opposing any expenditures not already included in the current budget. They're worried about tuition increases."

Cassandra's breath became labored as she reached the opposite corner of the building's basement and again climbed the stairs. "Not everything the Deaf Studies group has asked for costs a lot of money. It's more about staff time and shifting resources. The software and new technology are the expensive parts."

"People in that parent group say these kids are already pampered private school students who don't need every new technology as soon as it becomes available."

She stopped on the landing of the fourth floor to catch her breath. "From my research, Morton's public address system is pretty far behind what most other schools have. I'm not even sure we comply with current federal law." Her heart thumped against her chest wall and her legs felt like rubber bands. It was a great indoor break from sitting at her desk. "I'm worried this is going to get worse before Wednesday's meeting. Maybe I should ask Dr. Winters if they'll reschedule the board meeting to a more private time and place."

"Won't it seem like the board is hiding something? Not transparent enough?"

She hadn't even thought about an opposition group. Should they get the two groups together ahead of the board meeting and see if they could all work together? Pre-empt controversy? "Summers already had his hands full with security and logistics. Who knows how many more people will show up between now and next Wednesday." Except that was probably Dr. Winters' role, not hers.

"Why are you breathing like that? Are you at the campus gym?" Fischer asked. "Or are you just excited to talk to me?" His voice lowered into a sexy rumble.

It was such a silly thing to say and so unexpected. Cassandra busted out laughing. Already struggling from the exercise, laughing made her even more breathless. After five seconds, she bent over and held her stomach. Tears rolled down her eyes. Finally, she got control of herself. "Woo hoo. Sorry. No offense." She wiped her cheeks and took a huge breath. Standing up, she felt much lighter.

"Gee. None taken," he said flatly.

"Really! I mean it. I haven't laughed like that in weeks. Seriously, thank you." She'd arrived next to the Student Affairs door and stopped in the hallway.

"Your humble minion," he said. "Talk to you later."

Cassandra ended the call and remained in the hall a few seconds to swipe under her eyes and straighten her outfit.

* * *

Near the end of the workday, Cassandra gave up waiting for her boss to handle the protest situation and texted a few key people for an impromptu meeting. Even though the Deaf

Rights Coalition group's presence today was mostly just distracting, sitting around writing her report wasn't helping. She had to take action.

She arranged the chairs in her office to face around the coffee table, brought the snack basket from the outer office and placed it in the center. Cassandra's phone rang, and she spoke to the caller for a couple of minutes before thanking them and hanging up. Next, her phone buzzed with a text from Lance. "Thought you'd like to see the signs we made."

In one photo, the student advocacy group had made a hand-lettered poster that said, "Stop Language Oppression." The second photo was a poster of SpongeBob holding a sign that said, "NO FAIR."

The students knew about her not-so-secret SpongeBob affection. Cassandra laughed out loud while she recited the protest chant from the TV show in her head. *Standing at the concession, plotting his oppression.* There's a SpongeBob episode for nearly any situation.

The worst part about this week was that Cassandra's natural loyalty to supporting students' success directly conflicted with her administrative role. She believed in free speech but would feel horrible if it disrupted students' ability to study and do well in their classes. There was no good vs. evil dichotomy, just two sides with opposing priorities.

Within a half hour, Cassandra sat next to Meg on the leather loveseat facing Dr. Bryant and Fischer and opened her journal. Between the campus security issues and his new dog, Andy was unable to join them.

"Thanks for coming on short notice. I haven't been able to talk to Dr. Winters today." Cassandra tried to keep the frustration out of her voice. They were all friends here, right? "I just wanted to make sure we're all on the same page this week."

Bryant handed her a printed document scribbled with red ink. He signed and Meg spoke, "I've made a few suggestions on your diversity and inclusion summary for the board meeting. You did a good job laying out the benefits of adding text-based emergency systems. I added a paragraph about how stakeholders will notice improvement in communication at all levels of the college. The board won't be able to say that this purchase only accommodates a few people on campus. Mentioning that we're seeking matching grant money should also get their attention."

"I agree." Fischer nodded. "The more I've learned about this whole issue, I'm excited that we can notify people about everyday situations in addition to emergencies. Like if we're closing a floor or building for extended maintenance and want to tell people to avoid an area. Or if a parking area is inaccessible due to weather or special events."

"Thanks for your feedback, Dr. Bryant." Cassandra said, "Have you been in touch with Coalition protest representatives? I hope they don't hijack our work with the board on Wednesday."

Cassandra didn't know how to interpret the look Bryant gave her. It wasn't openly hostile, but she still didn't trust him 100%. Probably the feeling was mutual. He signed, "I didn't invite them. I don't control their appearances. Other colleges and the public are watching us. The board's decisions will not go unnoticed by the national organizations.

Equal access is a civil rights issue and hearing people have been ignorant for too long."

"We've talked about this before. In order for students and faculty on campus to appreciate the diversity of others, they first have to get to know folks on a personal level. That's the whole point of Diversity Day. It's a central tenet of my presentation to the board."

"You've heard of racism and sexism? There's a thing called *audism*."

"Autism?" Cassandra asked, "You mean the autistic spectrum disorders?"

"Nope, it's audism with a 'd.' People who can hear think they are better than people who can't hear. They're unwilling to recognize their privilege as members of the hearing majority."

"Is that what I'm doing?" Cassandra had never heard the word before. "I didn't mean to—because, I don't think I'm better than—"

Bryant said, "Privileged people usually don't recognize they're doing something wrong until someone points it out, right? You know this from your own experiences. Every activity on campus and during Diversity Day doesn't have to be conducted solely in English. Why don't we get more creative and offer an event that's visual, or not English language-based? Like a performing artist who signs or gestures, an art exhibition, or movement-based icebreaker games."

Who was going to research and plan all of this? "You've got some great ideas. Assuming the board and Dr. Winters vote to keep the Diversity Council going at their meeting,

I could use some help." Her early mentors had taught her to keep your opposition close in order to convert them to your way of thinking. "Dr. Bryant, how would you like to be co-coordinator of Diversity Day?" Cassandra guessed he'd be flattered by the leadership position, but his face did not look pleased.

"Dr. Winters side-stepped the Council and appointed you to provide this diversity and inclusion report at the board meeting. She doesn't support Diversity Day or real change at Morton." Bryant shook his head. "I've got one more year before I go up for tenure. I'm not climbing aboard *that* sinking ship."

That was not the answer she'd expected. She took a breath and changed tactics. Could she count on him or not? If Cassandra was going to battle for her principles, she wanted to go down fighting.

Cassandra glanced at the executive summary still in her hand. Even with Bryant's changes it seemed . . . dry. "I know Winters wanted me to give the presentation at Wednesday's meeting, but I have an idea." One that would get more attention than burying stodgy white men with statistics and bullet points. "I think part of this message would be more impactful coming from the students. A learning moment for them, and a chance for the board members to experience Morton's bright and engaged students."

Surprise and respect grew on his face and Bryant nodded slowly. "Not a bad idea."

Fifteen minutes later, they'd hammered out the details for who was responsible for the last few slides of the presentation. Bryant said his goodbyes and left her office, and Fischer got up to follow him out.

Cassandra turned to Meg, "Could you and Fischer stay for a minute?"

Fischer frowned and closed the door. "You seem kinda jumpy. Worried about the snow forecast?"

Her head turned towards the window where gently falling snowflakes looked harmless from this side of the glass. "Not at all," she fibbed. "It will probably stop soon, right?"

"If I wasn't an interpreter, I'd be a weather person." Meg laughed. "I could be wrong 70% of the time and still have a job. Last night on TV they said we could get up to six inches overnight."

Cassandra felt the blood drain from her face. Maybe she'd ask Meg to pick her up tomorrow on the way to work. Meg checked her watch and stood.

"I know you need to hurry home, Meg. I can make this quick." Cassandra steadied herself and faced them. "I think I know who hurt Rachel Nagle."

Fischer folded his arms and leaned against the door.

Meg gasped, "Why didn't you tell me?"

"I am telling you! Several people I've asked about Dr. Kovar remembered him and Susan Peters, including Dr. Hansen."

Fischer pointed a thumb to indicate Hansen's office next door. "You mean old man George Hansen?"

"The hermit?" Meg asked. "I thought he retired."

"He still comes to work a few days a week." Cassandra wiped her sweaty palms on her wool skirt. "He's a grouch, but he's still here. Anyway. Dr. Hansen and Swanson, the reporter, said everyone knew that Kovar fooled around with students. Susan Peters was one of them."

"I thought we were talking about Rachel Nagle, not her grandmother?" Fischer's eyebrows came together into a deep frown. "Are you saying old man Hansen pushed Rachel?"

"No, not him." Cassandra took a deep breath. "There's one other person who knew Susan Peters. Who coincidentally seems to be nearby when Rachel has an *accident*."

Fischer and Meg eyed each other skeptically, but Cassandra kept going. "Here's the kicker. Right before you came to my office, Susan Peters' mom called me. She told me that the night Susan Peters crashed her car into the tree, she'd left Dr. Bergstrom's house after one of his Sunday Salon house parties. No one mentioned that before or in the police report."

"Whoa there, wahine," said Meg. "You're all over the place. I don't like where this is going. We've been down this road before with Dr. Winters, and you were wrong. Is everyone over the age of 65 automatically suspect?"

"Meg's right." Fischer shook his head. "Where's your evidence?"

How could they not see the obvious? Cassandra tried to control the exasperation in her voice. "Who claims he 'found' Rachel down near the football field?" Cassandra wanted to trust him. He was her mentor. Beloved by students.

"Bergstrom. He called 9-1-1. Then performed first aid."

"Right." Cassandra nodded. The facts all pointed at his involvement. "And who did I see in the library walking away from the smoke-filled area when Rachel ended up in the medical clinic for smoke inhalation?"

Meg's shoulders raised up, "Bergstrom? Really, I didn't know that. Hmm."

No one else had the means or motive to get Rachel out of the picture. "Wasn't Susan's death very convenient for Professor Kovar? The Bergstroms were close friends with the Kovars. Now, if Rachel leaves Morton because she fails her classes or gets hurt, who won't need to answer for his role in whatever happened in the 70s?"

Cassandra had counted on these two for support, but their skeptical expressions were discouraging. "Bergstrom needs to face justice for what he did then and now. I thought you two would help me get evidence against him."

"Andy Summers tried to find evidence that someone pushed Rachel, but there wasn't any." Meg put on her coat and hat. "You're guessing Bergstrom and Kovar had a hand in Susan Peter's death? No. There was already an investigation forty years ago."

"How carefully did Summers check all the security camera footage on the grounds?" Cassandra persisted, "There must be something we've missed."

Fischer pursed his lips. "What are you planning?"

Looking down, she picked at an invisible piece of lint on her skirt and fibbed, "Nothing."

Cassandra felt Fischer's eyes bore into the top of her head for the space of several seconds. When she looked up and met his stare, his eyebrows lifted. He didn't believe her but didn't challenge her either.

Meg gently squeezed Cassandra's arm. "That's for the best, Cass. You have enough to worry about. Let the past go."

Cassandra nearly laughed. An ominous dread settled over her after they left and the rest of the evening. People thought she was courageous for moving so far away and pursuing her dream career. Without her friends' support, she was a coward who resisted believing the facts right in front of her face. As if the impending snow wasn't enough. She had to accept that someone she trusted was willing to hurt a student to hide the truth. Why did Bergstrom do it? For loyalty to a friend? For his legacy? Letting the past go wasn't as simple as just moving on.

Chapter Twenty-Four

Cassandra had been in the dream so many times the past eight years, she knew it by heart. The long maze of Kapiolani Medical Center's hallways, industrial carpet squares underfoot, soft beeping of equipment as she passed each room and glanced in at the beds. Into Paul's room, the still, wax museum-like figure instead of her laughing fiancé. Fear.

Oxygen, a breathing tube, the IV port taped to his hand. Mom and Dad and his younger sister always in the room, whispering in hushed tones. Regret.

Days spent in a confined space that smelled of disinfectant, body odor, and fear. The doctors' urgency, the nurses' efficient care. The turning point, the hopelessness, preparing for the worst. Grief.

Drifting awake, Cassandra rolled over in bed and gathered the familiar sorrow around her like an extra blanket. Over time, she'd been able to morph the dream sequence to begin with the worst but return to better early days. More often than not, she'd awaken with a sense of nostalgic calm instead of grief.

Tonight, the darkness persisted. Cassandra stood crying in the hospital at the end of the bed, unable to act. Paralyzed.

Blonde hair splayed on the pillow and a bandage circled the head. The parents huddled in the corner weren't Paul's parents. Cassandra had entered the wrong room. Rachel belonged with that blonde hair and those parents. Cassandra hadn't done enough to prevent her death. She gasped for air like she had fallen from a window flat onto her back. Suffocating darkness.

She had to find her people. In the doorway, bumping into the doctor, he placed his hands on her shoulders. His eyes glared, his mouth moved, "Why did you wait so long? You should have come earlier." His warm hands burned deep into the muscles of her shoulders. Guilt.

Gasping, her eyes opened immediately to force the dream to stop. Heart pounding, she knew it was false. All except the crushing hopelessness that was as real as the clammy sweat beading across her forehead. Intellectually, she knew Paul's death wasn't her fault. But no matter how much she wanted to forgive herself, she couldn't.

Picking up her phone, the time appeared on the home screen. 3:16 a.m. Paul's time of death.

Slowly turning onto her back, Cassandra rested her palms on her ribs, willing her breaths to slow and deepen. With each inhale and exhale, her heart gentled, her panic soothed. She felt the knobs of her hipbones and the valley of her stomach.

Before she'd gone to bed, Cassandra had known her sleep was doomed. How could she rest comfortably when she had to face Dr. Bergstrom? He probably imagined his actions serving some greater good. No matter what excuse he came up with, she'd have to focus on getting justice for Rachel.

Just like one of his comic book heroes. His obsession with superheroes and philosophy had seemed kind of frivolous to Cassandra, but she had figured to each his own. If academia found his research topic worthy, who was she to say it wasn't important.

She had no proof against Bergstrom. Summers had checked the video feed in the library before the smoke alarm went off, but the affected corner was out of the camera's coverage area.

Surprisingly, she wished she could ask her former boss, Dr. Nielson for advice. He tended to talk too much and made her eyes cross sometimes, but he had the best interests of Morton at heart. The Diversity Council had had Nielson's full support. Dr. Winters seemed bent on protecting Morton's reputation and traditions at any cost. She would not be pleased by more negative scrutiny.

Her breathing finally returned to normal, but the earlier anguish lingered. Paul's spirit had warned her with this twisted dream. He'd sent her a sign. If Cassandra failed to stop Bergstrom, Rachel could end up hurt or dead. Missing the window to act in time to save Paul was an experience she never wanted to repeat.

Although supporting students was her official job, this time it was personal. Letting go of the past didn't include forgetting the lessons she'd learned from past mistakes. She'd made a promise to have Rachel's back. Today.

At four in the morning, Cassandra decided it was late enough to get out of bed. She tried the poses with her usual yoga video in the darkened living room. The sound of ocean waves crashing against the shore didn't center her breath. She slowly teetered over twice during tree pose, unable to focus on one distant point.

Calling upon her ancestors and the energy that must have come from Paul, she meditated until mindfulness and calm settled over her.

* * *

When daylight broke, Cassandra peered out the window in the front sunroom at the crystalline beauty blanketing her front yard. Powdery snow filled the nooks of the trees along the street and dusted the shrubs in her yard.

After breakfast, she'd stayed home past seven and called the college's information number anonymously to ask if school was cancelled. The laughing man on the other end had assured her that if she didn't like the weather this morning, she should wait a few hours and it would change. She'd hung up on his patronizing attitude.

Pulling on furry boots, hat, and gloves, she headed for the garage. Ignoring the cold, she was excited about her first snow shoveling opportunity. The first few times she scooped and heaved the snow off the driveway, her feet slid on icy patches hidden beneath the layers. It took several passes in front of the garage before she became comfortable planting her feet wide and keeping her body centered.

An even bigger problem loomed further down the driveway. Her neighbor's tree branch had broken off the main trunk and landed across Cassandra's driveway. She was stuck.

By the time she'd cleared a wide swath from the garage to her back door, her fingers had numbed beyond feeling and she went inside for a break. Drinking hot cocoa, she wrapped her fingers around the warm mug and made a game plan for getting to work.

Although she lived only two blocks away, walking on snowy, icy sidewalks was out. Calling someone like Andy to pick her up seemed like a sellout. When she had moved to Nebraska, she knew she'd have to deal with snowstorms. Calling in sick wasn't an option either.

Besides, she'd spent the last five hours talking herself into meeting with Bergstrom to set things right. What seemed completely sensible at three-thirty in the morning now gave her pause.

Revived by the cocoa, she'd bundled up again and stomped outside to inspect the tree branch. About eight inches wide, the whole thing was long enough to block her driveway. She could lift the top half, keeping her eyes squinted half-closed to protect them from pokey little branches. She heaved it slowly around until it was almost parallel to the driveway. She'd have to drive onto the yard to get around it.

She was breathing hard, hands on her hips when Mr. Gill, the neighbor, came out wearing his heavy flannel shirt and jeans. With his bare hands, he helped her shove the whole branch around and back into his yard. "Sorry 'bout that. My son's coming later with his chainsaw. We'll have it cleaned up before you get home."

"Thanks so much. I really need to get to work."

"I'll finish your driveway with my snowblower. Take me just a bit to get over there."

"I'd be so grateful. Thank you." She had to stop herself from calling him Uncle out of respect. Old habits die hard.

* * *

About thirty minutes later, Cassandra faced Dr. Bergstrom's office door and looked up to compose her thoughts before knocking. Years ago, students had stuck a large painted cardboard yellow and black Bat Signal above his doorframe. Time and fingerprints had wilted the edges and marred the surface.

Her day had already been long. The dream, the snow, pushing the tree branch had left a small scratch on her face, and backing out of the driveway, she'd groaned when icy rain drizzled on the windshield. Luckily, her street had been empty while she slowly puttered to campus.

She rapped three times on the door. Blew out a big breath. Read the printed class schedule taped to the wooden surface. No answer. Frowning, she knocked again. He didn't have class this morning. The small white marker board where professors often left handwritten notes like "Be back in 10 minutes" was blank.

Turning towards the department office, the rubber soles of her wet boots squeaked down the hallway's ancient linoleum.

"Can I help you?" asked the apricot-haired woman her gran's age who was seated behind the reception cubicle, when Cassandra entered the office.

"I'm looking for Dr. Bergstrom. Do you know when he'll be back?" Snow globes lined the top shelf along the back wall. Silver tinsel was taped in swags along the front partition and a small reindeer dish full of candy rested next to a plastic Santa Claus holding a ho-ho-ho sign. Someone had altered the sign with black permanent marker that read, ho-ho-hell.

"Dr. Bergstrom isn't in yet, dear."

But Cassandra, carrying her large tote bag, had carefully shuffled on the sidewalk sprinkled with green—she was guessing "ice melt"—pellets all the way from the administrative parking lot to Bryan Hall and up the stairs to the bat cave. Her voice rose, "What do you mean he isn't in yet?" If *she* had made it to work this morning, surely people who'd lived here for decades could deal with the weather, too?

"He called and said he was taking the morning off. He'll be in after lunch. If you want to come back then."

No, she didn't want to come back then! She had shoveled. She'd moved a tree. She wanted to talk to him now. "Thank you, ma'am."

Reversing her path from Bryan Hall and back to her car, she threw her bag on the front seat and crawled inside, arranging her coat and buckling her seat belt. Her breath puffed in clouds inside the cold car.

A wiser person might have gone into her warm office and waited until after lunch. But Cassandra was tired of always doing the sensible things. She'd started this day with a mission, and nothing would stop her. Cassandra had gone rogue.

Turning the car on, she flipped the switch to clear the windshield. The wipers didn't move. The sleety rain had stuck to the window while she'd hiked across the tundra on her wild goose chase. Now a thin layer of ice made visibility zero. Reaching under the front seat, she pulled out the ice scraper oven mitt combo thing and mentally thanked Cinda.

She blasted the heater to high, pulled up the fur-lined hood on her parka, and climbed out to scrape the ice from the windshield. A few staff parked and said good morning while they carefully walked by, but no one she recognized or acknowledged with more than a grunt or a wave.

On the way to Bergstrom's house, Cassandra's tires spun and the Honda fishtailed when she pressed the gas pedal, so she slowed down to under 20 mph. By the time she'd reached the tree-lined boulevard of Professors' Row, ice chunks caked her wipers and Cassandra hunched forward peering through a small square of clear windshield to pull into a parking spot in front of his house. Opening her car door, she'd stepped onto crunchy frozen sludge on the street. Her next step broke through the ice and into a deep cold puddle that slopped over her black suede ankle boot, seeping into her socks.

Three steps up his snow-covered driveway, her foot shot out from under her center of gravity, and with a "Woof!" she was airborne briefly until landing on her right hip. Cassandra laid there a couple of seconds to see if any sharp pains told her she'd broken something. Tears of frustration streamed down her numb cheeks, mixing with falling snow and clouds of breath from her open mouth. That made three forms of precipitation, which was just one form too many. Cassandra was over this day already.

Gingerly, she stood and limped to the front door. When no one answered her knock, she tried the knob. Finding it unlocked, she let herself in. Michiko Sato would not approve of her haole behavior. However, crossing fingers, she'd never know.

Chapter Twenty-Five

Cassandra squirmed on the leather chair in Bergstrom's library where heavy curtains covered the oversized windows. Her right hip throbbed. In hindsight, she should have listened to Meg and Fischer.

Behind his desk, Bergstrom's weary face was wreathed in dim light from one small banker's lamp. In front of him lay an open file folder and a half-empty snifter of what looked like brandy. Musky tobacco scents seemed embedded in the furniture. Maybe she'd been a tad impulsive.

Ten feet away in the kitchen doorway, Liz stood wearing a long, white sweater over lounge pants and a silk shirt, her hair pulled back into a loose ponytail. Raising both palms out to her sides, she shrieked, "What kind of degenerate tracks muddy puddles through a house uninvited?" Her words slurred together enough that Cassandra guessed she'd already had a few drinks.

Cassandra peeked at her watch. 9:30 a.m. and 31 degrees. Why were they already drinking? Had she interrupted an argument?

Cassandra pushed a dripping lock of hair off her forehead and leaned forward. She gasped in surprise at the wet, brown footprints she'd left on the expensive white carpet under her ankle boots.

Her mother would die of mortification if she saw Cassandra at this moment. Arriving at the house uninvited, making a huge mess, and disrespecting her elders. What a disgrace.

"I came to talk to Dr. Bergstrom." Cassandra held up a hand like an oath. "I'll clean up the mess after we're done." She'd love an ibuprofen.

The gloves in her hand were sopping wet and she unzipped the top of her winter coat. Squinting at her sleeve, she saw white cotton poking through the tear near her elbow. Stupid ice. Why couldn't crises happen on nice sunny afternoons?

"Why don't you pull up a chair, dear, and join us." Bergstrom gestured to the other armchair next to Cassandra. "You look a little tired, and this might take a while."

Liz frowned at him for several beats. Backing up, she dragged a tall chair from the wall to the space where she'd been standing. She looked from her husband to Cassandra, her hands fidgeting restlessly.

Cassandra had trusted her instincts in the past and had been correct. Cassandra wiped her forehead. "Look, I'm sorry for barging in like this. I seem to have interrupted you two..."

Bergstrom folded his hands on the desk in front of him. Belatedly, Cassandra felt a moment of uncertainty. His shoulders hunched forward and his normally twinkly eyes looked resigned as they surveyed her messy hair and wet face. "My eyesight isn't what it used to be, but even I can see you have something to say. Why don't you just skip the formalities and get to it?"

Good. He knew she'd figured it out and he was ready to talk. "I know what you did. I just can't figure out why. Maybe there were extenuating circumstances. You could turn yourself in. I can't let anything else happen. It has to stop. Now."

His fingers steepled together in front of him like he was gearing up for one of his wise lectures. "Everyone has secrets. Everyone has things they'd rather not relive. Perhaps," he raised an eyebrow, "even you? Surely you can understand the need for discretion?"

Trying to right the wrongs of her past was a big reason Cassandra was here right now dripping slush on his chair and carpet. Maybe she could appeal to his inner philosopher. "The Buddha taught that each person is responsible for his own life decisions and karma will decide his fate in the future. Until you accept responsibility, you can't move forward."

Bergstrom looked towards the darkened window. "Blessed are the merciful for mercy shall be theirs."

"Which philosopher wrote that?"

"Jesus Christ," he replied.

She blew out a big breath. "Didn't Jesus also say you have to confess your sins before they can be forgiven?"

"Technically, no. But his followers did." He looked at Liz. "Maybe some things are unforgivable." The eyes behind his wire-framed glasses shifted back to stare into Cassandra's.

"Are you saying *I* need to forgive someone?" Cassandra looked between him and Liz. Or was he asking for *his wife's* mercy?

Cassandra needed to hear him say the words. He was responsible for hurting Rachel and she couldn't let anything more happen. "I just want you to tell me the truth." To her own ears she sounded self-righteous, but she couldn't stop herself even if she'd wanted to.

"You don't want the truth. Even my wife doesn't know everything about me."

Liz's voice was steely. "You overestimate yourself. You may be able to fool a bunch of young coeds, but you haven't fooled me. I've loved our life together here. I've loved bringing the students into our home." Bergstrom didn't look surprised to hear Liz's vow of loyalty. "Tell her what you did, Mike. Just tell her."

Cassandra tamped down a flicker of regret for confronting him.

His head bowed and in that pose he looked like he was praying. Raising his eyes, he said, "I don't know how you found out, but yes. It was my fault."

Her eyes opened wide with the thrill of being right.

"What you need to understand is that Dr. Kovar and I were good friends. We started at Morton the same year as graduate teaching assistants. Our wives were friends. Alec and his wife had their first son right away. We played cards together or talked politics. We took weekend vacations together at a cabin in Michigan. There's something about that bond you develop with people your own age during your first real job. Anyway, the new family took its toll on Alec."

Bergstrom sat back in his chair, warming up to his story. "Susan Peters started off as the Kovars' babysitter. She'd stop by his office to set up the schedule or catch a ride to his house. The exact details are irrelevant, but he told me later that their affair just happened. He'd even considered leaving Anna to be with Susan. I thought he was acting like a fool."

He sipped from his brandy glass. "Anyway, back to 1975. After a few months, Anna got wind of it and told Kovar to end the affair or they were over. So he ended it with Susan. A couple months later, Susan told Kovar she was pregnant with his baby. He was as relieved as anyone to hear her adoption plans. She moved home during the spring semester, and I heard she had a girl. Kovar never mentioned her again until she showed up on campus the next fall."

Cassandra unzipped her coat the rest of the way and shifted onto her other hip. His story was mesmerizing.

"Why did Susan come back? That question has haunted me all these years. Out of all the colleges in the state, why did she return to Morton? She must've known there was no future for her and Kovar. Didn't it hurt her to remember their mistakes every time she saw him?"

Bergstrom frowned. "You need to know how much Alec loved his family. He wouldn't leave his wife for a twenty-two-year-old girl. Why couldn't Susan understand that? I was only protecting my friend. Kovar was finishing his dissertation, with a wife and kids to support. Susan turned up at our Sunday Salon and drank too much. Heck, back in those days, drinking was part of the culture. She hinted to Kovar that she regretted giving up the baby and could petition to get her back. He was distraught. He knew that parenting the baby with Susan would destroy his marriage. His wife had been willing to forgive a small indiscretion, but a baby was just asking too much."

Cassandra glanced at Liz who had stood up and leaned against the kitchen doorway, her arms folded across her chest.

"I tried to convince Susan to leave Alec's family alone. I offered to help her enroll at another college, that I'd send a good recommendation." Bergstrom shrugged helplessly. "We quarreled in the entryway. She was too drunk to listen to reason. I told her it was better for her to leave and avoid a scene. I practically pushed her out the door. I stood there on the porch and watched her drive away in the snow and ice."

Tears glistened off his cheeks. His gaze focused on Liz, "I'm the reason Susan got in that car and drove off in a drunken rage. It was my fault she died. I never told anyone. Not Kovar. Not even my wife. For forty-three years." Stubby fingers swiped the wetness off his face.

Liz stepped away from the doorway and out of Cassandra's sight. Cassandra's disappointment seeped out of her lungs like a balloon whose air slowly deflated until there was nothing left except a shriveled clump. "You never forgave yourself after all this time?"

If she were kinder, she would feel sorry for him and the years he'd spent paying for his perceived sins. If she were more truthful, she'd admit that his years of beating himself up over mistakes of the past served no purpose except to cause him pain.

Cassandra couldn't undo his past. Or hers. She felt empty because the emptiness was easier than feeling pain. She tired of carrying the pain around inside her for eight years. The emptiness was a blessing. She wanted to feel nothing. It hurt less that way.

Wiping tears from her own cheeks, it was time to do her job and hold him accountable for his actions now. "No one would have known any of this, if you'd just left Rachel Nagle alone. She was only interested in her family's genetic history. You didn't have to hurt her. I have to tell the authorities."

Bergstrom frowned and raised his palms in front of his chest. "Liz—"

A cold voice slowly said, "I will not have it!"

Cassandra's head swiveled towards Liz who had returned to the library door. She leveled a small dark gun at Cassandra's torso with surprising steadiness. Cassandra jumped out of the chair and backed up several steps. A sharp pain started in her hip and shot down her leg. "Whoa—"

Liz looked at Cassandra but spoke to Bergstrom. "I told you years ago to get out of this God-forsaken place. You mope around like the weight of the world is on your shoulders. Give me a break. You promised me a retirement. We are selling this mausoleum, buying one of those 5th wheel campers, and moving to Arizona. And you, young lady, will not stop us."

Cassandra knew nothing about guns or how to disarm a drunk, retired woman. She thought about diving on the floor but wasn't sure how easy it would be to stand up again. Luckily Bergstrom surprised them both by standing, taking four long strides, and grabbing the gun from Liz.

Unmoving, Cassandra stayed near the window. "Put it down, sir. Put it on the desk." Her heart thumped. "I have to call the police. Let's everyone relax."

"I warned you not to put me on a pedestal. I told you I was unworthy. I merely study heroes." He held the gun by the barrel and laid it on the far desktop side away from Liz. "It was a good excuse to read comic books on the job."

She let out the breath she'd been holding. "Just admit the truth and you can start fresh." Maybe they'd go easy on him.

His lips pressed together. "I can't tell you what you want."

Can't or *won't*? The disappointment returned. Hands on her hips, Cassandra said, "I've missed my family so much since moving here and you gave me fatherly advice. I trusted you." She understood how Harry Potter felt when Dumbledore had hung him out to dry. Like he had some noble cause that Harry couldn't understand.

"I'm just an old philosopher circling the drain." Bergstrom slowly walked towards Cassandra, his self-effacing smile causing wrinkles to spider out from his twinkly eyes. "You either die a hero, or you live long enough to see yourself become a villain."

He was back to playing games. She'd ruined another pair of shoes, and it would take weeks of yoga to heal her aching side. Cassandra rolled her eyes.

"Two-Face. *The Dark Knight Rises*."

"I have a confession, too." She let out a big breath and did a palms up shrug. "I've never seen a Batman movie."

A long laugh rolled up from Bergstrom's belly. "Oh, that's a good one." Pivoting, he gestured to his wife. "Okay, Liz. You win. We're leaving Carson. Let's get packing."

Cassandra stared at him, speechless at how fast he'd changed his mind.

"I'll submit my resignation tomorrow," he said. "I've worked too hard for too long to destroy my good name and my wife's safety net. You want me to be the villain, fine. That's on you. You decide what you want to tell the Morton board and the police, but I'll never speak of this again."

"Nev-" Cassandra clamped her lips shut before she spit her rage right back at him. He thought he could hurt Rachel, scare her off campus, then drive off into carefree retirement.

Without his confession, Cassandra had no way to hold him accountable. She needed to track down that evidence. Even if she had to do it herself. Cassandra stomped out the front door, wet socks squishing in her ankle boots, trailing slush and dirt behind her.

* * *

Cassandra pressed a dry towel to her hair and stood shivering on the cotton mat in her bathroom. Her thumb skimmed her cheek, hitting a tender spot. Frowning, she wiped steam from the mirror and checked her face. A three-inch scratch started at the hairline by her ear and ran down her jawline.

Her smartwatch vibrated against the porcelain sink edge where she'd taken it off before gingerly stepping into the hot shower. She ignored it.

Weird that the scratch hadn't hurt until now. Of course, her aching glute from that fall on the ice trumped every other bodily discomfort. Twisting to the side, she examined the baseball-sized bruise that had already formed. Bergstrom was literally a pain in her butt.

Cassandra had always prided herself on being a good judge of character. She studied how people acted, not only what they said. How could she have been so wrong about Bergstrom all semester?

When the smartwatch vibrated a second time, Cassandra blew out a sigh and wrapped the towel around her torso. Stepping into her bedroom, she scooped up her phone from the nightstand. Marcus Fischer. "Hello?"

"Where have you been?" His voice was loud.

She stepped around her neatly made bed with the heavy comforter she'd ordered online the previous week and stood in front of the window. "I'm fine, thanks. How're you?"

Blown snow covered the bottom portions of the windowpanes, and the gray sky hung low. "Worried you'd slid off the road into a ditch." Around six inches of snow had settled onto her deck railing and back yard. "I stopped by your office, and Lance said you never came into work. I've called you four times in the last three hours."

Weird, she'd had her watch on all morning and hadn't noticed it ringing. Sitting down on the bed, the worry in Fischer's words hit her. "Pretty sure there's no ditches between the college and my house," she joked, hoping to lighten the mood.

"Please tell me you were out shoveling and making snow angels and lost track of time?"

"Uh, that would be a big no. I went to Dr. Bergstrom's house where he admitted to feeling responsible for Susan Peters' death forty-something years ago. Oh, and his wife may have held a small gun on me for a few seconds."

She could practically hear him cross his arms in that judgy way he did. "A *gun*?"

She couldn't tell if Fischer was skeptical or as surprised as she'd been when Liz had stepped into Bergstrom's library. "Bergstrom took it away from his wife and no one was hurt." An icy shiver ran up her back and she tightened the towel under her arms. Maybe she'd been in a smidge more danger than she'd originally realized. "I wanted him to tell me why he'd hurt Rachel Nagle, but he wouldn't say. He's submitting his resignation letter and says they're retiring to Arizona."

"Here I thought you'd crashed in the snow and ended up in the hospital." Fischer blew out a loud sigh. "Didn't know I had to worry about you bleeding out from a gunshot."

Cassandra smiled. "No hospital-level catastrophes. Just licking my wounds. Having a moment." That scratch on her face was going to need some thick concealer. "I'll be in the office after lunch. Hey, why were you trying to get ahold of me earlier?"

"I just had a feeling something was wrong. Wanted to make sure you were okay. It's been a weird couple of weeks."

He had that part right. She went back over what he'd said. Aww. Fischer had been worried about her.

Chapter Twenty-Six

Thanks to the wonders of modern pharmaceuticals, a long hot shower, and two cups of Kona coffee, Cassandra felt excited to face the day Wednesday morning.

She checked the phone's weather app while standing in her walk-in closet. Eight total inches of snowfall yesterday and overnight, but the sun was predicted to make an appearance by noon. Deciding on a wool pinstriped pantsuit, Cassandra questioned how anyone in Nebraska dressed professionally during winter storms. She packed her navy pumps in a tote bag and wore her warm, rubber-soled boots for the ride to work. Keeping her hair down and pulled to one side, it partially covered the tree scratch she'd layered with concealer.

Driving the two blocks from home at about 10 mph, she had taken the turn into the staff area behind the Osborne Building at a crawl to avoid sliding into parked cars. She couldn't believe they hadn't closed school and cancelled the meeting.

By 7:15, she was in her office chair sipping a third cup of coffee from her Morton travel mug. Just in time for the board of directors meeting, the *Omaha Daily News* had published a follow-up article summarizing Derek Swanson's report from last week. They rehashed the Deaf Studies advocacy project, Rachel's deafness and her first injury, her family's adoption story, and the Morton administration's resistance to funding a large technology update. Even the fire alarm in the library and the Deaf Community's national push for equal access to emergency and text-based event notifications were included. All in one neat, full-page package.

A side panel included new quotes from Dr. Bryant touting Cassandra's assistance to the Deaf Studies students and their advocacy project. Bryant had even mentioned how she'd invited the students to speak at the Morton board meeting.

Cassandra nearly spit out her coffee. The reporter's slant made it seem like she'd sided with the students and turned her back on her job and the administrative team. She saw herself as a liaison working for the ultimate good. But being mentioned in multiple news articles connected to disrupting the status quo meant she'd be the easiest scapegoat, if any heads were to roll.

In addition to Dr. Bryant, Swanson had interviewed parents, those both for and against the technology purchases. Chairman Hershey was quoted, "Normally our meetings only draw a few bored spectators, but I understand we're expecting a record turnout. We have a long agenda for our last meeting of the calendar year and may not get to all the topics we had planned to discuss."

She'd gathered data and studied ways Morton could improve in diversity and inclusion. If today went well, the Diversity Council would be fully reinstated, and the emergency management system would be funded. If not, she'd look frivolous and inexperienced. The worst part was that the needs of students like Lance, Rachel and their classmates would be ignored again.

The scene in Dr. Bergstrom's library kept popping into her head, but she refused to dwell on it. She couldn't prove his role in Rachel's "accidents," but she didn't want him to dodge justice. It was tempting to pity him for the years he'd spent agonizing over his role in Susan Peters' death. That part was complicated. But the way he tried to cover up the past by scaring Rachel away from Morton was unforgivable. Cassandra had liked and respected him, but she'd been mistaken.

It would be easy to blame Bergstrom, the students, or the board for her situation. Bergstrom had started this whole decline by hurting Rachel, then denying any involvement. The students had pushed their changes too quickly, putting the board on the defensive.

Professional integrity demanded she get over the defeat and focus on making sure the board presentation went well. Plus, it was the middle of Dead Week and students needed quiet, undisrupted time to attend class and study.

She pulled out her phone and tapped a few buttons.

Andy Summers picked up on the third ring. "Good morning. Any stray animals camping out at your office?"

Cassandra laughed, "Are you always this chipper in the morning?"

"Only when I've had enough coffee. Are you ready for today?"

"I was going to ask you the same question," she said. "The newspaper article made it sound like parents, students, and other groups might attend the board meeting. Is the meeting room even large enough to hold extra people?"

"Usually there's about five guest chairs, but when I looked yesterday, they'd set up more along the walls. The VIP parking area security checkpoint is ready, and a few off-duty officers are coming in to make sure the public stays in designated spaces within the building."

"Wow, you really did put in a lot of extra planning this week."

"Just trying to be ready for anything," said Summers. "You seem down. Want me to bring Buckley over so you can pet him?"

"Buckley?" She was confused. "Oh, you named the dog. Are you keeping him?"

"Once I cleaned him up, he snuggled onto my lap while I was working at my desk. He's a good dog; he has some basic obedience training already. The hospital in Wahoo offers a therapy dog class. I signed us up to take it after winter break. He could come to work with me. I bet the students will love him."

"You have such a big heart." She hadn't meant to say it so wistfully, but it was the truth.

After a few moments, he said, "I'm a sucker for strays of all kinds."

After they hung up, she thought, hmm, had she been included in his definition of a stray? The idea of two men interested in her was scarier than facing a line of protestors and the board.

* * *

Shortly after the office opened, Lance and Rachel stopped by. Cassandra stood to talk with them because sitting hurt worse.

Rachel's eyes shone and the volume of her voice raised above the copier working in the corner and the space heater next to the receptionist desk. She signed and spoke, "I think a bunch of kids from my Deaf Studies class are coming to the board meeting. Should we divide up the presentation or just have one of us do it?"

"One person is better." Cassandra signed. "You'll only get a few minutes. I gave you that document we can hand out with numbers." Frustrated by her limited ASL vocabulary, Cassandra grabbed her phone and typed, "The board has a long agenda, and this is just one item on it. Practice your speech a few times so you can keep it under five minutes. Make eye contact and be yourself. Students pay the bills around here. You have power, too." She showed it to them, then held two thumbs up.

Lance and Rachel looked at each other, seemed to come to a decision together, and he typed, "What if the national protestors come back?" Yesterday they'd stayed away probably because of the snowstorm.

She typed, "If anyone behaves badly, the Deaf Studies advocacy project will get blamed." And by extension, if Cassandra publicly supported them, she'd be sunk, too.

"We haven't done anything wrong." Lance typed. "We want our chance to change the system. They're just support-ing and promoting our work."

"If this initiative is going to pass, you have to be subtle. Fifty-year-old men don't like being forced to do something by a bunch of twenty-year-olds. Be respectful, please." Cassandra looked meaningfully at Rachel. "And be careful."

Rachel seemed as excited as if she were preparing to attend a party or stage performance instead of a business meeting that would decide the fate of several people's jobs. "We're going to get some breakfast and then a bunch of us are making protest signs! See you later."

Cassandra nodded, slowly turned on her left leg, and limped into her office.

* * *

Cassandra dreaded the moment when Dr. Winters read the *Daily News* article. Or what she'd do in response to Dr. Bergstrom's resignation, assuming he went through with his promise. She didn't have to wait long. Within thirty minutes after Lance and Rachel left, Julie called her to come over for a talk.

Entering Winters' office, the effect of the white walls, rug, and furniture combined with the snow's reflection out her picture window made Cassandra want to reach for her sunglasses.

Dr. Winters matched the mood of her office, wearing a loose-fitting pantsuit several shades darker than her wavy hair. She met Cassandra just inside the door and gave her a firm handshake. "It's a big day, Dr. Sato! I love meetings like this where critical issues are discussed and decided. Makes me glad I came out of retirement. Way better than sitting around playing Bridge all afternoon with the old ladies down in Arizona."

"I'd take Arizona's weather today over Nebraska's."

"I do enjoy playing golf year-round," Winters agreed. She retrieved a business envelope from the top of her spotless desk. "Apparently, Dr. Bergstrom has similar aspirations. He's submitted his resignation. I know you're close. I thought you'd want to be the first to know."

Cassandra locked her hands behind her back and stood up tall. She was still at least six inches shorter than Winters. "Right now? Before the end of semester?"

Winters said, "Bergstrom says he already wrote the final test, and he's arranged for his grad assistant to score them. His resignation is effective immediately."

If she was going to level any accusations against Dr. Bergstrom, now was the time. "Did Dr. Bergstrom happen to mention a reason for resigning?"

"You mean other than the fact that he's been collecting Social Security for three years already?" Winters made an imposing figure with her hands on her hips, her graceful neck smoother than most women her age.

"Dr. Sato, you probably aspire to a bigger job than this someday." Winters hadn't invited Cassandra to sit. "Morton's reputation has been tarnished the last two months, and as its steward, I will not allow another black mark during my watch. It's time to put the past behind us."

Thinking of the students and staff who just wanted to be able to read the public announcements, Cassandra asked, "What about justice?"

"You've spent too much time with Professor Batman, haven't you, dear." She laughed, "Look, our problem today is keeping current students from running amok. Let Bergstrom take some much-delayed time off, while we get this whole Deaf Studies advocacy thing settled without any bloodshed, okay?"

Winters stepped close enough to place her hand on Cassandra's shoulder and steer her towards the door. "I'm counting on you to put Morton College first in that little journal of yours today."

Within moments Cassandra found herself standing outside the office door while Winters gently shut it behind her. For a woman who seemed on the brink of confusion half the time, she'd noticed Cassandra's bullet journal. Maybe Cassandra had underestimated her.

* * *

Cassandra skipped lunch. Her stomach was too fluttery to keep anything down. Shortly after noon, Dr. Bryant knocked on her door with Meg close behind.

His dark eyebrows nearly met over the bridge of his nose. He signed, "I just came from Dr. Winters' office."

Meg closed the door behind them and walked around the desk to stand near Cassandra. She nodded at Cassandra, her eyes conveying the frustration she couldn't say out loud while she was working.

"What happened?"

Bryant signed and Meg spoke, "She gave me a warning for failing to adhere to expectations of ethical teaching and for violating Morton policies regarding insubordination or otherwise unacceptable conduct."

"Seems kinda vague," said Cassandra. "Did she tell you why?"

"Because I talked to the reporter about the board meeting. She thinks I'm behind the Deaf Rights Coalition's interest in our little civics lesson." His head shook and his hands rested on his hips like he wanted to punch something.

Cassandra fiddled with her necklace. "Yeah, probably you meant well, but the way I read the article it seemed like we were trying to use public pressure to get our way with the board. I don't know if it helped the situation."

His eyes dropped to the floor and he pursed his lips. "I guess you're not going to support me then, huh?"

"I didn't say that." She put up one palm. "I just don't think you made our task easier today." Cassandra said, "Besides, my opinion isn't very popular in Winters' office either. You might be better off getting other people's support instead of mine."

"If they fire me, I'm suing them for discrimination."

Whoa. Cassandra didn't know how to explain that her academic politics approach was far less confrontational than his. She'd always gotten more accomplished with cooperation than threatening litigation. "Let's try not to get fired today, okay?" Cassandra placed her hands together like praying. "I finished unpacking a month ago, and I'm not really up for moving again yet. Can you please talk to the Coalition people and keep them contained?"

"You're just like Winters," Bryant signed. "I didn't invite them here, and they don't answer to me. We've stumbled into a national issue and if the board ignores the deaf students' request, there will be consequences. If you won't stick your neck out for the students, I will."

Before Cassandra could respond, he turned and left her office. Which had become a bad habit of his.

Once again, there was a surreal moment of awkwardness while Cassandra and Meg stood facing each other, and Cassandra reminded herself that Meg didn't necessarily agree with everything she had to say while she was interpreting.

Meg stepped around to the front of Cassandra's desk and sat in the armchair, her hand on her baby bump.

"Hey, are you feeling okay?" Cassandra panicked. "Are you having contractions?" Grabbing a bottle of water from the mini fridge, she pressed it into Meg's hands.

"Thanks." Meg took a generous swallow from the water bottle. "No contractions, but all this arguing is giving me a headache."

Cassandra dug through her top desk drawer and handed her the Tylenol. "Should I call Connor? Do you need a ride home?"

"I'm fine." Meg smiled. "I'm almost five months hapai, sistah. We get one long time to wait. Don't hover, eh?"

"Okay, brah. I'm chill." Cassandra sat in her desk chair and held up her Morton travel cup for a toast. "Let's get this party started."

Chapter Twenty-Seven

Walking over to the Student Center, Cassandra wore her winter coat unzipped. The afternoon sun had melted the ice, the sidewalks were dry, and the only evidence remaining of the snowstorm were piles of dirty snow on the grass.

Turning to Meg, her voice full of wonder, Cassandra said, "What a nice day." Gee, one snowstorm and her whole perception of nice and warm had changed completely.

Lance and Rachel stood on the far side of the building's entrance sidewalk, signing with a few other students. Meg pointed towards them. "I'm working with the students outside. A different interpreter is assigned to the board meeting."

Cassandra didn't need to go inside early, and since it wasn't cold, she didn't mind standing outside with Meg.

Some of the twenty people loosely gathered on the sidewalk in front of the center wore jeans and fleece sweatshirts, others wore business clothes like they'd come from working in an office.

One cluster looked like a bunch of middle-aged moms in trendy sweaters, pants, and boots.

These people weren't too loud or unruly. Cassandra was relieved. "Are these the protestors?"

Next to her, Meg studied the area. "I don't see any signs. No one's chanting."

A few minutes before one o'clock, a black sedan pulled up to the full VIP lot and stopped at the checkpoint. Two uniformed officers wearing navy jackets that said Security in yellow on the back spoke to the man driving. They allowed the car through and it parked near an Omaha TV truck.

As if a switch had flipped, another car parked a block away and four men wearing business suits climbed out, dug a few large signs out of the trunk, and walked purposefully towards the others on the sidewalk.

Cassandra blinked. "Is it just me, or are these folks much older than college-aged kids?"

The students arranged themselves in a line along the edge of the group, holding more of their home-made signs: "Stop Language Oppression" and "Can You Hear Us?"

Behind them stood a handful of Coalition members, chanting, "Deaf Rights Now!"

Cassandra couldn't control the off-campus groups, but she was proud of the way the students behaved. They'd felt ignored and instead of shouting and swearing, they approached opponents non-violently. With any luck, this would be over soon, and everyone could get back to studying in peace.

Cassandra elbowed Meg when she noticed Dr. Bryant alone about fifteen feet behind the students, quietly holding

Lance's SpongeBob sign that read, "No Fair." Wearing dark sunglasses and a full smile, he remained in the background.

Meg discreetly snapped photos of him and the students. "This is fun. It's like MLK!" She quoted, "'Hate cannot drive out hate: only love can do that.'"

So much for impartiality. Cassandra liked MLK as much as the next person but would rather poke a fork in her eye than monitor a campus protest.

"Let's do this every week," Meg gushed.

Cassandra said through her teeth, "Let's do this never again."

Chairman Hershey and another man in a suit made their way slowly from the parking lot towards the Student Center's main doors.

The pack of women pointed and rushed towards him. Voices carried to where Cassandra and Meg stood watching.

"That's Hershey!"

"You, there! Our kids' safety is priority number one!"

An elegant woman with dark hair piled onto her head in an elaborate updo hurried alongside Hershey and his companion, speaking loudly, "Don't walk away from us. These are our children we've entrusted to you! We can replace you, you know."

A fresh-faced reporter thrust his phone towards Hershey's face, "Chairman Hershey, do you have anything to say to this crowd before the board meeting?"

Hershey held up a hand and grimly shook his head, not a hair out of place despite the slight breeze. He tried to walk past the group, but by then the business-suited men from the car had caught up to the cluster of protestors and the board members were surrounded.

At first Cassandra thought the businessmen might be accountants or finance staff members here for the meeting, but they too held signs saying, "Fiscal Responsibility for Morton," and "No Tuition Increases."

Meg did a low whistle, "Ho-ly Mary, Mother of God. It's the Helicopter Moms versus the Tightwad Dads!"

Cassandra was betting on the Moms. Didn't the bean counters know better than to upset a bunch of peri-menopausal women protecting their young? She turned to Meg, "Tell Rachel I'll text her when it's our turn to present. Let the games begin."

The main doors opened, and Andy Summers broke through the circle that had formed around Hershey and the other man. Like a linebacker, he ushered them back to the door and into the Student Center leaving behind the three groups of protestors. The TV camera crew darted around taking footage while the reporter pulled representatives aside to interview them.

Meg went over to interpret with the student group, and Cassandra walked to the top of the stairs. Before heading inside, she paused to look back at the assembly. They looked and sounded nothing like the violent, shouting groups you see on the news. Nebraskans were under control even while having a raging disagreement. How odd.

Cassandra's heels clicked on the hallway tile as she found her way to the third floor board Room. Teak wooden benches were placed on either side of the double wooden doors where a few business office staffers and Winters' assistant Julie were seated with file folders or tablets.

Cassandra didn't know the protocol for when she should go inside. The preliminary agenda listed her Diversity and Inclusion Report second after the quarterly financial report. Sitting next to Julie, she watched more people file into the room. Cassandra whispered, "Is Dr. Winters already inside? Should I wait out here until they call me?"

Julie smiled at her and handed Cassandra a paper copy of the agenda. She'd also dressed her best today, wearing a long sweater over matching pants and a patterned top, rings on every finger and long earrings dangling to her shoulders. "You'd better wait inside. I doubt it will take very long to get to you. Save me a seat, I'll be there in a few minutes."

Cassandra found two chairs together along the back gallery which had mostly filled up with people who looked like the parents gathered out front. Dr. Winters was in the front right corner, next to Dr. Gregory from the Business Office. A woman wearing black sat to the left in the front row. Cassandra remembered her as Meg's coworker in the ASL interpreter office. Turning, she nodded at Dr. Bryant, who was seated in the far corner of the back row.

Cassandra's stomach clenched, and she breathed deeply a few times. She'd been in high powered meetings many times before, and she was prepared.

Within a few minutes, Mr. Hershey banged a wooden gavel gently on the table—they actually used a real gavel? —and announced, "The quarterly meeting for the Morton College board of directors is now open." He glanced around the large teak table at the seven men and one woman seated in plush velvet chairs. "All members are present. You have the agenda and the September minutes?"

Cassandra wished she was a few inches taller. Her back as straight as possible, she still had to crane her neck to see between the two rows of people seated in front of her. Bright sunshine spilled into the room from large windows along one wall, and the rich scent of fresh coffee lingered over the refreshment credenza that was also set with a tray of cookies and a large glass water dispenser. Cassandra's stomach growled, reminding her she'd skipped lunch.

"I propose two changes to the agenda," Hershey announced. "Skip Stevenson from the insurance company needs to leave early, so let's move him up to the first slot after the financial report. And since we have so much on our plates this afternoon before the year-end, I suggest tabling the Diversity and Inclusion Report until our next meeting in March."

Cassandra felt a whoosh as the calm air inside her lungs rushed out as though she'd been punched in the stomach. *Was Hershey joking?* She'd spent the last two weeks holding departmental focus groups, pouring over employee and student demographics, and researching emergency management systems so he could just wave them aside with one sweep of his shiny gold pen!

The ornate clock with Roman numerals hanging on the far wall of the room ticked loudly as no one spoke for several seconds. Several board members' heads were down while they made notes on their agendas.

Cassandra would have to text Rachel and Meg that their whole presentation was scratched.

The female board member Cassandra had noticed earlier raised a hand. She was in her late-forties, thin with dark brown hair cut into a simple bob hairstyle. She wore little makeup, but had a graceful, quiet power that must have earned her position with these guys.

"I'd prefer to keep that report on today's agenda. I believe that's why those people outside and the extra security today are present, correct? Shouldn't we discuss topics in order of relevance to current issues? Whatever has caused so many people to feel compelled to attend makes the diversity report more relevant than . . ." Reading glasses perched on the bottom of her nose, she perused the agenda, ". . . say a discussion about the Solar Panel Renewable Energy Initiative in 2025. Couldn't the solar panels wait until March?"

Heads raised around the table and pens were laid down. Hershey made eye contact with several members as though he'd previously warned them of his intention to delay the discussion and avoid the distraction from the extra circus happening outside.

Finally, a short, wide man with triple chins spoke up. "Ms. Hermson makes a good point. I'd also like to hear the report today."

Cassandra held her breath.

More nods around the table.

Hershey scowled, his large head swiveling as he looked around for a consensus. "So be it. We will hear the diversity report after the insurance report. All agreed? Fine. Next let's review the minutes . . ."

Stars flashed in Cassandra's vision as she let her breath ease out slowly. While the board reviewed the minutes and moved on to the financial report, Cassandra discreetly rose and stepped into the hallway.

She texted Meg, "Almost cancelled my report. ugh. We are up third on the list. In twenty minutes, come wait in the hallway by the board room."

Less than a minute later, Meg replied, "Got it. Oh Captain, my Captain!"

Cassandra laughed out loud in the hall.

Back in the meeting room, her eyes soon glazed over as she stared at the clock facing her, willing the minute hand to move faster so she could get her report done. She'd preloaded the PowerPoint on a flash drive and submitted it to be cued up when Cassandra started speaking.

She rehearsed her opening lines in her head. *Good afternoon, Chairman Hershey and board members. President Winters charged me with gathering data about Morton College's current climate regarding diversity and inclusion.*

The insurance guy was refreshingly brief. He passed out a rubric comparing two student insurance policies up for renewal next semester.

Cassandra heard voices in the hallway and turned to see Meg had arrived with the students. Her heart thumped as Mr. Stevenson finished speaking, gathered his coat and briefcase and excused himself.

Hershey said, "Next up, Dr. Cassandra Sato with the Diversity and Inclusion Report."

Cassandra moved into the empty chair to Mr. Hershey's left side and addressed the board.

"Good afternoon, Chairman Hershey and board members..."

She made eye contact, spoke slowly and clearly. Out of the corner of her eye, she saw the ASL interpreter signing to Lance, Rachel, Dr. Bryant and the other students who had filed in along the back wall of the board room watching the meeting.

"Institutions that want diversity must practice inclusion. Inclusion is simply treating individuals as insiders in an organization, while also allowing them to retain and feel comfortable expressing their unique qualities."

"Diversity isn't limited to admissions quotas or placing x number of minority faculty on decision making committees. Inclusion is not about what you say. It's about what you do."

Cassandra used the mouse on the table to thumb through the slides on her PowerPoint that were displayed on the large LED screen over the wall behind the table.

She spent three minutes summarizing the focus groups and current numbers. She wanted to leave time for the students.

"This semester students from an Introduction to Deaf Studies class were tasked with developing an advocacy project taking on an issue they identified at Morton. Their highest priority item was purchasing an emergency management system that allows students to receive text-based updates to their devices during weather, maintenance or safety events. Students would also be able to report emergencies to the security's dispatch center by texting. Some of those students are with us today and would like to share their learning experience with you."

Cassandra stood off to the side and waited while Rachel walked closer to the table in front of the board. Dressed in a black dress with patterned tights and knee-high boots, her wavy blonde hair falling down her back, she looked nervous, but excited. Patty Nagle proudly observed her daughter from the back of the room with the students and a few other parents.

Rachel carried one paper folded in half and glanced down at it before beginning. Cassandra advanced the slide on their presentation to a photo of Morton taken the previous day with the sidewalks covered with ice and snow.

"Good afternoon. My name is Rachel Nagle and I'm a freshman biology major. I became deaf a little more than three years ago—"

Dr. Winters stood up in the front row of the public seating section and slowly raised a finger in Rachel's direction.

Rachel looked confused. "—when I was in high school. I started learning American Sign Language last year and I'm in Dr. Bryant's Deaf Studies—" Rachel's voice trailed off.

Winters' face was white, and her other hand came up to cover her open mouth. She looked afraid.

Rachel stopped talking and the board members turned their heads to see where she was staring.

Cassandra's stomach dropped low as Winters broke out in a sweat and her finger shook. "What is SHE doing here?!" Winters demanded. "You all see her, can't you? I did the ritual. I sent her back to her realm, but she won't go away."

Cassandra made eye contact with Meg. For some time, she'd known something was wrong with Winters. The strange emails at all hours. The forgetfulness. The mood swings.

Julie lunged out of her seat and clasped Winters' elbow, placing a hand behind her back. "Dr. Winters, how can I help you?"

Winters flailed her arm free of Julie. "Why are you following me? I saw you talking to George Hansen about me. What lies did he tell you?"

Rachel backed up two steps, shaking her head, her eyes wide. "What? I don't—"

"Don't you play coy with me!" Winters stepped closer, clearly agitated. "I thought you were dead the first time!" Winters shouted, "What do I have to do to make you go away?"

Several people gasped.

Rachel's lower lip quivered. "I, –I know that voice!"

Winters' mouth set in a hard line.

Patty Nagle had made her way to Rachel's side and put her arm around Rachel's shoulders. "What's wrong with that woman?" she said incredulously. She glared in turn at Hershey and the other members. They all sat dumbly watching the scene unfold.

Cassandra glared wide-eyed at Meg, who mouthed, *What the heck?* Stepping around to Winters' other side, Cassandra spoke calmly, "What did you mean by 'the first time?'"

"The first time." Winters shook her head, confused. "In the snow. I followed her home from the party and bumped the back of her car. She was *dead.*" She pulled at her hair, making her look as deranged as she sounded.

It all fit together in Cassandra's head. Rachel really did look exactly like her grandmother, Susan Peters.

"Yes, I remember you!" Tears ran down Rachel's cheeks. "Before you pushed me on the ice, you yelled at me... You're messed up, lady."

Andy Summers and another officer entered the board Room, hands on their batons.

Cassandra held up a hand to stop Summers momentarily. She patted Winters on the back and spoke to her like a child. "Do you mean Susan? Did you kill Susan the first time?"

Winters quieted some. "She had his baby, but he loved *me*! I just wanted her to leave Alec alone." She tossed her head towards Rachel. "She's been following me around all month! I saw her at the library. I did the cleansing. I told her to go back to the other side, but she won't leave me alone."

Winters' legs gave out, and Cassandra and Julie helped her slide down into the chair. "Ma'am, you're going to have to go with Officer Summers, here."

Winters hunched down even more, shrinking before their eyes. "Just give me a few more minutes." She reached under her chair for her white tote bag and began digging inside. "I don't need anyone's help. I can find my keys. Let me call Charlie."

Cassandra squatted next to Winters and kept an arm around her back. Looking down at her feet, Cassandra felt tears spring to her eyes. Just like when her Gran got confused, it was so hard to watch a person betrayed by their own brain.

Chapter Twenty-Eight

Friday morning, Cassandra gathered herself for the difficult moment ahead. Standing on the porch, she knocked on the front door. Heavy footsteps approached on the other side. Waiting, she turned around and surveyed the front yard and now dry driveway. The bruise on her butt had turned a sick combination of green and yellow, and Cassandra still had to sit down carefully.

The door opened and Liz Bergstrom's face showed the surprise Cassandra had expected her visit would bring. Hair pulled back in a ponytail, minimal makeup on her face, Liz wore a matching sweatpants and zippered hoodie outfit and held a roll of gray duct tape in one hand.

Her baleful stare amplified the squirmy feeling inside Cassandra. "Mrs. Bergstrom. I—"

Without even a hello, Liz stepped back and opened the door wider. Walking away, she left Cassandra standing in the entry hall alone. Cassandra removed her shoes, closed the door, and peeked left into the living room. Large white sheets covered the sofas and chairs. A stack of brown cardboard boxes was neatly placed by the door, labeled Kitchen and Christmas. In the back of the house where the kitchen was, Cassandra heard voices and plates like more packing was underway.

Turning right, she stepped into the library. The dark draperies had been pulled back and the space was decidedly brighter and cheerier than the last time she'd been there. Dr. Bergstrom sat on a low footstool surrounded by books in piles on the floor. Looking up at her, he smiled. "Dr. Sato!"

Grateful he didn't growl at her to get out, she said, "Cassandra, please."

He nodded.

She stepped in front of him and sat cross-legged on the floor. "I owe you an apology, Dr. Bergstrom."

"Mike, please," he said. "I'm just plain Mike now."

Her eyes filled. "I thought you were the person who hurt Rachel Nagle," Cassandra folded her hands in her lap. "I wanted to hold someone accountable so badly that I blamed you instead of waiting until I knew more facts."

"Well, I was keeping secrets, just not the ones you suspected me of hiding."

"You wished you could go back in time and do things differently. Batman wanted to right the wrongs of the world because of his past. Without your past, maybe you wouldn't have become the same professor you are today."

"Cassandra!" he laughed. "You told me you'd never seen a Batman movie."

"No, but I'm a Google keyword rockstar." She shrugged. "I am so sorry for doubting you, my friend. I'm seriously glad that you weren't the bad guy."

"Speaking of which, how is the Wicked Witch Winters doing?"

Cassandra bowed her head. Dr. Winters had caused Susan Peters' accident, then carried on as if nothing had happened for forty years. It was unfathomable. But she also felt sorry for Winters and wouldn't wish dementia on anyone, no matter how evil their energy.

"Andy Summers met with the county prosecutor and the family. The statute of limitations on the car accident passed long ago. They won't charge her for Susan's death. I wouldn't be surprised if Rachel's family pressed charges though. The board's Executive Committee removed her as President."

"Winters and I were friends once. She had to sense how devastated I was after Susan died leaving my house party." Bergstrom shook his head, staring at the book in his hands. "She let me think it was my fault all these years."

"Yeah, about that," said Cassandra. "Can I convince you to stay a couple more weeks? Long enough for a proper retirement party. There's no reason for you to slink off into the sunset anymore."

"Only if Julie promises to bake her famous carrot cake."

"That can be arranged," she agreed.

Cassandra had stayed several minutes longer while Mike told her about their planned trip to scout RV communities in Arizona. They'd stop in Denver and the Grand Canyon before heading south for the rest of the winter. Cassandra envied him for spending the cold winter in the South. He offered her to visit them when she couldn't take the cold anymore.

He promised, "It'll happen. You think the snow is all beautiful and seasonal now but come February you'll be looking for any excuse to get somewhere warmer."

She left him feeling sad that she'd miss him, but glad they knew the truth now. Bergstrom seemed lighter, happier and looking forward to his retirement.

* * *

Rachel and Lance sat next to each other in the executive conference room; Rachel's mother was across the table. Cassandra spied Lance squeezing Rachel's hand under the table which answered Cassandra's question that Rachel and Lance were now an official couple. From the silly smiles on their faces, Cassandra guessed their attraction went deeper than easy communication because Rachel could sign ASL.

Rachel bit the fingernails of her other hand.

Meg sat next to Patty Nagle while Cassandra waited in the doorway.

Soon, Julie—who no longer had an official boss because Chairman Hershey had taken over the role until the end of the year when a new interim President would be named—escorted an elderly couple down the hall towards Cassandra.

The man was once tall, but now hunched over a walker with tennis balls on the bottom of the legs, shuffling along the carpeted hallway. His white dress shirt and light plaid suit jacket were topped off by a jaunty brown bowtie. His wife looked like Mrs. Claus with a full head of wavy, gray hair and wire-rimmed glasses. She wore a long navy skirt, support hose and orthopedic shoes, walking alongside him as Cassandra imagined they had done for more than sixty years. They were adorable.

Cassandra ushered them into the room, "Welcome Mr. and Mrs. Peters. I'm Cassandra Sato. We spoke on the phone. Thanks so much for meeting here. It's so much closer than going all the way to Omaha. How was your drive?"

Mr. Peters' slightly cloudy eyes gazed in Cassandra's general direction.

His wife answered, "Good thing the snow melted. You look different than I pictured, Dr. Sato." She looked expectantly around the table.

Ignoring the comment, Cassandra gestured around the table, "May I present Patty Nagle, her daughter Rachel, Rachel's friend Lance, who is deaf and uses sign language to communicate, and our interpreter, Meg."

Mrs. Peters greedily examined Rachel's face, then turned to Patty and nodded, smiling sweetly.

"Please sit down." Cassandra pulled out the nearest chairs. "Can I get you some water or coffee?"

"Coffee please, for both of us," she answered.

Mr. Peters' thick white hair was parted on the side and neatly combed. Eyes behind dark framed glasses shifted between Patty and Rachel.

Cassandra poured them coffee from a carafe on a side table and placed the china cups in front of them.

"You look just like our Susan! Like in that newspaper story," Mrs. Peters faced Rachel, then turned to Patty and studied her more. "I see Merlin's nose in you, dear."

Patty hadn't spoken in five minutes. It was the quietest Cassandra had ever seen Rachel's mother. When she opened her mouth, a little croak came out first like she was talking over a lump in her throat. "Grandmother!" Patty's eyes filled. "Did you have any other children besides Susan—my mother?"

"No, just our Susan." Her fingers covered her mouth and she sighed. "We should have tried to meet you sooner. We're sorry."

Mr. Peters held his coffee cup in his right hand, but it trembled so much Cassandra wanted to leap over and steady it before coffee splashed in his lap. Slowly he raised his left hand, cradling the cup with two hands before sipping through his dry, cracked lips. Then he smiled broadly at Rachel and nodded once.

"I should have looked for you. I only requested my birth certificate a few years ago when Rachel asked about it. I never knew your names." Patty swiped wetness from under her eyes. "I didn't know that you had lost your daughter."

They talked happily until the older couple seemed tired and ready to go. Mrs. Peters reached into her handbag and pulled out a tissue paper wrapped bundle and a beat-up light brown teddy bear. "This belonged to your grandmother." She handed it to Rachel. "She kept it on her bed throughout high school and college."

Rachel scooped it up and hugged it to her. "Thank you, Mrs. Peters," she whispered.

Lance gently rubbed her back.

"Everyone calls me Lily. You can call me Grandma Lily. I've always wanted someone to call me that." She pulled a wadded tissue from the wristband of her sleeve and wiped her eyes.

"Thanks, Grandma Lily," Rachel said through a teary smile.

Next, Mrs. Peters handed the wrapped gift to Patty. Carefully Patty Nagle unwrapped the tissue paper, revealing a baby's small plastic brush, comb and mirror set. Her face melted into tears until Meg reached into a pocket and handed her a few tissues.

Pressing the bear to her chest Rachel said, "Can I . . . can I hug you?"

"I'd like that, dear."

After hugs all around, it took several minutes for everyone to pull themselves together enough to end the meeting. After the goodbyes, the old couple shuffled back down the hall toward the president's office.

* * *

Back in her office, she and Meg both blew their noses and checked their eye makeup in the small mirror behind Cassandra's door. Meg had just sat on the couch and opened a water bottle when Cinda knocked on Cassandra's doorframe and came inside.

"Oh my God, Cinda!" Meg said, "Those two were so sweet, *I* wanted to go home with them and call them my grandparents."

"I don't know how you can interpret those types of meetings and not bawl like a baby," said Cassandra.

Meg was still patting her face dry, "I don't know either. I was three minutes away from ugly crying."

They told Cinda about the meeting between Rachel, her mother, and Susan Peters' parents.

By the end, Cinda was dabbing her eyes too. "Well, something good came out of this whole mess after all, bless their hearts."

"When I promised Rachel my support and help, I had no idea it would lead to all of this. For a while, I seriously questioned why I moved here. It felt like I did all the wrong things for the right reasons."

"You made a difference for a lot of people, Cass. You convinced those board members to accept your recommendations." Meg said, "Even Dr. Bryant was happy when they approved the monthly subscription software package that enables the text-based alerts."

"That's a temporary solution until the budget allows for purchasing new equipment." Cassandra's shoulders wiggled in excitement. "And we're going to apply for a federal tele-communication grant together. I wonder if he'd tutor me in ASL. I wish I could talk to him more directly." She laid a hand on Meg's arm. "Not that I don't appreciate your help."

"I assume you're going to reinstate the Diversity Council now that you have no boss again," Cinda said.

"Yeah. About that," Meg said. "To recap, this semester's presidential revolving door began with No-Nonsense Nielson, the good old boy who first invited you to our lovely campus. Have you heard from him, by the way?"

"Just a postcard from the Florida Keys showing Nielson holding a giant fish and wearing one of those fishing caps with the dangly lures stuck all around the brim. I doubt he's coming back any time soon."

"And in only one month, Dr. Winters managed to shove a student, attempt arson in the library, and have a complete mental breakdown," said Meg. "I wonder who we'll get next."

Cassandra raised her bottle. "A toast to the future Morton College President."

They clinked water bottles together.

"And no, I'm not applying for the job. One thing I've learned is that I still have a lot to learn. I'm planning to do better in the work-life balance department."

Meg wiggled her eyebrows up and down a few times.

Cinda said, "If by 'work-life balance' you mean you're finally getting some action in the dating department, I'll drink to that."

* * *

For a change, Cassandra arrived home before complete darkness fell. She threw her laundry down the chute to the basement and took the time to make a real dinner. The rice cooker's timer chimed just as she moved to the stovetop and gave the garlic shrimp and vegetables one last stir before turning off the burner. Plating the food, she set her china on the table and relaxed into the chair.

She was ready for a quiet weekend.

In the middle of hand washing the dishes, Cassandra's laptop beeped from the desk in her converted dining room-office. Rushing to hit Open, her parents' faces appeared together on the screen.

"Hello Cassandra!" her mother yelled, always certain that 4,000 miles away meant Cassandra wouldn't be able to hear her normal inside voice.

Cassandra sat down on a stool and centered her head in the camera frame. "Aloha Mom and Dad!"

"You get someting on your chin," her mother held out a wadded tissue towards the camera as though she could reach through and wipe the spot off Cassandra's face.

Cassandra did a sigh, "Hey Daddy. I shoveled snow this week! But it melted the next day. Maybe next time I'll just wait for it to melt and save myself the trouble."

Her father's lips moved, but Cassandra couldn't hear him because suddenly the room was filled with enthusiastic barking. A little fluffy white dog growl-barked at Cassandra, stopping arm's length away. She scooped him up, but his paws stuck out stiffly. He looked soft and cuddly, but his personality was standoffish.

Her father frowned, "you dog-sitting for da neighbor?"

She shrugged and tried to pet the squirming animal. Finally, she had to let go before he fell.

"Kinda," she said. "It's a really long story, but my new boss, Dr. Winters? That's her dog, Murphy. Dr. Winters had to quit her job as President because she found out she has early stages dementia."

This was the long-distance parent sanitized version of events.

"Oh, that's very sad, yeah." Her mother agreed.

"Anyway, this morning I went for a walk because it's pretty nice outside. Dr. Winters lived a few houses down from me, and there was a moving van in her driveway. Her daughter was packing up Dr. Winters' things to move her into a memory care facility. The daughter lives in a no pets allowed apartment and has a new baby, so she couldn't take Murphy."

Murphy heard his name and growled again on cue. Glancing down at his bared pointy teeth, Cassandra realized she forgot to ask Winters' daughter if Murphy was a biter or just grouchy.

She faced her parents again. "When I started walking to my house, Murphy followed me. I carried him back to Dr. Winters' house. The daughter asked if I would adopt him so she wouldn't have to bring him to the animal shelter."

One long look at those brown melty doggie eyes and Cassandra had been willing to forgive the time he scratched her leg, drawing blood. She'd do this for Dr. Winters. Because losing your mind one memory at a time was a really horrible thing. Cassandra thought maybe she could bring Murphy to visit Winters at her new memory care place to make the transition easier.

"He's one cute dog," Her mother elbowed her father. "He gonna make shishi all over the house. Good luck keeping that clean."

Her mother was right. Cassandra rubbed her temple. She'd never owned a dog and didn't particularly like them. Murphy didn't seem to trust her either. But she'd made a promise, and now she would find a way to keep it.

Next in the
Cassandra Sato Mystery Series

Dead of Winter Break, **Book 3 Coming Soon!**

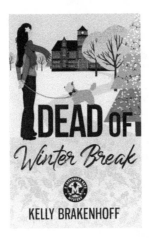

Reach Kelly at her website at **kellybrakenhoff.com**

Like Kelly's Facebook Page to get the latest updates:
https://www.facebook.com/kellybrakenhoffauthor/

*Sign up for periodic emails with Kelly's special offers, recipes, and book
recommendations here:*
http://eepurl.com/ggOkvP

DEAD OF
Winter Break

BOOK 3 IN THE *CASSANDRA SATO MYSTERY* SERIES

Chapter One

December in Nebraska was best left to poets droning on about the dubious merits of frosty icicles and face-freezing temperatures. Inside the stuffy Performing Arts Center, Cassandra Sato felt sweat rivulets slide down her back under her academic regalia. Easing the light blue velvet sash a few inches away from her throat, she crossed her ankles and inhaled deeply to slow her heartbeat.

Moments earlier, while the Fall Commencement speaker—an economist who had graduated in the 1950s—launched the concluding salvo in his uninspiring remarks, Cassandra had glanced across the stage at Board of Directors Chairman Alan Hershey, Master of Ceremonies and owner of an age-defying head of hair that never fell out of place. Hershey had raised two fingers of his right hand and dipped his chin in a subtle greeting to someone in the audience.

Cassandra had followed his gaze to the parents and guests in the lower level seating that curved behind the Morton College graduates. The center's Gothic interior resembled an old European chapel. Except instead of a central altar, a stage was flanked by two levels of box seats. Decorative carvings on the pillars and ceiling continued the impression of an old, stately theatre.

She smiled at the families wearing their finest clothes, pride in their new graduates obvious as they snapped photos of every aspect of the auspicious day. She loved commencements. Poignant endings and eager degree candidates brimming with promise for the future made her heart swell.

Cassandra had met a small number of parents in her four-plus months as Vice President for Student Affairs. As her eyes slid down a row about halfway up the section where Hershey had nodded, she hadn't expected to recognize any of the faces.

Which was why her heart had lurched so suddenly.

With narrowed eyes, she confirmed the tall, thin, gray-haired man with the unruly eyebrows was indeed her former boss. Why was Dr. Gary Nielson sitting in the commencement audience instead of floating in a fishing trawler off the Florida coast wearing the goofy hat he'd posed in for the postcard Cassandra had received less than two weeks ago?

She racked her brain for a good reason why Nielson would end his sunny retirement trip so abruptly and return to wintry Carson, Nebraska. The skin on his face was several shades darker than the pale complexions he and his wife had sported in early November upon departing to begin their new life. His unexpected exit had thrown Cassandra's office into a bit of chaos while the administrative departments divided up his duties and the board of directors hired an interim president.

That had not worked out as anyone had hoped. Now they were back to a vacancy, with Chairman Hershey making important decisions while pursuing a suitable replacement.

Just minutes before spotting Nielson, Cassandra had daydreamed of the time when she would become president of a university and it would be her duty—no, her deepest pleasure—to impart her own wisdom while standing before a crowd of beaming graduates and well-wishers.

The rest of the ceremony had passed in a distracted rush of excited motion and frustration while Cassandra waited to corner Chairman Hershey. The ending bars of Pomp and Circumstance echoed in the main hall while the stage party and graduates marched out to the lobby.

Unzipping her black outer gown, Cassandra left her floppy velvet tam in place so she wouldn't mess up her hair. "Mr. Hershey, a moment— "

"Dr. Sato!" Hershey was only a few inches taller than her in heeled knee-high boots. "Glad I caught you before the reception. Dr. Nielson has changed his mind and will be reinstated as president for the spring term, giving us ample time to search for a permanent replacement."

Six weeks of retirement under his belt and Nielson had changed his mind. Who does that? Disappointment pinched a nerve in her temple. "Reinstated? He just left in November—"

"You well know the past two months have been controversial," Hershey nodded. "Donors have complained. Parents have encouraged their children to transfer. Dr. Nielson was kind enough to oblige us on short notice."

One student's death, another violently attacked, campus protests, and media controversy had made for an exhausting first semester. All Cassandra wanted for the next four weeks of Winter Break was to watch mindless TV, wash every surface of her house, and write a telecommunications grant proposal.

Nielson's reappearance seemed too coincidental. "But sir,—"

Hershey's hair-sprayed head leaned closer to her ear. "Personally, I wish you had the age and experience to apply for the president's job," he said. Parents and audience members streamed into the lobby to meet up with their graduates. "Although I feel obligated to mention that it's doubtful you'll be seriously considered for the job here, no matter how mature or experienced you become. You, um . . . well, you don't fit the Morton presidential mold . . ."

Without a trace of malice in his voice or expression, Hershey had just dismissed her aspirations as easily as one casts off a pair of shoes because she wasn't the right style or color. Cassandra squinted and squeezed the heavy cardboard program in her hand until it bent in half. How dare he?

Cassandra's face reddened and she'd just opened her mouth to reply when she felt a strong hand grip her elbow and an arm settle on her waist. She was steered away from Hershey and hustled off to the alcove leading to the women's bathroom.

Cassandra yanked her arm away. Shaking out her poufy green striped velvet sleeves, she directed the indignation she'd felt towards Hershey at her friend Meg O'Brien instead. "Why are you pushing me?"

Meg held both her palms up in mock surrender, flipped her wavy red hair over one shoulder, and glared back at Cassandra using a stink eye so authentically Hawaiian that Mama Sato would have been proud. "Is that how you thank me, wahine?" Meg's index finger came up between them and hovered just inches from Cassandra's chin. "I saved you from making a scene in front of all those people."

If Meg ever used that look on her ten-year-old son, Tony, he'd probably turn to ash. Cassandra batted Meg's finger away. Her face was inches from Meg's, and she stage whispered, "I wasn't making a scene! That patriarchal good ol' boy just assured me I'd never get the president's job here."

"I overheard that part," said Meg.

Cassandra backed away from her best friend and opened the bathroom door. They stepped around the corner into the lounge and huddled together on a chaise, out of range of others using the restroom stalls and sinks. "Does he think I'm too female or too Asian to fit the Morton presidential mold?"

Meg had worked at the commencement in her role as Morton's ASL Interpreter Coordinator. A cantaloupe-sized baby bump protruded from her black sweater dress. Black tights and black boots made her outfit funeral-ready, but that was her standard uniform for stage events. "Mr. Country Club Helmet Head wasn't trying to piss you off. He thought he was giving you friendly advice. Hershey likes you, Cass, although he's oblivious to how backward he sounds. Didn't you tell me after the fiasco with Dr. Winters that you won't be applying for the vacant president's job?"

The ladies lounge door banged open and Cinda Weller zeroed in on Cassandra and Meg in the corner. "I'm not wearing your ridiculously heavy outfit, but I'm still dying in this overheated mausoleum." Cinda fanned herself with a souvenir program while her bouncy, blonde hair wilted into frizz. Morton's Counseling and Career Services Director was practically defined by her dry humor and oddball Southern sayings. Several years younger than Cassandra and the mom of two young sons, she'd quickly become Cassandra's friend.

Cassandra adjusted her robes. "I love the costumes only slightly more than I love commencements. I only get to wear mine twice per year."

At the same time Cassandra and Cinda said, "It's old school." One of them meant it as a compliment, the other did not.

Cinda wore navy slacks with a Morton blue blazer and minimal makeup. She shook her head. "Did you notice that line of students who marched down the wrong aisle and had to double back around to their seats?"

Meg shrugged. "Dr. Bryant was their line leader, but don't blame us for the mix-up. We did our jobs. That whole scuffle with the air horn was distracting." Dr. Shannon Bryant was the Deaf Studies professor who Cassandra had recently gotten to know a little better. Meg worked with him often. Pointing towards the bathroom stalls, Meg said, "Mommy bladder."

Cassandra had heard air horns several times throughout the program in disregard for signs at the entrance listing commencement etiquette do's and don'ts. An announcement had been repeated during the ceremony requesting that the audience refrain from unruly behavior and everyone had complied. Except for one. Finally, Bob Gregory, the Business Office Director, had beelined over to a well-dressed woman and her disheveled friend in the left seating area and told them to leave.

The young woman had tossed her dark, tightly waved waist-length hair and loudly protested. "We're cheering for our friends! We aren't hurting anyone. Don't be so uptight!" After his stern beckoning gesture, they'd shuffled over the legs of ten people to exit the row.

There's at least one smartass in every audience.

By the time she and her companion had crawled their way to the aisle, the eyeballs of most males in the vicinity were fixed on the young woman's long legs, short skirt, and pretty face. She repeated apologies to each person she stepped around. "Excuse me. Thanks. Hey, how are you? Good to see you. Hi, Professor." The guy with her was dressed in jeans and a wrinkly t-shirt under a black leather jacket. He stood quietly in the aisle waiting for her until Gregory ushered them both out.

Some people had noticed the disruption, but the incident took only half a minute and the ceremony had continued smoothly.

As soon as Cassandra returned to the lobby, Bob Gregory appeared by her side. "Those air horn people were removed by campus security." His nose wrinkled in distaste. "I tried to calm the young lady down and was willing to let her stay for the post-commencement luncheon if she agreed to relinquish the offending device, but she refused." The way Gregory said lady made it clear he did not consider her worthy of the title. "Apparently her mother is some dip-lomatic la-ti-da and she threatened to complain about her treatment today. Frankly, she was quite disrespectful." His large stomach heaved upwards with his breath and his lower lip formed into a small pout. "Most of these young folks are nowadays. Disrespectful." He nodded to himself as though Cassandra's opinion was unnecessary for the conversation.

It was all she could do not to roll her eyes and tell him, okay, Boomer.

"Thanks for letting me know. I'll take care of it from here."

Pulling her phone out of her blazer's pocket, she sent a text to the campus security director, Andy Summers. "Hey Andy. Are you still with the couple from the graduation? Where are they now?"

While waiting for a response, Cassandra moved among the luncheon tables, congratulating graduates she recog-nized and meeting their parents. Small private colleges like Morton had a leg up on the chaotic busyness of her former college, Oahu State, because of intimate events like these.

Her phone vibrated with Andy's response. "Back at Picotte Hall. Student believes staff shamed her by singling her out."

Cassandra looked up towards the baroque chandelier and pressed her lips together. She typed back, "Hang on there. I'll be over in a few."

Cassandra scanned the crowd until she found Cinda Weller. She waited near the doorway for the luncheon buffet line to thin down while chatting with a student and his family.

Cassandra stepped into Cinda's line of sight, nodded her head to the hallway twice, and waited for Cinda to join her outside. "Would you mind going with me to deal with the students who were removed from the ceremony?"

"What was Sela thinking? I could hardly hear the graduates' names with all that racket!"

"You know her? Is she a troublemaker?"

Cinda looked around the lobby and stepped closer to Cassandra. "Not exactly trouble. More like high maintenance. Her mother works in DC for an embassy or something fancy pants. The guy is Daniel Leung, but I haven't had any problems with him." She made a big exhale. "Sela Robert can be a long day."

"Great. Well it might be an even longer day if she raises a stink about being called out." Cassandra often walked the fine line between enforcing rules and letting students express themselves in productive ways.

They claimed their heavy winter coats from the cloakroom. Cinda said, "It's colder than a well digger's butt out there."

Indeed.

Dr. Bryant walked out the main doors the same time she and Cinda were leaving. He made the sign for cold and then pointed to us and towards the luncheon as though he wondered why we weren't staying to eat.

Cassandra typed into her phone and showed it to him. "Checking on the students with the air horn."

Bryant laughed and pointed at his ears. "Didn't bother me," he signed in ASL.

Cassandra laughed and nodded. They waved at him and turned down the main walkway traversing brown grass covered common areas sprinkled with crunchy leaves.

Picotte Hall was one city block away from the Arts Center, but a stabbing pain on Cassandra's right pinky toe formed halfway there. Cassandra had assumed that her dress boots with 3" heels would be a perfect fit for the ceremony. Since moving to Carson, Cassandra had experienced several catastrophic footwear events, but she wasn't giving up her love of beautiful shoes. No knockoff flats or clunky snow boots yet.

When Cassandra and Cinda made it past the security desk to the residence hall's lobby, Andy Summers was waiting alone, thumbing through his phone, one hand resting on his thick black utility belt.

"Hey Andy. Where did the students go?"

His eyes broke away from the phone and slowly traveled from Cassandra's boots to her face, then lingered on her head. She was still wearing the graduation tam. "We had a friendly chat. I think I convinced them not to file a complaint."

About her age, military-cut blonde hair now covered by a thick navy stocking cap, Andy probably could stand to lose twenty pounds around his middle. Not that she was judging. Because not everyone had inherited their metabolism from Cassandra's parents who moved constantly like worker bees and never gained a pound over their healthy weight.

"My ears are still ringing," Cinda snorted. "I should file a complaint."

"You could have texted us before we walked all the way over here."

Andy's ears flushed red. "They literally just left the lobby before you arrived. I thought you'd appreciate not having to deal with Sela and Daniel."

"Okay." Were they really so difficult to handle? "Thanks for the assist. While we're all here, I need to ask you something else." Cassandra stepped to a seating area and perched on the edge of a large ottoman. Andy and Cinda rested on the nearby couch and chair.

"Did either of you see Dr. Nielson at the grad ceremony?"

Identical expressions of skeptical confusion appeared on their faces.

Cinda said, "How much of that Kona coffee did you drink this morning? Dr. Nielson? He and his wife are in Florida."

"I wish," Cassandra breathed quietly to herself. "I didn't see his wife, but Dr. Nielson was in the parent section, all dressed up and enjoying the show. Afterwards, Mr. Hershey told me that Nielson is coming back to work as president for the spring semester."

Andy Summers blew out a soft whistle. "That's good news! Nielson's a good guy."

"Hope nothing is wrong with his family," Cinda said. "Maybe they're in town for the holidays."

Adjusting her boot to relieve the pinch in her shoe, Cassandra stood. "Let's stop at Nielson's office. I don't want to wait until Monday to get the story."

Fifteen minutes later, Cassandra swiped her key card to open the administrative suite and they entered the president's office area. The reception area and large desk where the president's assistant normally worked was quiet, grey light penetrating the wall of windows.

Cinda paged through the piles of paper on the desktop.

"Don't snoop, Cinda!" Cassandra stage whispered.

"How else would we find out anything?"

Cassandra's high heels sunk into the plush carpet as she slowly pushed the heavy wooden door separating the entry area from Nielson's old/new office. Finding it unlocked, she opened it wide enough to see the overhead lights were on. Cassandra knocked. "Hello, is anyone in here? Dr. Nielson?"

No one answered. Was Nielson's key card still valid or had Hershey given him a new one already? Both women pushed inside.

Mismatched furniture and cardboard boxes sat where they'd been since the previous occupant's hasty departure two weeks prior. Cassandra made a circuit of the room, noticing a banker's box containing awards and framed diplomas on the white desk chair. Maybe he'd brought some of his old things from storage and begun unpacking already. A cup of pens, a blank desktop calendar, a Morton College coffee cup, a commemorative keychain, and a pad of yellow sticky notes were the only items on the desk. The top paper on the yellow pad had a few words printed in Nielson's trademark neat handwriting. He had been here at some point that morning.

"Should we check the men's bathroom?"

Cinda was taking this hunt too far and Cassandra hated wasting time. Cassandra's lips formed a line. "No, that's fine. Let's go back to the luncheon. Maybe Nielson is there meeting parents and hanging out with Mr. Hershey."

Turning off the lights and closing the door behind them, they headed downstairs and back to the Performing Arts Center. Cinda said, "Aren't you relieved that Nielson's back? Less work for all of us now that we don't have to do his job plus ours. I thought you liked working for him."

Cassandra had been looking forward to working at her own pace without anyone looking over her shoulder. She thought a minute before answering carefully. "Don't get me wrong, I'm grateful he took a chance and hired me. But Nielson can be . . ."

"Oh bless his heart, he's a sweet old coot."

Cassandra laughed. "That's one way of putting it. You didn't see him at the graduation this morning. His skin was tan like he'd been outside, but something was off. I need to talk to him." She nodded. "Then I'll adjust to having my boss back."

Acknowledgments

Dear Reader,

Thanks for your patience this year with my steep learning curve as I went from zero to three published books. Hurray, we made it! Work on the next book in the series is already underway. I'm writing this on Thanksgiving day, which is perfect timing to tell you I'm so grateful you took the time to read this story! The number of good books available is overwhelming. I know you have many options clamoring for your attention, and I'm thrilled you gave Cassandra's story a chance.

Again, I'm grateful to the NaNoWriMo community for believing that stories matter and in the power of creativity to transform people's lives. *Dead Week* was my November 2015 NaNoWriMo project. Thanks to the editing guidance and endless patience of Sione Aeschliman, it has undergone huge transformations. Michelle Argyle, thanks for another eye-catching cover that fits this story perfectly.

To my Deaf friends and coworkers, thanks for your willingness to share your experiences and stories with readers. I'm thankful for the fun times we've had, and the kindness you have shown me and my family. I look forward to bringing more of your original stories and books to life in the future.

Lori Ideta and Auntie Evelyn, we all miss you so much and hope to visit again soon.

Thank you to Abbey Buettgenbach, Pete Seiler, Ben Sparks, Elizabeth Cooper, Chris Timm, Jean Hinton, Carla Engstrom, Lori Ideta, and Jon Brakenhoff, for reading early sections or versions of this book. Mom, I owe you more fancy steak dinners than we could ever eat for reading multiple drafts and setting me straight when I went off the rails. Thanks Sherri Brakenhoff and Dad for your superior spell checking.

I'm grateful for the encouragement of writing friends, both online and in person like Macie McIntosh, Patty Krings, Shane Kennett, Fr. Winter, Jeff Walker, Laura Chapman, and Tosca Lee. Thanks to the Sisters in Crime and the Guppy Chapter for their awesome brainstorming and encouragement. Special thanks to Kaye George for the smudging idea, and Mary Feliz for getting me started on the back cover blurb. Shoutout to Morgan Hazelwood, expert moderator of the FB Pitch Wars YA group for holding us all accountable.

For friends whose names, character details, or quotable sayings I borrowed, thanks for being good sports. I won't point them out, you'll know which ones are yours. Thanks to my Book Club and PPH friends who nicely ask what I'm writing, and kindly don't ask when I look stressed out. I'm so grateful to know you all.

Love to Joe & Claire, Jon, Kate & Colton, James, and Oliver for epic game nights and delicious Sunday dinners. Dave, thanks for being flexible with our new empty-nester lifestyle, letting me figure out when to write and when to put away the laptop. I love you all.

Thanks to family and friends in heaven for lifting me up and guiding me.

"Have no anxiety at all, but in everything, by prayer and petition, with thanksgiving, make your requests known to God." Phil. 4:6

About the Author

Kelly Brakenhoff is an American Sign Language Interpreter whose motivation for learning ASL began in high school when she wanted to converse with her deaf friends. Her first novel, Death by Dissertation, kicked off the Cassandra Sato Mystery Series. She also wrote *Never Mind*, first in a children's picture book series featuring Duke the Deaf Dog. She serves on the Board of Editors for the Registry of Interpreters for the Deaf publication, *VIEWs*. The mother of four young adults and two dogs, Kelly and her husband call Nebraska home.

CPSIA information can be obtained
at www.ICGtesting.com
Printed in the USA
FSHW011958141021
85498FS